"This Is How You Start to Di[...]
in stories told with both skill a[...]
stories without ready resolution[...]

—RONA ALTROWS, author[...]

"In these precisely paced and deceptively dark stories, Astrid
Blodgett sweeps out the dust bunnies of contempt and devastation
from the junk drawers of her characters' family homes. These stories
do what short stories do best: every word flexes its muscles, every
detail teeters on an iceberg of deeper meaning. This Is How You
Start to Disappear is a complex and satisfying compilation of
unsteady bridge crossings between our childhood and adult selves."

—SUSAN SANFORD BLADES, author of Fake It So Real

"This collection is an intimate embrace of the moments and
memories that define us. With pitch perfect prose and heaps of
tension, Blodgett pierces so deep into her characters' hearts and
minds you feel as if you breathe their same air. Beautifully
imagined and bursting with compassion, every story is a stunner!"

—FRAN KIMMEL, author of The Shore Girl and No Good Asking

"With compassion and acute observation, Astrid Blodgett writes
about events, large and seemingly small, that can change the
trajectory of a life. Familial fractures spread like cracks in winter
ice as Blodgett investigates those moments that divide her
characters' lives into 'before' and 'after,' whether they are loyalty
tests one sister demands of another or a father so preoccupied
with his new relationship that he can't see his young daughter's
struggles at a skating party. At times, Blodgett's characters
recognize a life-changing event only after it has swept past them,
but the reverberations will be felt for decades to come. These finely
wrought, multigenerational stories pivot around such moments,
as ordinary working people cope with the unexpected tragedy
and dislocating circumstances of their unfolding lives."

—RACHEL ROSE, author of The Octopus Has Three Hearts

THIS IS HOW YOU START TO DISAPPEAR

THIS IS
HOW YOU
START TO
DISAPPEAR

STORIES

ASTRID
BLODGETT

 UNIVERSITY *of* ALBERTA PRESS

Published by

University of Alberta Press
1–16 Rutherford Library South
11204 89 Avenue NW
Edmonton, Alberta, Canada T6G 2J4
amiskwaciwâskahikan | Treaty 6 |
Métis Territory
uap.ualberta.ca | uapress@ualberta.ca

LIBRARY AND ARCHIVES CANADA
CATALOGUING IN PUBLICATION

Title: This is how you start to disappear / Astrid
    Blodgett.
Names: Blodgett, Astrid, 1964– author.
Description: Short stories.
Identifiers: Canadiana (print) 20230451829 |
    Canadiana (ebook) 20230451918 |
    ISBN 9781772127133 (softcover) |
    ISBN 9781772127232 (PDF) |
    ISBN 9781772127225 (EPUB)
Classification: LCC PS8553.L558 T55 2023 |
    DDC C813/.54—dc23

First edition, first printing, 2023.
First printed and bound in Canada by
Houghton Boston Printers, Saskatoon,
Saskatchewan.
Copyediting by Kimmy Beach.
Proofreading by Mary Lou Roy.

A volume in the Robert Kroetsch Series.

University of Alberta Press is committed to
protecting our natural environment. As part
of our efforts, this book is printed on Enviro
Paper: it contains 100% post-consumer
recycled fibres and is acid- and chlorine-free.

University of Alberta Press gratefully
acknowledges the support received for its
publishing program from the Government of
Canada, the Canada Council for the Arts, and
the Government of Alberta through the Alberta
Media Fund.

Canadä · Canada Council for the Arts · Conseil des Arts du Canada

Albertan Government

for Bronwen and Charlotte

Contents

These
People
Have
Nothing

TOM AND I stayed behind in the ditch when Dad went for the gun. Ferdinand lay on his side panting, hot, his tongue out. His eyes staring into nothing. I thought there would be blood, but there wasn't any. Did you see blood, I want to ask, all these years later. Tom's just arrived at my apartment with fixings for dinner, with beer, always beer, and this is what I want to talk about. This is what I've been thinking about all week. Was there blood.

We were driving to Evansburg, a hamlet above the Pembina River famous for a population count that includes one grouch. Tom was up front and I was behind Dad, reading the shopping list from Mom. Hardly anything today: two-inch wood screws and potatoes. The list was so short I read it again. Two-inch wood screws and potatoes. Would we go for ice cream before or after getting the stuff, I wanted to know. I would get butterscotch ripple this time. Because I always got strawberry and Tom teased me about getting the same flavour every time.

When we turned off our gravel road onto the secondary road, Tom rolled his window down and yelled, "Go on, boy!" There was Ferdinand, running along beside the car. "Go on back!"

We had four or five dogs over the years, mutts and strays, and for some reason Ferdinand, who was not a mutt or a stray, was Dad's. The others were Mom's. Her dogs never went past the gravel; they chased our car as far as the secondary road and then turned around and went back to the cabin. Ferdinand was an Alaskan husky Dad'd bought the year before and spent months training. Dad named him for the bull who sat in the field eating flowers and not fighting. You'd think a dog you named from a story and took to dog school would know how to listen. Not that dog. He kept running beside the car. Dad sped up a bit and Ferdinand disappeared behind us. A few seconds later he was right up to Dad's window. Dad slowed so the car hardly moved. I rolled my window down, too, and told Ferdinand to go back. He still didn't listen. He was too focussed on Dad.

"Go on, boy!" Dad yelled.

Ferdinand lowered his head, whining, and flopped away from our car. A blue pickup truck coming the other way smacked right into him. Ferdinand yelped and flew across the road behind us. The truck sped up and roared away.

"Oh, Christ!" Dad yelled and hit the brakes. "Bastard!" He ran to Ferdinand, leaving the door wide open. Tom and I got out and watched him carry Ferdinand to the ditch and kneel down and put his hand on Ferdinand's belly and his ear against his chest. Ferdinand lay on his side twitching and panting, the tip of his fat pink tongue resting on the dry grass.

Dad grabbed his head. "Oh, no. Oh, no, no, no. He's not dead," he said. Like Ferdinand should be dead. "He's hurting. No. No." He ran his fingers through his hair and looked at us with buggy red eyes, then up at the trees and back at us. I didn't know if he was confused or angry. "Jess. Tom. Stay here. I'm going to Harold Jamieson's. He's got a gun."

Dad had never used a gun. We'd never seen one. But the Jamiesons were farmers; farmers grew things and had animals and guns. We were just city people who came to our cabin in summer.

Dad turned the car around and drove off.

I looked up from the ditch when I heard a truck. It would be the driver who hit Ferdinand coming back to check on him. He'd say it was an accident and tell us he was sorry. Ask if he could help. He'd probably gone as far as the first turnaround and come back.

But it wasn't that driver. It wasn't even a truck. It was some old woman in a little blue car. We could just see the top of her head, her big round sunglasses and red baseball cap.

It was so hot the air over the road shimmered. We were surrounded by buzzing flies and bees and the agitated rasping of grasshoppers. Hundreds of grasshoppers sprang up around us. They jumped on Ferdinand and he didn't try to eat them. Silly dog didn't even flick his tail.

Tom crouched down and put his hand on Ferdinand's side. I wanted to touch him too. I had never been close to anything dead. Except bugs. A mouse, once. Nothing big. I moved my hand a little toward Ferdinand and then pulled it back. Tom crossed his arms over his knees and sank his face into his arms, crying. I tried not to look, but I couldn't help peeking. When he saw me looking, he jumped up and kicked the ground near Ferdinand's belly, spraying him with dead grass and bits of dirt.

"Stupid dog!" Tom yelled. "Why'd you have to run into the road? Huh?"

Ferdinand whimpered.

"Tom! Stop it!"

"Idiot!" Tom kicked the ground again. "You deserve this for being so stupid."

"He does not!"

Ferdinand's body shook and he closed his eyes. Tom stomped near Ferdinand and I pushed him down. "Crybaby!"

I could call Tom almost anything but crybaby. He grabbed me and then I was on top of him, pounding his chest and trying to pull his hair. After about thirty seconds he stopped. I was eleven and he was only ten, but he was stronger and always gave in when we fought. Because I was a girl. I kept pounding. I was angry. Not just angry but boiling mad. I thought, later, that we were always fighting that summer. The flies didn't stop buzzing, the grasshoppers didn't stop leaping and making that rasping sound, like matches striking. Every single day was burning hot. Ferdinand lay in the ditch, panting, then not, panting, then not. A few minutes ago he was running. And now he couldn't get up.

Dad was back. The gun was long and brown and looked old. I got off Tom and we scrambled a little way along the ditch and hid behind a shrub so we couldn't see Dad or Ferdinand. We closed our eyes and covered our ears. I willed the insects to be quiet for a few seconds to let Dad shoot Ferdinand in peace. Another car passed, then a truck. I held my breath. I flopped on the ground, face down, eyes squeezed tight, hands over my ears, and waited.

At dinner, Mom said, "The dog would have suffered. He would have lost the leg. It would have cost a fortune at the vet."

"Oh, stop," Dad said.

"I bet that chicken farmer hit the dog," Mom said.

"What chicken farmer?" I asked.

"Ernst Wesgeber." Mom took a long drink of beer. We didn't have a fridge, but we had a cooler, and until the ice ran out we had meat and milk and beer. "He stopped me on the road one day when I rode the bike to Marge's for eggs and told me our dogs've been going after his chickens and eating the eggs. Said he'd shoot them if they came back. No way it was one of our dogs. More likely it was a stray or a coyote. I'll bet Ernst hit the dog. On purpose."

"He would have lived." Dad was looking at his fork, not at Mom.

Mom didn't say anything. She didn't like Ferdinand. Tom and I knew it the day Dad brought him home and told us he was going to take him to dog school. "That is one special dog," she said, sounding angry, and I felt funny, trying to piece together how she hated something that was special to Dad.

The next day, we all drove to the Jamiesons' and the grown-ups talked. Dad and Mom stood side by side. There was enough space in between for me to slip in, maybe Tom and me both. I thought of it because June and Harold were so close you couldn't squeeze anyone in between. They leaned in to each other a little and looked right at Mom and Dad and you could tell by the way they looked that they were listening, really listening.

I want to ask Tom if he thought of that too. Then I will ask if he knows what that feels like, being that close to someone.

∗ Harold and June Jamieson were the only neighbours we knew near our cabin. They were tall and their faces were tanned from working outside every day. There's never a day off on a farm, Mom once said. But we knew the Jamiesons took Sundays off and drove to that little white church in Evansburg, Home of the Grouch. Some Sundays we passed them on the secondary highway, when we were driving home to the city and they were returning from church. Dad and Harold stopped in the middle of the road and rolled their windows down and talked until a car came along. Harold could talk with a long stalk of wheat between his teeth. The rest of us heard only what Dad said. They could make a conversation about the weather or what Harold was growing in his fields last for ages.

Harold and June had two children, about the same age as Tom and me. At their place, everything happened in the yard. It wasn't like a city yard, with grass and trees; the yard was the place to park. The grass was on the other side of the barbed wire fence, where the cows and the horses were. Sometimes Tom and I got out of the car with Mom and Dad. All four of us kids hung about not knowing what to say or what to do with our hands while the adults talked. I kept hoping we'd be invited inside. I was dying to know what the inside of the house looked like.

All the days blurred in summer and all the visits were the same. Except one day, a while before Ferdinand was hit. Eliza came out of her house and ran right back in. I thought I might as well go wait in the car. But then she came out and ran up to me and showed me two books. I took one. *From Anna*. She lifted the part of the fence that didn't have the electric charge and we crawled under. We lay on our stomachs and read and read and read. We didn't say anything, but I knew she was there, reading. Eliza and I were in a tiny, warm nest.

Eventually Mom called to say it was time to go. I gave Eliza the book.

"Do you like it?" Eliza asked.

I nodded.

"You can have it. I've read it a thousand times."

"A thousand?"

"Okay, maybe only a hundred."

"Thanks." I ducked under the barbed wire and sat in the car and read while my parents said goodbye to the Jamiesons.

When she got in the car, Mom said, "Where'd you get that book?"

"Eliza. She's already read it."

"You can't take it."

"She said I could. She's read it a hundred times."

Dad had just started to drive. He stopped. "You heard your mother. It's not yours to take."

Eliza wasn't inside yet. She was standing beside Brian watching us drive off. I ran to her and handed her the book.

"You don't want it?"

"I'm not allowed."

She looked down at the ground. "Oh."

"Don't ever do that," Mom said when we were back on the secondary road again.

"It was just a book," I said. "She gave it to me."

"It's not just a book," Mom said.

I puzzled over this but couldn't unpuzzle it. "I gave it back, didn't I?"

"These people have nothing," Dad said.

Tom was confused too. We thought they were rich. They had land that we thought went on for miles in every direction. They had horses and cows and chickens and pigs and dogs and cats. They grew fields and fields of wheat and barley and alfalfa. The lies started after that visit. We used to wander in the bush, sometimes out of boredom, sometimes because when our parents weren't talking to each other they didn't want to talk to us either, and not long after that visit we walked over to the Jamiesons'. Eliza and Brian would probably be doing chores, because that's what you did on a farm. We could help. But when we arrived, they were just about to have lunch on the front porch.

"Why don't you join us?" June Jamieson asked.

"We ate. At home."

We hadn't, of course; we'd slept in and had a late break-fast. Our parents wouldn't want us to stay for lunch. We didn't know exactly why, but it would be like taking the book. So we left, and instead of walking along the rutted lane, we went down to the creek that flowed from their land through a giant culvert under the secondary road and eventually into our bushy bit of land on the other side. On a slope near the culvert, on the Jamiesons' land, we found a massive white puffball, the biggest we'd ever seen. It was twice as big as my head and still fresh. The Jamiesons were suspicious of things that grew in the wild and didn't eat them. But Mom would be thrilled. Mushrooms were her wonder food. They cured all ills. And our family had a lot of ills. I wasn't sure what ills were, but I knew we had them. I knew it in the way Mom and Dad spoke to each other, the way Mom said *your dog* instead of Ferdinand, the way Dad went for walks alone at the cabin or retreated to our house in the city whenever he could.

"We should take this," Tom said when we saw the puff-ball. "Mom would love it."

"She'll say we stole it. Stealing a mushroom is probably worse than taking a book." But he was right, she would love it. She would be so happy. Making her happy seemed more important than anything else.

Tom picked it. "We'll just say we found it on our land."

We walked through the culvert shouting, to hear the echo: *Bo-ring! Weee! Haaaate! This! Plaaaaaace!* It was so dry that year the creek was just a trickle. Still, we soaked our runners.

Mom was excited, just like we thought. She'd never seen such a huge mushroom. "Where did you get it? Where there's one, there's more, that's how it works. The spores spread." She talked faster and faster. "Near the road? I'll go there tomorrow."

Tom and I stood side by side, shifting from one foot to the other in our wet socks and trying to be as vague as possible even though I could clearly see the slope above the creek and the short grasses around it. I couldn't get that picture out of my head. I didn't know any place like that near our cabin. There were too many trees and shrubs.

"In the woods somewhere," I said slowly.

"Across that way." Tom pointed in the direction away from the Jamiesons'.

"We were walking all day, so we don't know exactly," I added.

The happier Mom looked, the worse I felt.

Mom sautéed part of the mushroom for dinner and made a great display of serving it in the crystal bowl she sometimes used. I waited for her to say what she said every time she used it: Your dad and I bought it in that pretty little village in Austria on our honeymoon. But tonight she didn't. Tonight she just offered the mushrooms.

When Dad didn't look up, though, she said something. I don't know what. Maybe Tom remembers. She held the bowl out to Dad with both hands and her eyes looked bright and wet.

"This bowl? For a puffball?" Dad said.

"We hardly ever use it. Let's use it," Mom said.

"It's for fruit. Or dessert. Or"—he held up his hands in frustration, the way he did when something was obvious to him—"just to look at." Then he shook his head and put up his right hand, palm down. We knew he didn't really care for puffballs; he thought they were watery and bland. So she didn't serve him any. Tom and I let Mom put some on our plates but didn't eat much of it. She probably noticed, but she didn't say anything.

Mom's excitement about the giant puffball made us uncomfortable, even a little scared. Later we realized that it was because we were showing an interest in her interests. We were on her side without knowing we needed to choose.

✳ Tom cracks open a beer and offers it to me. He opens another and takes a long swallow. He's put the rest of the beer in the fridge. The bags of groceries are on the counter. He whistles quietly while he unloads. Our dad died three days ago. My son, Jack, is at his dad's.

"You like stir-fry?" Tom says. "Shrimp? Garlic?"

"Yes." I lean against the counter, sipping. Scout flops at my feet and watches Tom carefully. I don't see Tom often, but he seems to know when to make an appearance: my wedding, Jack's birth. When André left. And now.

"Cutting board?"

I pull open the drawer and Tom finds the one he wants. "Knife?"

I show him the two good knives and he takes one. In a few minutes, he has chopped a small pile of cilantro and a smaller pile of hot peppers. Now he slices onions, carrots, yellow peppers, asparagus, quickly, non-stop, smiling the whole time. The kitchen has come to life.

"Five-star," he says. "Nothing less."

I am elated that he's here. He gives something to a space that I can't, maybe don't want to. I am like my father, handing my mother a wrench or holding a board in place, but not knowing what's being built. I know I can hand Tom anything, a cast-iron frying pan, a bottle of olive oil, a shot glass, and he will make something of it. Something good.

"You'd make a good chef." I've said it before, but his face lights up anyway. He has wide lips and a wide nose and his hair is pulled back in a man bun.

"First time I was down there," Tom says, meaning his home, southern Ontario, "I heard the strangest sound." He covers his mouth and puffs out his cheeks and makes the low rumbling of a bullfrog. Scout's ears flip back. He growls at Tom, then lumbers into the living room and flops down in front of the couch. His tail flicks up once. "Sadly, you don't have bullfrogs out here. But you have. Let's see. You have." Tom stares around the kitchen and living room, tips his head toward the open window, his hand cupping his ear. A car drives past and gives a long beep. A siren wails. He laughs. "You have the sounds of Edmonton at night. Hallelujah! What are you doing living so close to down-town, anyway?" Before I can say anything, he says, "Don't answer. What did we hear at the cabin?"

"The cabin? I have no idea. We only spent three summers out there."

Tom snaps his fingers. "Owls! Hell no, more! More than three summers. Once, in all those years, I heard an owl. And cranes. Remember the Sandhill cranes? And the wolf?" Tom gives a long, deep howl. Scout runs to him and barks three times.

"Grasshoppers," I say. "It's okay, Scout." I want to ask about Ferdinand and the gun.

"*Grass*hoppers?" Tom tips back his beer and drinks.

"Yes. Everywhere. That last summer we'd step in the grass and about a hundred of them would shoot up."

"That time the swans came, flying so low we could feel the air moving?" Tom's almost manic. "I couldn't believe how heavy they were."

I miss Tom so much.

"Does Mom know?" His voice is soft now. He means about Dad.

"I don't know."

Tom slides the onions into the frying pan with the knife blade. They sizzle and spit oil at us. My eyes sting. I take a step back and inhale the sweet, sharp smell. Mom lives in Seba Beach, a village west of Edmonton. She moved there and opened a thrift store when Tom and I finished school and left home.

Tom goes to the fridge for another beer and holds it in my direction. I shake my head and raise my half-full can. He drops shrimp into the frying pan one by one, grinning, and we watch them splutter.

"I'd like to go to the cabin," he announces.

I make a face. "It's probably long gone."

"I'd like to go."

"Huh. When do you figure you'll go?"

"We could drive out tomorrow. Maybe even tonight.
We'll have light till at least eleven. Twilight could go on
even longer."

"Tonight?"

"Have you been back since?"

"Since they sold it? No. Have you?"

Tom shakes his head.

I was close, once. When Jack was five and we were
living in Red Deer, André and I happened to be along the
secondary highway that runs near the cabin. André had
just bought a jeep that he was proud of and we'd driven
to Edmonton, both to escape kitchen renovations that had
been going on far too long and to visit old friends of his.

André's friends persuaded him to take Jack to the
"secret" swimming hole on the Pembina. It wasn't far from
the summer cabin, but when we drove past the three-quarter-
mile gravel road that led to our always-under-construction
cabin in the bush, I didn't point it out. Nor did I point out
the long laneway up to the Jamiesons' when we passed it a
minute later. The lane was still full of deep, muddy ruts, but
there was now a huge arch where the gate used to be with
the words "Reese & Suzanne"—in green—blazoned on an
ornate, heart-shaped piece of wood at the top of the arch.
The letters were already fading. I didn't even comment on
how gaudy it was. I had stopped pointing out so many
things by then. I knew, now, what it was like to be looked at
and not be seen. I'd known for a while. I just didn't know
what the next steps were. I was surprised at how close their
lane was; it felt like ages waiting for Dad to come back with
the gun.

Tom sprinkles the cilantro over the shrimp and asparagus. "Have you wanted to go back?"

"Yes."

"Good. Plates?"

I open the cupboard and take down two.

"Chopsticks?"

"Forks."

"It's a clear night. Nearly a full moon. No chopsticks?
Let's just eat and go. Leave the dishes for the house elf."

A little before seven-thirty we pile into my hatchback,
Tom up front beside me and Scout in the back.

"The sun's still up! Hallelujah!" Tom shouts when the
car is pointed straight west on Highway 16. "I miss this
about prairie summers."

The sun is not just up, it's high and almost blinding.
I turn down the visor and put on my sunglasses. "The place
is probably a wreck, Tom. Unless the new owners tore it
down and rebuilt. It was never really finished anyway."

"It was too, finished. Mom just liked to tinker."

He's right. She tinkered, she sawed, she sanded, she
hammered. For ages, even after we stopped going, after it
wasn't ours, she told me she did all of it, sawed every two-
by-four, pounded in every nail, by hand. Years ago when
I was visiting Dad he shook his head when I told him this.
"No," he sighed, "no." But he didn't say more.

"It was her place, Tom, wasn't it," I say.

"Yup," he says, quiet. "But she wanted it to be theirs."

Tom is right about that, too. At dinner once Mom said,
"I'll build a porch and when we're old we can sit on the
porch and watch the sun set and listen to the coyotes." And

Dad said, "You can't see the sun set from here. There are too many trees."

"You remember the crystal bowl?" I say.

"What crystal bowl?"

"Mom put that mushroom in it once."

"Oh, that puffball. The one we, ah, appropriated from the neighbours."

Mom told me once, "Your dad went out to the cabin after it was sold and took the only thing worth anything, a crystal bowl we picked up on our honeymoon in Austria."

"Mom." I said. "Why did we have a crystal bowl in a one-room cabin with no power or electricity that was never really finished?"

"God only knows," Mom said. "I wish I'd smashed it."

When I asked Dad why he went back for the bowl, he said, "Crystal has a certain perfection. Your mother and I, for a time, were perfect together."

Dad put the bowl in a niche in the wall opposite the bathroom in the new home he bought with his new wife in a new city so that, he told me, every morning when he stepped out of the bathroom he could take it in. There was a time, he said, when he wanted his life to be just like that bowl: precise, clear, infinite. "What a strange and confused creature I was then," he went on, slowly. "I see it as a measure of how far I've come." He made a sound like a grunt and a chuckle. "You can have it when I'm gone."

I puzzled over how Dad thought they were perfect, even for a little while. Their tastes, their pursuits, never seemed to be in the same place. On long summer days, when she had the time or wanted a change from sawing and hammering, Mom made weavings. Not the sort of weaving you'd see at a craft fair, neat and with a recognizable image. Usually she started with a piece of willow she found and bent into a circle or an oval and bound together; she ran tight rows of strings from one side to the other and then wove in bumpy, colourful yarn or fluffy, unmanageable wool or pieces of birch bark or red willow or dogwood branches she found on her walks. Feathers, too, and twigs with dried berries sometimes, red or white cranberries, dark purple saskatoons. Sun-bleached pieces of bone from a mouse or a vole. Her fingers always moving.

"Very nice," Dad would say. He wanted to understand this impulse, but he didn't. His hands were often at rest, one above the other.

"This is so surreal," Tom says when we see the Highway 43 turnoff. "I never thought I'd go back."

"Me neither."

"Everything changed the day Ferdinand died."

There it is. That's how he sees it, too.

"What do you figure Dad would have done, if Harold Jamieson hadn't been home?" Tom asks.

"Dunno." Now, finally, I can ask. "Who shot Ferdinand?"

Tom turns to me. "Jesus, Jess. Is this a trick question?"

After that summer, after Ferdinand was hit, Dad moved out, first to a condo in Edmonton, and later to Calgary. Mom went from one full-time job to another: Safeway, Zellers, the Bay. Sometimes she gave art classes in the evening. Tom and I ate a lot of peanut butter and jam sandwiches and wore cast-off clothing from Mom's friends.

"No. It's not a trick question."

Tom doesn't say anything. We pass the Fallis Country Store. Soon we'll see the turnoff to Seba Beach.

"Ferdinand must have known," Tom says. "Just like we must have known."

"What did we know?"

"Come on, why did Ferdinand chase our car that day? Why didn't he go back?"

"Why did Dad want his own dog so badly anyway?"

"He wanted something that was his," Tom says. "You know that thing that happens when you get married? What's yours is mine and what's mine is mine. He didn't feel like anything he touched was his."

"How do you know this? And how are you the expert?"

Tom never married. He once told me he preferred his lovers unattached. He would rather leave them before they left him.

"Years of keen observation," Tom says flatly. "Remember that fire right after? I mean a week or so after? Along the road allowance?"

"What fire?"

✳ The shot, when it came, echoed through the thick, still air. Every last insect must have heard it because for a long, heavy minute, even they were quiet.

Dad grunted like he'd been punched. Tom and I were still behind the shrub, face down, hands over our ears. We waited, for a minute or maybe two, then crept out in the long silence that followed the echo. Harold Jamieson and Dad stood beside Ferdinand. The gun was on the ground between them. Ferdinand had stopped panting.

Through the stalk of wheat bobbing between his teeth Harold said slowly, "Want to bury him at your place?"

Dad shook his head.

"I have a spot or two," Harold said, just as slowly. Like if he spoke too fast Dad wouldn't get it.

"I'm very grateful to you." Dad's eyes were red.

They wrapped Ferdinand in a blanket, hoisted him together and carried him to the back of Harold's truck. Harold put his hand on Dad's arm. "You need anything?"

"No." Dad looked like he'd gone a long way inside himself. I didn't know what was worse, seeing Ferdinand's shape under the old green blanket or seeing Dad disappear.

Harold reached into his chest pocket and pulled out a small silver flask. He passed it to Dad and Dad took a sip, then another. He closed his eyes, opened them. They shook hands. Harold nodded, and Dad nodded back. I waited for them to talk about the weather or the crops but they didn't say anything.

Tom and I got in the car. We knew we weren't going to pick up screws or potatoes or get ice cream. Dad drove back to the cabin. I went to the swing Mom had rigged up between two poplars and spent hours on it. I tried to understand how a person could be sad and angry at the same time and what I was angry about. Tom took out his jackknife and sat by the fire pit, slicing long strips off a willow branch and crying without making a sound. We stayed outside because Mom and Dad were inside, talking loudly.

The next day we went to the Jamiesons'. June called Tom and me out of the car and invited us into the house with

Mom. I had been hoping for this since I met Eliza but I didn't want it to be today because I knew it wasn't a day to hang out with her. We left our shoes along with the others lined up in the front entrance and sat at June's kitchen table. It had a plastic cloth with a yellowish flowery pattern and a doily in the middle with white salt and pepper shakers and a small white pot with sugar and the tiniest spoon I'd ever seen. June put out cookies and juice for Brian and Eliza and Tom and me. She made tea for Mom. We sat quietly and tried not to make crumbs. I hoped nobody would talk about mushrooms.

"They won't be long," June said. "Harold has done this before."

"I'm sure he has," Mom said. She looked out of place. June wore a dress with an apron and her hair was short. Mom was wearing old shorts and what Dad called a hippy shirt, one of her loose colourful tops, and her long hair was braided.

"The sun is going to hold out for several days," June said. "That should be nice for you kids."

Tom and I looked at each other. We didn't know if we were supposed to say anything back.

Then she said something that confused us. "We've enjoyed having you as neighbours."

✳ For a long time I was angry with June and Harold for being so nice. Then I was angry with Mom and Dad for not having figured out how to be together. The way June and Harold Jamieson had.

✳ "I think they're done," June said from the window.

"Already." Mom set her teacup down.

Eliza and Brian got up. Tom grabbed one more cookie, and we followed them outside.

In a grassy area down a slope, the way we'd walked to get to the culvert, was an oval-shaped mound of dirt. Dad and Harold stood near it. Mom stayed behind, but the rest of us went over to Dad. From the mound Tom and I could see the place we found the giant puffball. We tried not to look there. Dad threw a clump of dirt on the mound. Nobody said anything.

Eliza stood beside me and took my hand in hers. "Sorry about your dog," she whispered.

✳ I turn north onto the secondary road. Several miles down is the turnoff to the cabin. Before that is the road to the river. That day I'd come with Jack and André was unbearably long. Jack was bored. André complained that the place was farther than his friends had led him to believe. I pretended to follow the hand-drawn map his friends had given us, not letting on that I knew where we were. That I'd been to the secret swimming hole. Back then, it had a couple of unlit, smelly wooden outhouses whose doors didn't latch properly, always low on toilet paper (or completely out) and full of spider webs and flies. There was a tiny playground with a wobbly teeter-totter and two swings in the shade of massive spruces. The playground was dark and cold and buggy. We didn't care about any of that; we came to swim. The day André and I went, there was a modern playground with slides, red saucer swings, a blue climbing gym; the big old spruces had been cut down; and there was a new toilet building with running water, lights, and even a changing area. There were people everywhere. We thought Jack would love it. Only he didn't. He was out of sorts and whiny and afraid to go into the river.

Tom is as content as I not to say anything for the moment. I drive slowly, taking in the fields and muskegs and scattered farmhouses. Not much has changed. On one side of us, a grazing field, and on the other, an alfalfa crop. In the distance, mixed spruce forests. I turn onto the three-quarter-mile road and stop after a few car lengths.

The road is still gravel. That hasn't changed either.

"Why you stopping?" Tom says.

"Let's get out."

We stand side by side and I point. "That's where Ferdinand was hit."

"No." Tom shakes his head. "It was farther up the road."

I gesture toward the grassy slope near the car. "That's where Dad put him."

Tom shakes his head again. "Over there." He nods to the other side of the three-quarter-mile road.

This makes me chuckle. "We can't both be right."

Tom just smiles.

"Was Mom there? Who shot Ferdinand?"

Tom looks hard at me. "This *is* a trick question!"

"We were on the far side of the car. Behind some bushes." I look around, but I can't see the ones in my mind. Everything is different. "We waited and waited for the gunshot."

"You attacked me. Lord Almighty, you were strong."
He says it playfully, lovingly. I miss him. I miss ten-year-old
Tom.

The day after tomorrow we will make the long drive to
attend our father's funeral. I knew he died before the call
came. Three weeks ago the crystal bowl arrived in the mail.
Dad was ill for more than a year, so it wasn't unexpected.
But I nearly dropped the bowl when I pulled it from the box.
I hadn't thought about it for years. I held it long enough to
feel the deep grooves against my skin. Then I put it in the
cupboard I rarely open. Stupid bowl.

I hugged Tom when he showed up at my door, unannounced. I want to hug him now, but I don't; we're not a
huggy family. It's as if we haven't learned how to hold on to
each other. But I let my hand brush up against his and keep
it there.

"It wasn't very long," Tom says. "Waiting."

At the time I had no idea why Ferdinand was buried at
the Jamiesons'. I was too slow to see what was happening.
I hadn't seen that our parents were about to sell the cabin
and the land. Dad hadn't wanted to leave any part of
himself there. I hadn't seen any of it coming.

Standing beside Tom, now, I can see my father patiently
handing my mother a bow saw or a wrench, the same
way I handed Tom spices and cutting boards in my apartment. And I see what I hadn't seen before: Mom. She must
have come, she must have walked down the three-quarter-
mile road and taken the gun from Dad, Dad who had never
used a gun and didn't want to. And after, she must have
held it out to him, the way she held out the mushrooms,

imploring him to see her, to see her great kindness. Doing for him what he couldn't do. Look what I've done, her eyes must have said. Look what I've done for you. Now it's your turn.

It's a quiet evening. The sun is a great ball just above the trees casting a yellowish glow on the fields and the road. The air is gentle on my skin, like Tom's warm hand.

"He was still alive, you know," Tom said. "Ferdinand. I felt him." He shook his head. "He would have lived. Dad knew it too."

Devil's
Lake

BETH SAYS Dad's *downright giddy*. "You look downright
giddy, Paul," she says. She's smiling, like she's teasing. She
shouldn't do that.

Dad's focussed on my laces. They're about a mile long.
He makes the part near my toes way too tight. The next bits
he makes too loose. He even skips a hole. Then he wraps
my laces around my ankles three times and pulls hard. It's
the same with the second skate. He squeezes my toes and
makes the middle too loose and then pulls the laces around
my ankles.

"Dad. The skates are too small."

"Go on." His cheeks are red. "Go skate. Catch up to the
other kids. We're here to have fun, not complain." He looks
at his watch. "Where's Glenda?" He's not asking me. He's
asking Beth.

Beth makes a funny half smile and lifts her eyebrows up,
meaning "I don't know."

When I get up from the bench my ankles flop in and next
thing I know I'm face down on the hard snow. The tops of
the skates cut into my shins and my toes are on fire. The
bench helps me up. For maybe half a minute I stand and tell
my ankles *stay straight, stay straight*, and then I look at my

toes and take tiny steps to the lake. Now I look up. The lake is huge. There's a rock in my stomach. Snot slides over my top lip.

"Go on!" Dad shouts. "The ice is great!"

He's still at the bench doing up his skates. He can't see the ice. The ice isn't great. It's bumpy and full of gigantic cracks. But he's getting angry now. So I take one step onto the ice, and another. Thunk! I'm on my back. My head whacks the ice even through the helmet.

"Just get up." Dad yanks my arm. The other kids are zigzagging all over, fast. Dad shouts "Glide!" But I don't glide. My legs don't move along like everyone else's. "Just do it." He zooms off.

Dad was up early, today. He's never up early. But there he was, pulling the covers off me, saying, "Hey, Willow, get up. We're going skating."

"I don't have skates."

"We'll rent. The ice is just right. I've called Jim and Beth, I've called Paramel and Mika, and we're all meeting there this afternoon. Glenda too. This is going to be a good day. Today—hey, why aren't you dressed? I picked up hot dogs, I picked up buns, the works, we're all set. Get a move on!"

Dad's never organized. Usually I'm up first and have to wait forever for him to get up and then he doesn't want to do anything. He was like a puppy at the skate rental place. And weird. He smiled so hard his face turned red and then he looked worried and then he smiled again. His eyes skittered all over, to my feet and the wall of skates and the guy helping us but mostly his phone.

"Her first time on skates," he told the guy. "Her first time. Hard to believe, huh."

I already knew at the rental place the skates Dad picked were too small. But Dad didn't listen, the guy didn't listen, he was helping too many people. We got them anyway. I hate it when Dad acts strange, because when he starts off weird, he's even weirder if the day doesn't go right. Weird and mad and then quiet and sad. Same every time. Sometimes he won't even talk to me after. That's okay. Today I'm going to show him I'm the best skater there is. And tonight at home we'll sit around the table like he does with the dads, Paramel and Jim, and I'll talk like I know all about stuff too. Mostly when the dads come to visit I can't get a spot because they hunch over the table with their elbows poking out and their legs spread a mile wide so you can't even get another chair in. They wear jeans and those checked shirts and sometimes baseball caps, even though nobody plays baseball. And they're loud. I can hear them from the couch or my bed down the hall. It's all: "Too bad about Devil's Lake. Too much snow on the lake this year. The ice has to be just right. It has to be cold enough at night for the ice to freeze up thick, one good cold snap is what you really need, huh? And smooth. Yeah, smooth. Oh, oh, remember crack the whip when we cracked Brad's head? That was great. And that time Cole went under, when the ice was rotten? That was really good."

Those growly sounds they make. Like bear cubs. Tonight I'm going to push my way in no matter what.

"I called it, didn't I?" Dad says. He's beside me again.

27

THIS IS HOW YOU START TO DISAPPEAR

"The ice is good and thick. Smooth as glass. Just a skiff of snow. Blue sky. You couldn't ask for a better day. I called it."

Everybody else is on the far side of the lake. I could walk there. But it would take me all day to skate there. After three steps I trip on a crack and fall, harder than before. Now I'm a long way from the bench. Mika comes and pulls me up and skates away. There's ice and snot on the mittens Gram gave me. My fingers are cold. The little bones in my feet are breaking into a thousand pieces. Nobody told me how tippy skates are. Nobody told me skates hurt. I take one step, stop. Two steps, stop. Three steps, stop.

The fire ring and picnic tables aren't far from the parking lot. I could walk there easily too. The kids all skate there in a flash and before you know it they're somewhere else, disappearing around the island. Like it's nothing. I'm frozen now. Nobody else looks cold. Everybody's jackets are unzipped, and Dad doesn't even wear his mitts. I wish I was at Mom's. There's a community rink near her house, but we never go. And with Dad, we can only do something when everything's just right.

"It's not your fault," he said on the drive to the lake. "It's not your fault that woman doesn't do a damn thing with you all week. Doesn't do a damn thing period." It's not true about Mom. I've told him but he doesn't listen. "But it's never too late to learn. It's never too late to do anything, is it," he said. "This is your year, Ding Dong!"

My nickname is like bells, Christmas bells.

"C'mon, Willow!" says the girl with elephant ears on her hat. She's younger than me, only seven maybe, and even she skates faster than me. She doesn't have rentals. She has her own skates, black ones, like the boys. "Come with us!"

"She's coming, Hare-brain!" Dad says. And I remember Dad saying, "What kind of hare-brained name is Harley?"

Beth is here now, too. "How's it going?" she asks.

"She's fine, Beth," Dad says, frowning a little. "She's just fine."

"My feet hurt," I say.

Dad skates backwards away from us. "Come on, Willow," he says. "Glide. Just glide. You're not trying."

Harley's big brother zooms up to Dad and grabs his toque and takes off. Dad chases after him so fast his skates make hard scratching noises and send bits of ice flying.

"Like this," Beth says. Her voice is kind. She glides slowly ahead of me but not far, not fast. Then she skates back and takes my hand. "Bend your knees a little," she says. "Your legs are stiff as chopsticks!" She laughs. I hold her arm tightly and let her pull me along. She's strong and she can hold me for a long time and her laugh is not mean and she's never mad for no reason.

"Hey, I'm skating!" I laugh.

"You are," she says. "Let me guess." She looks at me. "You look like you are nine-almost-ten. Are you nine-almost-ten?"

"Yes!" I shout. Before I know it we're halfway across the lake. My face is warm now and my hands too. I'm getting the hang of it. I'll be skating on my own in no time. I'll show Dad.

After a while I smell smoke, from the fire the dads are making. It doesn't have that stinky garbage smell that comes from the big oil barrels behind the garage where Dad burns tomato soup cans and those Styrofoam take-out trays and other stuff he doesn't want to haul to the dump because of the disposal fees. Garbage smoke comes out spindly and black like a monster with long wispy arms and spiky horns and pokes its way up my nostrils and gives me a throw-up taste in my mouth. Dad tells me to go inside when I complain and I do, fast, before those smoky arms get close to me. I like wood smoke. It's nicer even than the dry grassy smell from Mom's cigarettes, the smell that says Mom's sitting down, she's not doing dishes or looking things up on her computer or sleeping and I can snuggle in beside her on the couch. Wood smoke is velvety and warm and cozy. Right now it means soon we can roast hot dogs, we can get off the ice and take off our skates and put on our boots and forget we were ever skating.

Beth and I skate toward the fire ring yelling, "Whee!"

Dad's tramping out of the bushes in his old black hockey skates. He's got a pile of sticks so big I can't see his face. He drops the wood in front of the fire ring and brushes bark and stuff off the arms of his coat.

"Dad, look!" I shout. "I'm skating!"

"Not likely. Beth is hauling you along!"

The skates dig in again, at my toes, around my ankles. Everything's on fire. I look at Beth. "I am too. Aren't I?"

"Don't just stand there!" Dad calls. "Go with the other kids. It's not time yet anyway."

"You are, Willow," Beth says.

Dad grabs the cell phone from his pocket. He shakes his head. "Of course. No reception out here." He shoves the phone back and steps onto the ice and glides over to Beth and me.

"She's doing great," Beth says.

"Once she's on her own, then we can say she's doing great."

Beth looks serious. "She's never skated before. Her skates are hurting her."

"She's fine," Dad says.

"They're too tight," I say.

"Skates are supposed to be tight," Dad says.

"I'll loosen them," Beth offers. "Then you can skate some more. We want you to have fun. We want you to come next time."

"I want to stop," I say.

"Just like her mother," Dad says. "Gives up the first try, if it doesn't go the way she wants."

"Are your boots in your truck?" Beth asks. I nod. She takes my hand and we glide back toward the parking lot. I don't want her to let go, no matter what Dad says.

Dad skates in circles around us.

"Have you told her?" Beth asks. Her voice changes to the way grown-ups talk to grown-ups.

"What, about Glenda and me?" Dad talks the same to everybody.

Beth nods.

"That's the plan," he says. "I'll take her." He grabs my hand, the one Beth is holding, so Beth has to let go. She looks at Dad for a bit and then skates away. Dad holds my hand tight and starts to skate, fast, and I hit the ice hard, face first. "Stand up, Willow!" he yells and yanks me up.

"And stop bawling! You've been bawling for an hour. You haven't stopped crying since we got here. I don't know why I bothered bringing you."

I pull my hand away from his and walk on my own. I want to be on the old couch beside Mom and smell her cigarettes and her flowery shampoo. I always try to put her out of my mind when I'm at Dad's. Because she always says she'll be fine, when Dad comes to get me. I'll be fine, she says, don't worry about me, go have fun. When she says it like that I know she's not going to have fun. So mostly I don't think about her. It's mean. Mean as you can get. But I want to be with her, on the couch. Even if she says she wants to stretch out by herself and not have me right in her face.

When we get to the bench, I plop down and Dad kneels in front of me and takes a skate in his hand. He pulls at the laces till they make big loops.

"Christ." He frowns. "Don't be such a baby. You haven't skated before. You just have to keep trying." He pulls off the first skate, not hard, but slowly. Everything unscrunches and opens and stops hurting. Dad loosens the other skate and pulls it off, and I feel it again, all my bones spreading out. Like the butterfly we saw come out of its cocoon at that butterfly house in the fancy garden we went to with Glenda. Dad takes my feet in his big warm hands and holds them.

"What about you and Glenda, Dad?" I've met her four times. The first time, she said, "Aren't you sweet! I can see your dad in you. How old are you? What grade are you in? Does she talk?" and gave me a frilly pink and yellow dress that was too small. Why did she think I would like anything frilly and pink and yellow? She should have asked. I would

have told her. Dad could have told her. But Dad squeezed
my arm hard and told me to thank Glenda and then he told
her not once but three times it was a beautiful dress, the
most beautiful dress anyone had ever given me, and we
all went to McDonald's. I hate McDonald's, Mom says it's
garbage food and we shouldn't eat there, but *Glenda* said it
so we had to go.

Dad doesn't answer. He gets up and walks to the truck
and shoves my skates behind his seat, then comes back
with my purple boots and kneels in front of me again.
He never helps me with my boots anymore. I'm too big.
I'm almost ten. I want to tell him I'm sorry about skating
because I want the day to be different, I want us to go home
and sit around the table talking about all the lake stuff and
making those growly noises and saying *yeah, yeah* together
about everything, our legs spread out and our knees
touching, but when he holds my foot in his big hands,
making it warm before slipping on my boot, so slow, then
my other foot, I know I don't need to say anything, he's
telling me everything's okay, I don't need to say anything.

Dad goes back to the truck and sits in his spot. He turns
his body so it faces out and takes off his own skates, then
holds them by the blades and looks at them for a long time
like he doesn't know what they're for. Finally he shoves his
skates behind his seat with mine, pulls on his big white
boots and walks back to the bench without tying the laces.
He takes my hand and squeezes it, not tight.

"Let's go," he says.

I squeeze his hand back as hard as I can and even pull his
arm. But when I look up at his face, he's looking somewhere

behind me like I'm not there. He yanks his hand away and starts to trudge across the lake toward the fire by himself, staring down at the ice. It's not okay, then, that I don't like skating. I knew things would turn out like this, back at the rental place, when he was so excited. When he didn't listen.

I walk through the shrubs beside the lake. It's a little longer and there's no path, but I am not going back on that ice, not for anything.

It's slippery all around the fire ring from everybody standing here. The fire makes the snow melt and freeze, melt and freeze. That's what the dads say. The icy spots are black and sooty from the burned wood that ends up there. The fire is huge now. Dad keeps adding chunks of wood. He brought his little saw and he's cutting up a big dead tree branch. Jim and Paramel stand by the fire. Mika and Beth sit at a picnic table drinking hot chocolate. In my mind Mom's there, too, drinking hot chocolate and talking and laughing like she's known them forever and they're her friends, too.

The kids are still skating. They would skate all day and night. Harley and her brother Dante are zipping around in small loops close to the fire. The two big boys, Charlie and Aiden, are at the far end of the lake, near the spruces.

"Slow down there, Paul," Paramel says. "You're going to burn down the whole damn forest."

"There's lots more where this came from," Dad says.

"When's it weenie time?" Dante calls.

"Is The Poet hungry?" Dad asks, not looking at Dante. The Poet is the dumbest nickname he ever gave anyone. Sometimes he says it the way he says "that woman" when he means Mom.

"He's always hungry," Jim says.

"Hang tight, Poet," Dad says. "We're working on it." Then he sees me. "There you are, Ding Dong."

When I turn to Dad I slip on the ice by the fire ring and fall on the black soot. It's as hard as the lake. Even through my snow pants I can feel it. I wipe the muck with my mitt but now my mitt is dirty so I stop.

"You okay?" Mika asks.

"She's okay," Dad says. "Ding Dong is a klutz, haven't you noticed?"

"Why do you call her that?" Harley asks.

"What, Ding Dong? She is a Ding Dong. Oh, for God's sake, Willow, keep out of the mud. Look at the back of your snow pants. Look at your mitts. I can't take you anywhere."

I hold my wet mittens over the fire. If I don't look at Dad and Harley, maybe they'll forget I'm here. I thought he meant Christmas bells.

"How'd you get a name like Willow anyway?" Harley asks.

"Her mother was on drugs." Dad makes a funny hissing-laughing sound through his teeth.

Mika says "*Paul!*" fast and hard, the way you talk to little kids or dogs when they're doing something bad and you want them to stop *now*. It was bad. Mom was not on drugs. She would have told me.

"It's true," Dad says. "C'mere, Willow." He grabs my shoulder and tries to pull me to him, but I don't let him get me too close.

"Let's start," Beth says in her talking-to-grown-ups voice. "She'll join us later."

"Right," Dad says. I'm so close to him that I feel his body change. It gets heavier. "Hey, Poet, go get the boys and tell them it's time to roast wieners." He gets his jackknife and rips open a package of hot dogs.

Now all the kids are here, pushing in, holding their hot-dog sticks over the coals. The other kids shove each other and laugh but nobody slips. Dante bumps into me and says, "Oops, sorry, kid." Because I'm not like them. When they shove each other, they don't say sorry or anything like that. The person who gets shoved just laughs and does it right back, but not so hard that anyone falls but if anyone does they just laugh and get up and no one says anything, not even the adults, not even Dad. I watch my hot dog blister and spit and crack and pretend the other kids aren't there. Dad helps me pull the hot dog off the stick and into a bun. The picnic table is piled with stuff he brought, the squirty mustard and a huge bottle of ketchup and relish and even sauerkraut.

"Glenda likes sauerkraut," Dad tells Jim. "Had to look all over for the stuff." He's joking but nobody laughs and while he waits for someone to laugh he turns red, right up to his ears, and then coughs and says, "Willow, look at your coat!" There's a huge blob of ketchup on my zipper. "She's covered in mud and ketchup. You see why I call her Ding Dong," Dad says to Harley. He makes a sound that's half a laugh, to get her to laugh.

But Harley doesn't. "You shouldn't call her that," she says quietly, not looking at him. "It's not nice."

"It's because I love her so much. She's my Ding Dong." Dad puts his arm around me again but I wriggle away and walk back to the fire. He was mean about Mom. He was mean about my coat. And mean about my nickname. It was a nice name, before.

"Willow, I'll bet you're an expert at roasting marshmallows," Mika says.

I pretend she's not here. I pretend it's just me and Mom and I'm invisible. I know how because sometimes Mom imagines she's invisible. She makes it so her body is there but the rest of her isn't and she's so quiet, so still, you almost can't tell if she's breathing and even if I poke her, gently, she doesn't look.

"There's a coupla bags in the cardboard box," Dad says. He cuts branches from the bushes and hands everybody a stick. He wants the whole day to be great, not just the skating and the hot dogs but even the marshmallows at the end.

I roast one golden brown and puffy the way Dad likes it. "Here, Dad," I say as nice as I can so he won't be so mean for a while.

"No thanks," he says, not even looking at it. Then he sort of tips his head and says, "Oh, all right," and pulls it off and pushes it into his mouth, all at once.

The parents stop adding wood to the fire and tell the kids not to put any more on. That means we'll be going soon. The sun is almost behind the spruce trees on the far side of the lake.

When the adults are tossing the hot dog wrappers and dirty napkins into the big metal garbage bin, Beth puts her hand on Dad's arm and says quietly, "I'm sorry."

"Yeah, well," he says. "Win some, lose some."

Dad chucks the leftover buns and toppings into the cardboard box he brought, and we go back to the parking lot. The kids still have their skates on, so they skate across. By the time I get there Harley and Dante are in the back of their station wagon, and the big boys are climbing into their van. They're already in their boots. I wait by the door to our truck while Dad says goodbye to the dads. There's always a long goodbye with grown-ups, especially the moms. They talk and talk like they're never going to see each other again. Dad and Jim and Paramel stand on Dad's side of the truck and stare down at their feet, kicking loose pebbles with the sides of their boots and mostly saying, yup, yup, and laughing at the same time. Beth and Mika are in front of the truck, talking quietly. I move over to them.

"I had a feeling she wouldn't show," Mika says. "I thought something was up when I saw her at the store yesterday."

"Oh geez, what?" asks Beth.

"Oh, hi, Willow," Mika says. She gives me a hug. "Hope you had a good time. Skating will get easier, you'll see. Maybe your mom or dad will put you in lessons if you ask. Beth, I'll call you later."

I get in the truck and do up my seat belt.

Dad gets in. The cab stinks of the hot dogs, the burned sugar from the marshmallows the big boys turned black for fun, the wood smoke. All mixed together it's like the stinky garbage smoke.

"Buckle up," he says. "We're off."

"I am buckled!" I look down at my purple boots and stomp them. He wrecks everything. The day wasn't about taking me to Devil's Lake to skate for the first time. It wasn't even about skating at all. He doesn't think I know this. But I do know. I do. I look at the road and then at him. "I wrecked your day, huh."

"What?" Dad looks confused. "You didn't ruin my day. Someone else did."

I turn to look outside so he can't see my tiny smile. I got him to say it.

Dad brushes his hair with his grimy fingers and it sticks up a little from sweat and not being washed. His face looks warm. "I had this idea," he says. "I actually had a—oh, you won't get it."

"Won't get what?"

"I had a ring. All right? I was going to give her a fucking ring. You get it?"

"Yeah, Dad." I try not to sound mad. Not just because he didn't think I'd get it. Because he didn't ask me.

"'Yeah Dad.' Of course you don't get it. You're too young. You're, what, eight? Maybe one day you'll get it."

He puts his hand on mine and squeezes it, but not hard. I grab his big hand with both of mine and squeeze as hard as I can and then harder, because I want him to know what it feels like to have his bones scrunched so hard you think they will break. I squeeze so hard I make a little growling sound. Dad laughs. He doesn't know it's not funny.

"Geez. I love you too, Ding Dong," he says.

Everything's Fine, Actually

KIM FELT IT when she was drying him after his bath. The lump was a small bulb at the base of Ben's skull, so small she almost missed it.

"Don't." Ben reached up and pushed her hand away.

"Does it hurt?"

He shook his head.

"How long has it been there?"

Ben lifted one shoulder up and down.

Kim grabbed his shoulders and squeezed gently. "Was it in summertime? Or after Kindergarten started?"

"I dunno."

She was about to give him a small shake to jog his memory but was stopped by something dark filling his hazel eyes. This look was never directed at Troy. Troy who could do no wrong. She sat back and watched him put on his pajamas.

Kim told Troy about the lump near the end of the ninth episode of the Danish murder mystery they had been watching since June.

"Where is it?" Troy asked, not looking away from the screen.

"Here." Kim pushed gently at the base of Troy's skull.

"Ow!" Troy lifted her hand away. "He probably whacked his head on the monkey bars and it's swollen. Or Oliver threw a dinosaur at him. Or a rock." Troy laughed.

Ben and Oliver had known each other since being dragged out of Laugh and Learn at the Idylwylde library before they were two. Kim and Tessa had told the story so often the boys told it themselves now, with embellishments, though of course they remembered none of it; they were still preverbal and basically prehuman. In the boys' version of the great escape, they were hauled by their big toes, or their ear lobes, or their pinkies, and screaming at the top of their lungs. The real version is that three minutes into the second Laugh and Learn, Kim scooped up Ben, who wanted to roughhouse with the other kids, and hauled him out (not by his toes, but in a what baby books call a football hold). When she deposited him in the sand under the swings, she saw that Oliver and Tessa were right behind her. Oliver wriggled free and began roughhousing with Ben. Kim was surprised to see Tessa was on the verge of tears. Kim might have cried too but she had no tears left; she'd cried her last cry long before Ben was born. It was strange, not being able to cry anymore. Something wasn't right about that. Tessa looked okay after a few seconds, and both of them started laughing. Now the boys were chasing each other. All of a sudden they stopped, looked at each other, and flopped onto the grass like happy dead dogs.

"He's a kid," Troy said. "I'll bet you any money it'll be gone in three days. I give everything three days. Maybe a week." He spoke quietly now. "Kim. It could be worse. Everything can always be worse."

She didn't look at him. "I'll call Dr. Garga in the morning."

"*Don't worr-y, be ha-ppy*," he sang.

✳ "Has the swelling gone down, Ben?" Troy asked over breakfast.

"Stop talking about it," Ben droned through a mouthful of cereal.

"The answer is no," Kim said. Before waking him, she'd touched the back of his neck. It could be growing. She couldn't tell. She'd also called Dr. Garga. The appointment was next week.

"Can Oliver come over?" Ben asked.

"What, today?" Kim said.

"After daycare." At lunch Ben and Oliver walked from Kindergarten across the small field and through the playground to the daycare in the community hall. Most days they traded T-shirts on the way over and Ben came home in Oliver's shirt. Sometimes a plastic velociraptor came home with Ben and went back the next day. Because that is what half-brothers do, Ben said. Your half-brother, he explained impatiently when Kim asked, was the brother you lived with half the time. Tell her, Dad, Ben had gone on, exasperated. She knows, buddy, Troy had said, but Ben had only looked skeptical.

"For a little while, if Tessa says it's all right," Kim said.

"No, wait, can I go to his house instead? He's got a better dinosaur setup," Ben said.

"Oh, don't tell me you're doing that already," Troy said. "Before you know it you'll be telling me Oliver has a car and you don't. What's he got?"

"No I won't. The wheels keep falling off his Tonka."

"All's well, then." Troy put his coffee mug in the dishwasher and sang, "*Don't worr-y, be ha-ppy*."

"Dad, I hate that song!" Ben covered his ears. But he was smiling.

"Since when?"

"Since you always sing it!"

"It's a good song. Words to live by. Trust me. You'll be singing them when you're old and grey like me, buddy." Troy walked to the back door and called, "See you after work."

"I don't go to work!" Ben called back.

"Yes, you do. Those places you take the dinosaurs all day. That's your work. Kid work." Troy kissed his hand and held it up to Kim and Ben, high and flat, like a stop sign. The love in Troy's eyes was intense.

Kim was certain she loved Ben. Not the way other mothers loved their children. Not the way Troy loved Ben. Her love was precarious, conflicted, and a little painful at times. Troy's gargantuan love was curious. There was no doubt he was the better parent. *There* was irony for you. His imagination, his attention, his patience, all of it was huge. Most days Kim felt like she had burn blisters on random body parts, outside and in. The rawness, the soreness. Occasionally the feeling went away for a day or two, but by the time she realized it was gone, it came back.

Kim took Ben to school, waited while he laboriously changed out of his outdoor shoes into his indoor shoes and scuffed into his classroom, waved him a kiss, and then drove to work. She worked in the children's section of the downtown library. She loved the space, though it had one odd thing: the big windows near the picture books abutted the bus shelter. This was the north side of the building; it was dark and dank in that shelter, sometimes gungy. Pigeons flapped in, splatted white droppings, flew out. People slept there. The first time Kim saw someone, the mound in her peripheral vision unmoving as she made her way along the low stacks shelving books, she'd thought the heap was clothing. Because people dumped things there, too, beside the big black garbage can. But the clothing moved and a man sat up, languidly, and turned to look at her. His long thick hair hung past his ears. It was an outdoors face, a face always in the sun and the wind. She stared from the other side of the two panes of glass, the library window and the bus shelter window, holding an oversized picture book awkwardly. What was it? *Cloudy with a Chance of Meatballs? Are You My Mother?* They stood so close they could touch. Not two feet separated them. It was the end of January. He must have felt the cold even in the marrow of his bones. After a few seconds he blinked, slowly, and looked away. Only then did she pull back. This was the man's home, his sanctuary. He was just waking up, after all.

In the bus shelter this morning were traces of last night: needles, used condoms, bits of burger and lettuce and half a bun strewn across the bench. In Kim's hometown, the library was a single room in a building shared with the real estate office. The street was so quiet sometimes she saw three cars in an hour. She thought of that library when a young mother with a small child came to her and reported the needles in the washroom and later when an emergency vehicle screamed past the north window. No one had mentioned any of this at library school, though it had come up during the interview here in the city. Every winter she thought of that man she mistook, for an instant, for clothes and how first she was startled, and then he, and how they both stood, so still, so close, two panes of glass between them, and so many worlds apart, while behind her, mothers quietly read to small children and, behind him, people strode past or stood waiting for the next bus. People all around. How she knew, in that tick before he turned away, how acute his loneliness was.

From time to time she considered asking for a transfer to the adult section.

✳ "Mom, you said I could go to Oliver's," Ben said when Kim met him at the daycare in the afternoon. "He went home."

Kim sat down on the bench by the shoe rack and pulled Ben onto her lap, ruffed his thick hair a little and kissed his forehead. She tried to let her fingers brush past the back of his head gently. He pulled himself free.

"I forgot to talk to Oliver's mom," she said. She'd forgotten the entire conversation, till now.

"Mom!" Ben slid to the floor beside her and pushed his feet into his outdoor shoes.

"Maybe tomorrow, Ben," Kim said. She pulled him toward her again, smelled his sweaty head. "I'll call Oliver's mom tonight and set something up."

After dinner Troy and Ben went to Ben's bedroom to play. Kim stood in the doorway watching. Troy lay on his side, legs outstretched, and Ben squatted and hopped around the plastic toys or flopped across Troy's legs and hugged them with one arm while sending a dinosaur flying with the other. Sometimes they yipped and howled like coyotes or squeaked like pikas. Troy was an overgrown kid. Did men generally not mature, or was it just Troy?

Kim left them and called Tessa.

Kim sometimes indulged in a mini fantasy about trading places with Tessa the way Ben and Oliver traded shirts or sent toys for a sleepover. A twenty-four-hour trade, say. What would that make Tessa? Her half-wife? Because Troy deserved better. After all she had put them through. And she thought she saw a smidgen of envy in Tessa when Tessa looked at her and Troy. Maybe more than a smidgen. Tessa had even gone as far as to say, once, that Kim and Troy did everything right. As a couple. As parents. Kim knew then how well she and Troy hid everything. She hadn't told Tessa what they had gone through to have Ben. She hadn't told a soul. The less said, the sooner forgotten. Was that a saying? Now, on the phone, Kim would ask about a play date and then she'd mention the lump, casually, like it was nothing. To hear Tessa say it was nothing.

When Tessa picked up the phone, she skipped the "Hey, what's up?" and said, "Kim. He was a prick. And he doesn't want children. Why didn't he say so in his profile?"

"That he's a prick?" Kim said.

Tessa laughed a little and Kim felt relieved. But then Tessa started up again. "This is my life. I come with a kid!"

"I know," Kim said.

"You and Troy." Tessa sighed. "You. And Troy. And Ben. God you three are lucky."

The way she spoke, Kim knew Tessa had been drinking. Kim had a feeling that whatever Tessa said next would either be completely wrong or a thing she felt deep down but was afraid to say when she was sober. Quickly, Kim said, "I have to go."

✳ Dr. Garga lifted Ben's hair and looked at the back of his neck. Her face remained neutral, though from time to time she said, "Mmm."

"I don't know what it is," she said finally. "I'm going to refer you to a colleague. It will take some time."

"This means she's not concerned," Troy said after they'd dropped Ben off at daycare. "If she was concerned, she would have pushed for an earlier appointment."

"She doesn't know, Troy. She told us she doesn't know."

"*Don't worr-y, be—*"

"Oh, stop. I hate that song too."

"Why? It's a great song."

It was November when they finally met with Dr. Anders. The doctor was tall and tanned, probably from going to places like Cancun or the Dominican Republic, and had annoyingly kind, warm brown eyes. He had age lines around his eyes and a short fat scar above his upper lip. Kim felt slightly happy about that scar. She imagined telling Tessa, but then remembered Tessa didn't know about the lump. Least said, soonest forgotten. That was how the saying went.

After the handshaking, Kim and Troy sat down. Ben crawled onto Troy's lap. A big photograph of Lake Louise

and its massive grey sentinels hung on the wall behind the
doctor. On his desk was a picture frame that faced him,
probably a photo of his wife or him and his wife and a child
or two, posing somewhere hot and costly and getting his
UV rays. There was a big window on the left, overlooking an
ancient mustard-yellow brick building with windows set
at disturbingly regular intervals, like an old psych hospital.
Thin, feverish snow whipped past the doctor's window.

"You've got a squirrel in this ear." Dr. Anders peered into
the side of Ben's head. "And a dancing penguin in this one."
The doctor had a slight accent. Scotland, north England;
Kim couldn't tell.

Ben laughed.

"And you've got a wicked kick!" Dr. Anders chortled
when he tapped Ben's knee.

Ben laughed harder and wiggled reflexively. Kim smiled.

Dr. Anders inserted the earpieces of his stethoscope and
rested the diaphragm in the general vicinity of Ben's heart.
Now he took Ben's pulse. Kim thought that would be it. But
Dr. Anders looked into Ben's eyes. Everywhere but the back
of Ben's neck. Now he was tapping Ben's knee again. (His
knee?) What a charade. To what end? So he could say, *There
was no need to come today, folks. Sorry to have troubled you.
Everything's fine, actually*.

Finally Dr. Anders sat back and said, "We'll send him for
an MRI. It will be a few days."

"A few days," Kim said. "What do you think it is?"

"I don't know yet." He turned to Ben. "Best you get back
to school, young man."

"It's my sharing time at school today," Ben told the doctor while Troy held out his puffy blue coat. "I brought my stegosaurus," he called on the way out the door. Ben talked all the way to the front entrance. "I like the doctor. Do you like the doctor? Are we coming back? When we come back, I'm going to show him my dinosaur book. I'll bring four dinosaurs. How many am I allowed? Dad? Dad? And my big book of fun facts. Are we coming back?"

Kim wanted Troy to say never, they were never coming back, but instead he said, "Don't know, buddy."

"Oh, man!"

✳ She was somebody else all those years ago, when their entire lives fit into that tiny one-bedroom apartment. She used to talk about children, or, more accurately, a *child*, and every time she did, he changed the subject. It took her a while to catch on; he wasn't obvious about it. The evening she finally did, she straddled him on the bed and cupped his cheeks and said she wanted a real answer.

"Get off me so I can breathe," he said through puckered lips.

This was before they were married. She rolled over and lay beside him. He turned to his side and bent his arm to rest his head in his hand and looked into her eyes. "I don't want a kid. Couldn't we just." He frowned. "Not?" He slid his finger up her arm. "I mean, I'm happy. Aren't you happy?" When she didn't answer, he said, "I'm just not cut out to be a dad. My dad. You don't know how he messed up. I don't want to mess up any kid."

"Oh, don't be silly." She tried to ignore how the hairs stood up where he'd run his finger along her skin.

＊ The evening before the second visit to Dr. Anders, Ben grabbed Troy's hand and pulled him toward the pile of picture books on his bed.

"Ben, give an old guy a break," Troy said.

"Dad!"

"All right, all right."

Troy leaped onto Ben's bed. Ben jumped up, slid toward Troy, and hooked his arm around Troy's head while his bare feet slowly worked their way up the wall.

"Dad," Ben said, "Dad, tell me this one. Dad!" He dropped his feet to the bed and shoved a book onto Troy's lap, then started bouncing up and down. "What's that?"

Troy chuckled. "You know what that is."

Kim watched from the hall. When Troy read to Ben, when they lay on the floor or the bed surrounded by plastic dinosaurs, they were in their own world. Their own little refuge.

"Tell me."

"It's an elasmosaurus," Troy said.

"This one!" Ben pointed.

"Plesiosaur."

"Now the fun facts." Ben flopped onto his back, his cheek against Troy's thigh, his feet flat against the wall.

"A dinosaur DOT-DOT-DOT," Troy said.

Ben sat up and blurted, rapid fire: "Is a Greek word and it means terrible lizard!"

"You got it. I'll try something harder. Birds descended from DOT-DOT-DOT."

"Theropods!" Ben shouted.

"Hmm. I'll stump you yet. The smartest—"

"Troodon!" Ben shouted and hopped off the bed.

"You are amazing!" Troy gave Ben a huge grin. There was nothing ironic in the way Troy spoke to Ben. Kim wondered, sometimes, if this was a form of atonement. Being the perfect dad. Why couldn't she atone?

"Are you mad about my lump, Dad?" Ben asked.

"What? No."

"You are. Mom is too."

"She's not."

"The doctor's mad."

"Nobody's mad," Troy said. Ben climbed onto his lap. Troy kissed the top of his head and stared at the carpet near Kim's toes.

"Read, then," Ben said, pointing.

"The dumbest—"

"Stegosaurus!"

"Ah, let me finish! The dumbest dinosaur had a brain the size of what?"

"A walnut! Puny!" Ben pointed. "Read about that dinosaur that can grow back its teeth."

"The diplodocus?"

"Yes!" Ben leaped in the air, a victory leap.

Kim went to bed. Troy joined her, late. They had done this before, stopped talking about things. So it was easy now, not to talk. She stared at the dark ceiling. Snow fell all night and blackness eventually gave way to grey. She didn't know what she felt. It was possible she hadn't known, really known, what she felt since Ben was born. At six in the morning she turned on the radio. The meteorologist was saying, *That's a feels-like temperature of minus forty-eight with the wind.*

"You will need all fourteen pairs of long underwear, young man," Troy told Ben at breakfast.

"I don't have fourteen pairs!"

"All thirteen then. Eat up, time to go."

They dropped Ben off at school and drove the snow-covered streets to Dr. Anders. The doctor looked even kinder than on the first visit. The quiet look in his eyes told Kim everything. She sat on the chair nearest him, on the edge. Troy sat beside her and took her hand.

First the doctor named it. Kim caught the word *malformation*. "It's been bleeding and will likely burst," he said. He looked from Kim to Troy and back to Kim. "Children with this condition don't live very long."

Troy squeezed her hand, hard.

Dr. Anders mentioned life expectancy. He gave a number, in months. The malformation, he went on, had begun in the womb.

He continued to speak, but it was too late; Kim saw his mouth move but didn't hear the words. Instead she stared at his lips, his clean-shaven chin, the few individual black hairs just below the skin on his also-shaved upper lip, the funny scar that she hadn't mentioned to Tessa, his straight teeth.

Now they were standing, shaking hands, moving through the open office door. She didn't feel her legs or her feet; somehow, she moved along the side corridor and then down the long hall to the automatic doors. They stepped outside and the icy air lunged into her, taking her breath.

"Not far," Troy said. "Three blocks."

They walked quickly through the sleepy residential streets, heads tipped into the wind. An inflated Santa bobbed drunkenly at them from the lawn of a blue bungalow. He was running out of air. Another Santa appeared again a few houses along, this one made of hard plastic and sprawled buck naked in a green tub.

In the car Kim's fingers were too stiff to buckle her seat belt. There was Troy, pulling her belt across, buckling, his cheek cold on hers. When he turned the key, the car whined and coughed a few times before starting. He went outside and scraped the windshield.

"Let's just drive for a bit," he said, when he was in the car. His breath a puff of white.

"All right," said Kim.

He drove and drove, first west to Highway 60 and then south. Thin snow blew across the pavement and the windshield. The roads were icy. These were the kind of roads that your guts tell you to stay off, to avoid at all costs. The kind of roads where you imagine sliding into the ditch or into an oncoming truck. Still, he drove and drove.

"I'm so cold," Kim said. Her fingers were stiff, her brain had frozen. The doctor's words sat between them like lead weights. Words like womb. Inoperable. Incurable. More words, things to watch out for: Dizziness. Seizures. Bleeding, internal. "What did he call the malformation?"

Troy took a breath. "Arteriovenous," he said slowly.

He finally stopped near Devon in the vacant parking lot facing the North Saskatchewan River. He left the motor running, the heat on high. The meteorologist's voice from the morning drifted through Kim's brain: *Air moving slowly. A feels-like atmosphere of purgatory. Periods of scattered dread.*

The bank opposite them was high and bare and wind-blown. The greyish ice on the river was broken up in massive chunks, stiff and unmoving, like the words lodged in her brain.

"The beach," Kim said, remembering. She'd never been here in winter. She'd come in summer, to swim, with Troy. Before marriage. Before Ben. Faces flickered in her subconscious, the two of them playing by the shore, discovering colourful objects. Floating toys thrashed by wind and water, plastic grocery bags, dog chews. Then, something green snagged in the branches of a downed tree. A small glass pop bottle with a note, a pen, and a cheap plastic ring. That day's date on the note. Disappointment that the bottle hadn't been travelling for months or years. Troy setting it back in the water like it was treasure, treasure they'd found and were sharing with the world. They'd spent hours there, just the two of them, in their own world, oblivious to everything outside it.

Troy took her hand again, held her with his eyes.

"Tell me again what the doctor said," Kim said. "How long."

What she wanted was for him to sing, all on his own, *Don't worry. Sing it*, she willed him. *Please, sing it.*

✳ After they married they moved into a two-bedroom apartment. She didn't know anymore who that person was, the one who wanted something so badly she ached.

"I just don't want to be a breeder," he said one day. A *breeder*. Later, thirty seconds later, he said he was joking, but it was too late. She wouldn't touch him or let him touch her. She walked around pretending she had a Plan B while her insides seeped out of her. She was a mannequin now, a body with clothes.

He blinked first. After a week of not talking, he came to her, not his usual goofy self but quiet, sober, and said, "All right. Let's."

She moved toward him, slowly, and shook a little; with relief, she thought.

"I'd do anything for you," he said.

At first, it was fun. But after a few months, it was awful. When they were done, they'd lie flat on their backs in the bed, out of sorts and confused. When she wasn't pregnant after a year, they reasoned that they simply had to try harder and more often. She had written a diary, before then. Religiously, the way a diary was meant to be written. She stopped around that time. If something wasn't written down, it could be more easily forgotten. It might not even have happened. When he came to her, she lay on her back, knees high, legs wide, and stared at the ceiling. They stopped looking at each other when he was inside her. They didn't speak or kiss or touch each other unless they had to, and then they turned away, embarrassed. Images of huge marionettes floated through her mind during the day. Lifeless creatures. One night he turned his back to her and made himself hard and forced himself inside her, and then went to the bathroom and puked. She pulled the sheet over herself and cried. When she miscarried, she cried, too, but with relief. She bled into the toilet, grateful that he wasn't there. If he was, she'd tell him she was sorry. They could stop. They should stop. Whatever it was she thought she wanted, she didn't anymore.

And then, a change. She went to her doctor, had it confirmed.

She found him sweeping the floor in the garage.

"We can." She looked away. "We can stop now. It took." She wanted to throw up.

"It took," he repeated, and she heard how odd the expression was. She'd heard someone say it once. It seemed the most expeditious but at the same time the most vague.

He hadn't shaved in a few days, his hair needed a cut and a comb, his skin was scruffy, and his eyes were sort of vacant. The words hung between them. *It took.* Took what? Took the life out of them, and then some, that was it. Took their pride, their affection, more. It took everything. She felt gutted.

"We can stop," she said.

✳ Snow, wispy like a threadbare blanket, blew over the top of the cold and naked sandstone cliff and slithered along the river. All of it, the river, the cliffs, the sky, stared gauntly back at them.

Kim saw her breath, little silvery puffs. The windshield fogged up. Her head hurt. It had a hungover feeling. Her mind tried to piece together a drunken Santa who couldn't hold himself up with a naked Santa in a bathtub. "He knows, doesn't he," Kim said.

"He fucking knows dinosaurs, that's what he knows." Troy smacked the steering wheel.

Across the river, on the cliffs, Kim made out shapes, battered by the blowing snow. A big spruce, so like a woman in a long, black-skirted coat.

Troy got out and scraped the windshield, then drove back up the side road to the main highway and north and eventually back to the city and their neighbourhood.

He parked in front of the community hall. From there they could see the playground and, beyond it, the school. Where Ben would start first grade with Oliver. It seemed right that tiny flakes of snow obscured it all.

The big room in the daycare was filled with activity stations: the giant dollhouse, the reading corner, the trains and blocks. Kim knew where to look for Ben: the round mat with the bin of dinosaurs. There he sat, feet flat on the floor, his knees up to his chin, sending his stegosaurus flying toward Oliver's T-Rex. There was no need to call out. One small head turned toward them and then toward Ben. Then another small head. And another. Turn, turn. No one said anything. It was the daycare telegraph system.

When Ben sensed the eyes on him, he looked up and bounced over to Kim and Troy.

"It's not time yet." Ben had worn his wolf hoodie in the morning. Now he was wearing the light blue sweater Tessa had knit for Oliver. Half-brother, half-wife. Kim felt immense relief.

Troy knelt and touched the sweater, squeezed Ben's shoulder. "I know, buddy. We just came to say hi."

"I need a hug," Kim said, crouching down.

"Oh man, you always need hugs." Ben reached out with his small arms. "You're freezing, Mom." He took a step back. "Brr, I'm not kissing any freezing cheeks. Hey, don't cry, it's just a joke. I'm a big joker like Dad."

"I know. Go back and play now," she said.

He galloped back to Oliver.

"The shirts," Troy said when they were in the car. "They traded. That's a sign."

Kim started to say, "Of what?" but stopped herself.

"Want I should drop you at work?" Troy asked.

Kim nodded.

The day she found Troy in the garage, she waited, expectantly, wanting him to look relieved or even a tiny bit pleased. Instead he wiped his lips with his hand and then ran his fingers through his unwashed hair and looked down at the dusty cement floor. After a long, sweaty silence he looked at her. He seemed thinner, smaller even.

"I guess you're happy now?" he said kindly. She wasn't sure later if she heard it or imagined him saying it but she nodded. She didn't say that for months she'd been hoping it wouldn't take. She didn't say that she hoped it would find a way to quietly disappear.

They moved, not long after that, into the little bungalow where Ben was born.

And now. And now. She did not know what to say, now, in the car, and so she said nothing. Troy dropped her off out front, near the bus shelter. The bus shelter that was a man's home, from time to time. She wanted to step inside it, just once.

"See you later," she said, from the curb.

The man wasn't there, today. He would return, she knew he would. And when he did, she would sit with him and

listen. Or simply sit and take in his breathing. They didn't
need to say anything. Least said, soonest forgotten. Whenever
she was in the picture book section of the library, she watched
for him. He didn't come. This went on for a year. Even after
she'd been moved to the second floor, she frequently made
her way back to the big windows and looked and still he
wasn't there. But by then she was so in the habit of
checking that she couldn't stop.

Alex
and Clayton
and Raylene
and Me

ALEX KNOCKED ME across the head. "Let's go," he said.

"Where's the dog?" I was on the floor. I'd just set up the Monopoly board. The dog piece was missing. I wanted the dog, but I used the boot now. Alex liked the top hat.

"Forget that. Let's go," he said again. He was out in the hall.

"Where?" I rooted through the box. I looked under my bed. I looked under Alex's. No dog. It was always missing. "Are we weeding?"

"Of course not, dumbhead."

Alex put his finger on his lips. For a few seconds we didn't move or speak or breathe. Grandpa and Grandma were having their nap. She was across the hall from us in the big bed and he was in the covered porch past the kitchen and we could hear the snoring. He slept there at night, too. I saw him once when I got up to go to the can. Only because I heard him first. He slept with his mouth open and his whole face loose and grizzly. Grandma snored, too, but not loud. More like a soft whistle. If we wanted to see her sleeping, we could. The house was so old everything had shifted and the bedroom doors didn't close all the way. The house has its own mind, Grandpa liked to say. "Nothing for it," he'd say. "Things get a certain way after a long time on this earth and there's nothing for it. Old house might just up and walk away one night." The gap in Grandma's bedroom door was about a foot wide. But we didn't look in because she was old or a girl or both.

We tiptoe-slid down the hall and through the kitchen. We knew where all the creaky spots were. Now we just had to get past Grandpa and out the porch door. Nobody ever used the front door unless they didn't know Grandpa and Grandma. It was dark over by that door and crammed with stuff. Sometimes a Jehovah's Witness came and rang the bell and we just froze wherever we were and held our breath and tried not to giggle till they left.

I kept my eyes on Grandpa when we crept past. Alex opened the screen door slowly so it didn't screech. He held it while I slipped past him, then closed it by putting his fingers on the door frame so it wouldn't bang. We were pretty good at that now too.

"We're not weeding?" I said, when we were away from the house.

"What weeds?" Alex asked, scooting ahead into the woods.

"Grandpa said to weed the potatoes."

In a squeaky voice Alex said, "Grandpa said to weed the potatoes." He turned around. "You can stay behind if you want. I'm going to have some fun."

He walked faster. I ran a little to keep up. The woods were shady but hot. Baking hot. I was sick of the garden too. And everything else. It was the same every summer. Right after school ended, Mom and Dad put us on the bus to Grandma and Grandpa's. Every day we did stuff. Moved rotten old fence boards. Sorted tools. Pulled nails out of boards. Saved stuff nobody would want. And weeded the gigantic vegetable garden. I didn't know why they did the garden. It was huge and things hardly grew because it was so dry up here. Today at lunch Grandpa said, "Been a drought so long we wouldn't know rain if it hit us in the face." Plus, after all that work, we had to wash and dry the dishes every night for Grandma.

"Keep yourselves busy, boys," Grandpa liked to say. "You'll make less trouble."

I used to spend ages asking myself how we could make trouble up here in the middle of nowhere.

"I'm getting a job next summer," Alex said. "Never coming back."

"Me too," I said.

We had to go single file in the woods. Alex stopped on the spot so I walked into him. He shoved me with his shoulder and snorted. "I don't think so, kid."

I grabbed a stick and whacked the dry grass. Alex was going to be fifteen by the end of summer. I was only eleven. Sometimes he made me feel like I was five. So I just followed. I didn't know where he was taking us; I never knew. Sometimes we walked around for a while on the animal trails trying to get lost. Alex always said you could walk for hours and not see anyone but there was no way

you could get lost up in this part of the world because
everything lined up. Everything went by road allowances,
barbed wire fences, fields, shelter belts, and maybe a creek
or a river. Sometimes there were big patches of trees, like
Grandpa had, and sometimes we didn't know the best way
back, but we never got lost, no matter how hard we tried.

Alex took us to the river. It was about a mile from the
house. We weren't supposed to go there without Grandpa.
He said it wasn't safe. But the water wasn't all that deep or
very fast, in most parts anyway. In some places it was only
up to my neck.

We flung our clothes on the grass in a heap and stood
buck naked pounding our fists on our chests and grunting
and howling.

Alex squeezed my arm. He didn't have to say it was puny;
I knew it was. I didn't have any muscles. Then he pulled
me into the water and dunked me under. He tried to keep
me down but I always got up. Because he let me. I climbed
on him and he threw me in, but not hard. He grabbed me
again and tried to push me under. He was really strong and
he knew how far to push. It was like he knew what was too
much but never went that far. That was how we played; it
was what I liked about playing with him, being that close,
smelling his smell, knowing he knew what to do. Knowing
he knew things about me nobody else did. I was crazy about
Alex. This was before I found the dog piece.

"Swamp creature." Alex splashed water at me and we
laughed.

Then we heard another laugh. There were two kids in
the short grass across the river from where we'd left our

clothes. The girl looked a little older than me, maybe Alex's age. The boy looked a bit older than Alex. It was the girl who was laughing. Not at us, but at the boy, at something he said. They took off their clothes too, except for their gonch, though the girl kept her T-shirt on, and then they were in the water.

Alex and I splashed over to the shore and put on our boxers as fast as we could. Then he started talking to the boy like he knew him. He's still like that. Before I knew it we were into a game of tag. Not normal tag. You had to grab someone's ankle and pull till their head was under water for them to be "it." After a few minutes, we only wanted to tag the girl. She laughed a lot at the boy and Alex, especially when she got away.

We stayed for hours. Grandpa was mad when we got back. Mad about us going to the river on our own, mad about the weeding. He was so mad we didn't tell him about the other kids.

When we went to the river the next day, Clayton and Raylene were there again. We got going in a game of tag right away, but they had to go pretty soon after we got there, so we left too.

"Are they brother and sister or boyfriend and girl-friend?" I asked.

"Brother and sister, pea brain."

"How do you know? Did he tell you?"

"He doesn't have to. I can just tell."

"How?"

Alex groaned. "It's how you do it."

"Do what?"

"Everything. You talk different to your girl. You do things to see what she likes. To see how much you can do."

"Like what?"

"They don't kiss. For instance. The rest you can figure out on your own."

Raylene and Clayton were there the next day and the next. Raylene stayed on the shore when we roughhoused even though Clayton tried to get her to come in. Sometimes he pulled her shirt so that if she didn't move, her shirt would come right off. So she had to come. Alex really liked it when she came in, but he didn't play with me as much when she was there. It was the same when we went through the woods on their side, exploring and climbing trees. Alex and Clayton tried to get her in a game. They wanted her to be "it" no matter where we were. It was like I wasn't there sometimes.

We didn't go to the river for a few days and the next time we did, they weren't there. I didn't tell Alex, but I was glad. I wanted to ask him again if he was sure Raylene was Clayton's sister. How could you tell when sometimes she didn't even talk to him? But he was too busy dunking me and throwing me in. It was almost like before. Almost, because he kept looking down the path they always came from.

The next day, before we left the house in the afternoon, Alex reached into Grandma's purse and pulled something out. She always left her purse on the counter by the toaster.

"C'mon," he said. We got into Grandpa's truck and he put it in reverse and made me help push it to the end of the lane.

"You can drive?"

"Nothing to it." Alex pulled a key from his shorts pocket and started the engine.

"Where are we going?"

"Been wanting to do this all summer."

"You're not wearing your seat belt."

"Anybody in this truck say you have to wear your seat belt?"

I didn't click mine either. It didn't matter, because there weren't any cars on the road. Alex drove all the way to the gas station on the highway.

"Wait here," Alex said. He went in for a few minutes and came out with four gigantic Slurpees in a box lid. "Hold this. Don't drink yet."

He drove us back to the house and halfway up the lane we had to get out and push the truck so we wouldn't wake Grandma and Grandpa. Then he took the lids off the Slurpees and poured something into each of them.

"This is going to be so good," he said.

"What's that?"

He looked into my eyes and said calmly: "Laughing gas."

We took off to the river. Clayton and Raylene weren't there.

"Now what," I said.

"Wait, dumbhead."

We went into the water with our trunks on and when we came up they were sitting on a big flat rock by the edge of the river with their feet in the water.

"Hey," Alex said. "Brought you these." He handed out the Slurpees.

"Hey, thanks," Clayton said.

The Slurpees were half melted, but I was so hot I guzzled mine. It was good, sweet but with a funny taste.

Raylene gave Alex a funny look. "What'd you put in this?"

"Laughing gas," I told her.

"It's pretty good," Clayton said. After a bit he said, "You guys from around here?"

"Sorta," said Alex. "Just over there." He looked in the direction of Grandpa and Grandma's. "You guys?"

Clayton nodded slowly and gave us a big smile.

I drank and drank and felt my stomach bulge like a gigantic pumpkin. I stood up and walked around shouting "Lookit my pumpkin! Lookit my pumpkin!" and laughing.

"Sam's got peas for brains," Alex said. He was giggling. He never giggled.

"He's just a kid," Raylene said to Alex. "He'll get sick."

"Make your T-shirt wet again," Clayton said to her.

"Shut up." Raylene flung her hair behind her. She had bright hazel eyes that looked like marbles.

"Then take it off. Take everything off." Alex took a long suck of his drink, and then he said, still looking at her, "Good, hey, Sam?"

"Good." I went into the trees to take a leak before I burst. I walked a little way in and kept my back to them. I watered the dry grass for ages. The trees were tilted. The laughing gas was making me giggle and I couldn't stop. Everything was funny and I was filled with love for Alex and Clayton and Raylene and Grandma and Grandpa and the whole world. I was bursting with love.

Clayton said, "Now Raylene will come in and play tag."

"Raylene will not play tag," Raylene said slowly. "Raylene will have a nap."

I turned around. Alex and Clayton were wrestling with her, not really wrestling, but tickling her and trying to pull off her clothes. First slow, then watching and waiting, and then suddenly quick, the way Alex sometimes roughhoused with me. I didn't say anything because my head was full of bees and flies. I knew they were outside my head but it felt like they were inside. On hot days you heard the bees and the flies, and today they were loud. I pushed at my head to get them out.

When I got back to the water, Alex, Clayton, and Raylene were tilted like the trees under the too-bright sun and moving from side to side. Alex held Raylene under the shoulders. Clayton held her ankles. She was giggling and trying to kick her legs but without really trying, like she was tired.

"Cut it out!" Raylene said, but smiling, as if she was joking.

"Sam!" Clayton said. "C'mon. We're—" he stopped, he was laughing so hard. "We're gonna show her a lesson. We'll hold her."

"Sam!" Alex called. "Come jump on her knees."

I went closer. They were still tilted and flicking and I was overflowing with love for them. They all shook hard from laughing, even Raylene. She had laughing tears sliding down her cheeks. The sun was so bright now it speared into my head like a bunch of knives. Raylene was too high for me to get on. She was nearly as high as their waists. I would have to climb up on her and then jump. Like on a trampoline. I wanted to do that, because I was mad about her being here even though I loved her and Alex and Clayton. I stared at them and tried figure out how to get up onto her knees. But I could hardly walk. I sat down, hard.

"Sam! C'mon," Clayton said. "Before I drop her!"

"Ow," Raylene said, kicking at Clayton and not laughing. He was squeezing her ankles. "Okay, you've had your fun, put me down."

"On the knees," Alex said again. "Jump on 'em. Time to teach her a lesson. Maybe break them."

"Cut it out!" Raylene said again, spitting in Clayton's direction. "Sam, they don't mean it. It's just playing."

"How about," Clayton said, "how about we dunk her instead."

Clayton and Alex walked with her to the edge of the deepest part of the river and swung her back and forth. "On three!" Clayton yelled.

"One!" Alex shouted.

Then Clayton: "Two!"

"Oh fuck!" Raylene yelled.

"Three!" Alex and Clayton screamed together and threw her in. They fell in, backwards. For a second they were up to their necks and sliding down the river on their butts and letting out whoops. I held my pumpkin belly and laughed so hard I had to piss again.

﹡ I have a daughter now. Lily is three. For a while last winter and into spring my wife and I had a babysitter named Char. Char lives in our apartment building. Bottom floor, north end. We needed someone to stay with Lily when Jen was at her massage course and I was at work. We needed someone close, someone who could get here on her own. We needed someone to help us, to see a way through for us. We needed a lot of things.

The first time I met Char, I felt funny and started to laugh at something she said when she handed her references to Jen and then felt embarrassed and stopped. It took me weeks to see why.

✳ Alex and Clayton and Raylene didn't get very far. They all drifted close together, or maybe they swam, or crab-walked, but when I looked up they were near each other. Probably Alex and Clayton were helping her. The water was almost up to their necks, not because it was deep, but because they were play-fighting or wrestling. They were doing something I couldn't see. In slow motion. There was not much of a current so they weren't even moving downstream. They were smiling in a funny way and not talking and their eyes were mostly closed. Except Raylene's. She was looking at them both, a glassy, dark look, and her lips were in a line. Whatever they were doing, they did it for a long time. I stopped laughing. Now I was really mad at Alex. I wanted it to be just Alex and me in the water.

They floated to a big rock and flopped onto it. I watched for a bit but I was so tired I fell back on the ground. After a long while I sat up. I knew it was a long while because the sun was lower and the air was a little cooler. Clayton and Raylene were gone. Alex and I looked at each other like we'd just woken up. When Alex took me in, his eyes got huge.

"We gotta go, kid," he said. He sounded worried, not mean. We put on our clothes and trudged back.

✳ This past year or so has been funny. I've hardly seen Jen because of her course and my work. We've arranged it now so one of us is always home with Lily. When we are home together, Jen's tired. Some days we don't talk about anything besides what Lily is eating and if we're getting low on diapers. We aren't doing it. Every day I ask myself if this is normal.

✳ Alex got a job, like he said. I went to Grandma and Grandpa's on my own after that. The first summer I went alone, I stayed close to the house. Grandpa wasn't like before, when he kept trying to get Alex and me to help, to keep us out of trouble. It was like he was too tired. Mostly he talked about his garden. He'd take a handful of soil and watch it slide, like dry sand, through his big, cracked fingers and say, "We need a good rain, Sam. A good soaker. We've had too many years of drought. We're due for a wicked forest fire in these parts." He'd kneel in front of a potato plant, root out three small potatoes and reach up with his other hand for me to help him up. Other days he'd look at me, his eyes clear, and say, "Some days you just put one foot in front of the other, Sam. That's how you make a life."

The last summer I spent at their place, when I was fourteen, I was afraid that one or both of them would keel over and die when I was there alone with them. I didn't know how someone died, but I imagined an old person might just stop breathing and slowly fall down. Maybe at lunch,

Grandma would just tip over onto her plate. Grandpa would collapse in the row of peas he was weeding.

If they died when I was there, I wanted it to be at night, when they were already lying down. Every night, though, I waited for the snoring. Once, when I didn't hear any sound, I peered through the gap in the big bedroom door at Grandma. Her eyes were closed, her mouth was open a little and her face was the same light tan colour of the soil that drifted through Grandpa's hands and so still I thought she'd stopped breathing. I didn't leave till I heard the whis- tling sound.

I found the missing Monopoly dog that last summer, near the end of August. It was in the small gap between the peeling lino and the wall beside Alex's bed. I was sure we'd looked everywhere. He must have hidden it on purpose. I put it on the small table between the two narrow beds and tapped it with my finger, going over in my mind how I'd tell Alex, casually, and see if he'd let slip that he knew where it was all along. I'd mention the gap between the lino and the wall. Maybe we'd laugh about it. Probably not. Probably he'd pretend he'd forgotten about it. He was like that. He had a way of turning things around to make me feel small. I wanted him to feel bad anyway.

I stopped tapping when I heard the funny sound, tight and cloggy breathing, and went out to the hall. It wasn't snoring. It was like someone couldn't breathe. I waited for the sound to stop, but I didn't want it to stop, because that would mean something worse. The breathing was hoarse. Wheezy. I ran out to the front porch for Grandpa. He wasn't there. I kept on, to the garden. Not there either.

I went back inside and tiptoed down the hall to the bedroom. The wheezing sounds had stopped. Everything had stopped. I stood still and wondered how long I would have to wait till I had to call someone.

After a minute, I heard talking. Grandpa and Grandma. Talking to each other. They spoke quietly, so I couldn't hear what they were saying, but they were both making sounds like giggling. Two old people, giggling! Like little kids. I peered in the gap and there they were in the big bed, close together, with just the sheet drawn up over them. When I looked at their faces, Grandma was staring straight at me, her eyes like the ice on the creek in spring, clear and blue and cold. But I felt hot all over.

∗ Grandpa and Grandma died last year, not of age, but on the highway, in a collision. They weren't very old. They just seemed old when I stayed with them. Old, and sort of peaceful. The way they walked through the house and touched each other on the arm or gave each other a certain look. Seeing Grandma and Grandpa like that only made me lonelier and wishing I was with Alex, who was somewhere else, with other people, having fun.

∗ The last time we hired Char was at the beginning of May. Jen was at her night class, I was at work. I got home first, around eight o'clock. I was bagged. As soon as I walked in I went for the fridge and grabbed a beer. Char was flopped on her back on the couch, flicking through stuff on her phone. She got up when I cracked the beer. Instead of leaving, she came to me and took the beer and guzzled. So I opened

another. She was wearing a plain white T-shirt like the ones
Raylene always wore. Underneath Char had on leggings.
She had a sort of glow. She strolled out to the balcony and
I followed. We sat on the wobbly wooden bench and talked
about Lily, the park Char took her to that afternoon, the
way Lily poured sand on Char's head. Ordinary stuff. I
could picture it. It was funny. Char must have been a mess.
A cute mess. Hearing about the sand made me want to take
Lily to the park with Jen.

After a bit I lifted Char's shirt a little. She looked
surprised, but only for a second or maybe even less than a
second, so I kissed her. I felt like if I didn't do anything now,
I never would. I wanted her to see me differently. Char. Jen
too. Mostly Jen. I wanted that feeling I used to get with Alex
when he wrestled with me and knew how far to go. I don't
know how he knew. I wanted to know.

Char and I didn't say anything. We were too focussed on
kissing and trying to touch each other and trying to breathe
normally but we couldn't really breathe and it was warm.
She seemed to expect everything: her shirt coming off,
then her bra, then my hands moving across her breasts and
down her front, her leggings coming part way down. She
didn't stop me. She just sort of watched, with her lips in a
long line. Like Raylene.

I was mostly on top of her when I heard the apartment
door open and close. Jen. I zipped and sat up.

Char pulled her shirt back on, yanked her leggings up.

The screen door to the balcony was closed and we hadn't
turned the outside light on but still, it was May, it was a
bit light out. Jen was looking down at something, a letter
maybe, and slowly making for the couch. She was just

about to flop down on it when Char flung open the screen
door and burst in.

"Oh, hi," Jen said. "Sam not home yet?"

Char didn't say anything. Her back was to me so I couldn't
see her face. I just saw that she stopped, then kept going,
faster. Her hair was mussed and her bra was scrunched in
her hand, in front of her somewhere. Then Jen turned her
head toward the balcony and saw me.

✳ Early in June, I take Lily to a lake. The day's a scorcher.
The lake water is frozen, not cold, but like in a painting.
Frozen. And grey, even though the sun is out. Jen's eyes are
that lake, the hot and cold of them. Like Grandma's that day
she and Grandpa were in their bed not dying. The warmth
that slid through me when Grandma saw me watching, I
still feel it. It's a thing, a living, breathing thing. It was there
the times I made love with Jen, in the shadows, waiting to
fling itself on me. It was there the whole time I was out on
the balcony with Char and later, when I told Jen about Char.
Jen didn't ask me to leave, that night. She didn't up and
leave either. I don't know why. This thing, whatever it is,
and Jen not leaving, they have a power over me.

The heat today is so heavy it owns me, it's got sweaty
paws in my skull even. I carry Lily along the sand. She
smells like sunshine. I kiss her mussed and wild hair that
makes her look like Jen till she turns to look at me, catches
my eyes with hers. You can tell by Lily's eyes that she's in
love with the world.

"Let me down, Dad," she says, wriggling off out of
my arms.

The whole time on the balcony with Char I was desperate to tell Jen about that summer, how my brother hung out with Raylene like I wasn't there. I saw now that it wasn't about Alex and Clayton hanging out with her. It wasn't tag, it wasn't wrestling. It was something more. It was how Clayton and Alex, without talking, without anything, kept doing things to see how far they could go.

Because Raylene wasn't Clayton's sister. Alex was wrong about that.

The other thing I wanted to tell Jen was how when Alex and Clayton were under the water, making out with her, I thought Alex would have the look on his face like she was the only person in the world for him. Like he was having the time of his life. Like he knew what to do and what she wanted. And he didn't.

Lily yanks off her T-shirt and shorts and flings them in the air, and next thing I know her panties are flying over her head and she is splashing though the skiff of water along the shore. She turns and runs back toward me, arms and legs whirling. Just before she reaches me, she spins away and shouts, "C'mon, Dad. Try to catch me!"

This Will
All Be
Over Soon

BRI WENT TO HER CLOSET and ran her fingers through her dresses. Tanya needed something nice, Bri said. Something swish. Tanya sat on Bri's bed, watching. Bri had all the stuff.

"Here." Bri held up a short yellow dress.

It was a Bri dress. Tanya wore jeans mostly. But she put on the dress. She looked different anyway. Maybe she could pull this off after all.

"It's so thin," Tanya said, turning to look at her backside in the mirror. "It's like I'm wearing nothing. Is it see-through? Can you see my panties?"

"Of course not." Bri shook her head. "Now, the hair."

And then the fussing began, too much fussing. Bri was on a mission.

"What you want," Bri said, "is that slightly windblown, just-brushed *au naturel* look."

"Since when?"

"Since now. Since it's the style. Trust me." Bri stood back, nodded. "Now make-up. The trick is to put it on so nobody knows you're wearing any."

"Whatever."

Bri sang parts of a song their dad liked to sing to them, the one about the sisters. She looked at Tanya from head to toe. Bri squinted a little as she finished with the mascara, her face close to Tanya's. "All these little tricks to get you just right. Stop moving your eyes!" She lah-lahed a bit. "That song. Something about one sister wearing a dress and the other staying home, something about caring and sharing, I don't know. Dad hasn't sung it for a while." Bri stood back. "Look at you." Then she reached under her mattress and pulled out a wad of bills. "Here." She pressed the wad into Tanya's hand and pushed down hard. "You're the best. Like I said, you're doing this for you. For you. Not for me." She puckered her lips, then moved in close and grazed Tanya's lips. Tanya stepped back. She didn't know what Bri was up to. She never knew. "Promise me you'll kiss him at least. Live a little." She gave a smirk and slinked out of the bedroom, slow and quiet, like a cat.

It wasn't true, that Tanya wasn't doing this for Bri. Tanya had wanted to stay home when Bri announced she was having a party. She'd stay in her bedroom all night. No, Bri said. No. She didn't trust some of the guys with Tanya. She'd seen stuff. She knew what to look out for; Tanya did not. Tanya said too bad, she was staying home anyway. Bri pestered Tanya non-stop for three days. "All you have to do is stay out till two in the morning. You owe me. Besides, you need a date. You are about to start your last year of high school. Have you even been on one date?"

Tanya had no answer. In a time when a person could be anything, she was nothing. Her friends knew they were straight or gay or bi or trans or exploring or whatever. She was none of the above. Nothing. But she couldn't tell Bri this; Bri would think she was a freak. Tanya gave in, finally, to get Bri off her back. And so Bri wouldn't think she was a freak. Tanya always gave in, and she always hated herself for doing it.

Tanya stuffed the money into her wallet. It wouldn't close. She took the money out. So many fives and tens. She shoved them into her purse (Bri's; it was nicer than hers) without the wallet and stood in front of her bedroom window. Bri was backing out into the street in their mother's Kia and driving away, making one last rum run. The kid across the street, Markus or Magnus or Malachy, tossed a ball at the hoop above the garage door. A small white dog chased Markus-Magnus-Malachy's heels and yipped.

The big elm out front was full and mostly green. A few leaves had gone yellow, even though it was still August. A Camaro stopped under the tree, right on the dot of seven-thirty. Russ stepped out. In a suit and tie. Tanya took a few steps back when he glanced up at her window. He looked pretty good. Of course he did; she had told him to dress up.

The doorbell rang and Tanya counted to thirty-three like Bri said before walking down to the front door, slowly, one bare foot in front of the other. *Don't look rushed, don't look too eager, don't run you'll sweat, you have all the time in the world.* She did. All evening, anyway. It was going to be a good time, like Bri said. All she had to do was nod a lot and go along with everything, maybe drink something strong to relax. Okay then. She'd figure out whatever she was supposed to figure out and after tonight, they would be a regular couple. They would go on regular dates. She wouldn't have to explain who she was. She wouldn't have to wonder who she was.

She opened the front door.

"Hey," Russ said. He stepped in, swinging his arms a few times before squeezing his hands together. Blotches of red appeared on his cheeks. "You look, uh, different."

"You too."

He grinned goofily. The pants were a little long, the jacket drooped a bit over his shoulders. They were probably his brother's.

She pulled on her pumps, also Bri's; Bri'd freaked out when she saw Tanya's old flip-flops. Her mother's red sweater was draped over the bench by the door. Tanya reached for it and then stopped herself. Dumb, wearing her mother's sweater. Besides, it was warm out.

Russ stepped to the side and Tanya walked past without looking at him. If she looked at him, she'd start giggling. She did giggle a little when he opened the car door for her. Only old guys like her dad held doors for people. When Russ looked embarrassed, she stopped. She reminded herself to be like Bri and go with the flow or be cute or whatever. Only she had no clue what that was. She didn't know what other girls did. She only knew that people had always wanted to be around Bri.

Russ got in and started the car, then lowered the windows a little. "Now will you tell me where we're going?" he asked. "So I know which way to go?"

"La Ronde! The fanciest place I know."

"The revolving restaurant?"

"Are you surprised?"

"Well, yeah." Russ started to drive. "Have you been to La Ronde?"

"Never. Have you?"

"Nope."

"All the seats are along the windows, and the restaurant goes around once every eighty-eight minutes."

"Eighty-eight? Why eight-eight? How do you know?"

"It was on the website."

"Let's time it."

For a few minutes they both looked out the window without saying anything. Finally Russ said, "So, uh, you looking forward to grade twelve?"

"Sometimes yes, sometimes no."

"How come?"

"After school's over—what then?"

"Don't know yet."

"I know. I feel done. For now anyway."

Russ pulled up beside a parking meter not far from La Ronde. When they walked, Russ didn't take her hand. Maybe he would if she walked close enough. She tried that, but he didn't seem to notice. Or maybe she should just take his hand. What would Bri do? Bri went on and on about how Tanya should kiss but not how to start.

In the elevator, Tanya remembered some of the words from the song Bri sang earlier. Something about sisters and sticking together. Tanya played the bassoon in band but could never remember words to a song.

A server, a skinny man with a white shirt and a ponytail and bored eyes, walked Tanya and Russ to a table and held out a chair for Tanya. There was that feeling again that she should feel ladylike or cute. Or something. But the dress wasn't quite right. It felt tight around her thighs when she sat down. Maybe Bri lied and it really was see-through. Tanya stretched out her legs and one shoe nearly slipped off. She wiggled her toes as far into the shoes as they would go and tried not to move her feet.

On all the tables were candles in glasses, already lit, and wine goblets with white napkins folded inside them. The whole space sparkled—the shiny surfaces, the glass, the cutlery, the huge window beside them.

The server showed them drink menus. Tanya scanned the list, pretending to choose. She wondered whether he would ask for ID. Russ had just turned eighteen; he was allowed to drink. He ordered the red table wine. (And had to show his ID.)

"I can't believe you're doing this," Russ said. He read the food menu. "A Nouveau Beef Wellington. Thirty-four dollars. Pan Seared East Coast Deep Sea Scallops and Prawns. Geez. The stuff people eat. And what it costs."

"The sky's the limit. I don't know what these things are," Tanya said. "Do you?"

"Nope. Here's something: Fine Herb and Spice Crusted Veal Chop. I'll have that. I know what a chop is."

"I'll have the halibut."

"You eaten halibut?"

"No. But I've had fish. Fish is fish."

"Twenty-four storeys up, huh," Russ said, turning to look out the window after they ordered.

They saw all the way to the fields south of the city. Below them, cars filed up into downtown or headed south to the suburbs. Everything was so far away: Tanya's parents, her sister, her home. She was floating over it all. Stretched out face down, seeing everything going on but too far away to talk to anyone. She wished she felt even a little excited. This was the place her parents went, for their anniversary last year. When they went, Tanya had asked when her parents would take her and Bri.

"It's not that kind of place," her mother had said. "Someday you'll go. With the right person."

Anybody could be the right person, Bri had said, as long as you made it that way. And then: Heck, just fake it. That's what most people do.

Fake it. Tanya sipped Russ's wine. He'd ordered a glass and didn't seem to mind her taking a sip whenever the server was out of sight. The wine got less sour the more she drank.

"You can have it all if you like. I'm not much of a wine drinker," Russ said.

"Me neither."

"I couldn't tell."

She didn't know if he was joking or not. "We're not going to tell anyone about this," she said.

"The dinner?"

"The wine!" She giggled; somehow, it seemed funny now. "Because I'm underage." Luckily, Russ grinned.

She drank some more. They both looked out the window. There were Bri's lips moving in toward her, then away; that was Bri, right up close, on the edge of creepy, and then gone. Bri was always there, even when she wasn't. Tanya forced herself to focus on Russ. Russ played the flute in band and had sat in front of her for years, meaning usually she looked at his back. Or mostly his hairs at the back of his neck. Sometimes they were trimmed a bit crooked, sometimes they stuck out in a funny way, sometimes they were thick and curly and sometimes they were greasy. Once in a while Tanya and Russ said hi. Now Tanya was looking at his face. He had probably shaved a bit. He had pimples. And there was Bri again, like she was sitting beside Tanya, going on and on about the way he flattened his lips on his flute, making the staccato with his tongue so fast Tanya wouldn't be able to breathe. Then: "That's how flute players kiss. Making a staccato. See, I know what staccato means. I didn't skip that much school. Everybody just thought I did."

"Your Caesar salads," their server said, setting plates in front of them.

The salads were the one thing on the appetizer menu they were both certain about. Russ ordered another glass of wine, because Tanya said to, and sometime later their meals came. Tanya found it funny, the piece of parsley planted on top of her perfectly shaped mound of white rice. Russ's chop and something green were perched on some mashed potatoes. Everything began to feel funny and slow; what a long night it was going to be. Tanya glanced quickly down at her watch. Not even eight-thirty. One or two of Bri's friends would be arriving by now to set up or get snacks out maybe; it was still so early. Their parents wouldn't call, not now; they were all the way at the other end of the country, where everything was three hours later.

Tanya sipped wine and poked at her food. Russ dug in heartily; he ate all of his and then finished off her plate.

"No point wasting it," he said. "This costs a lot. How can you afford all this anyway?"

"I'm not allowed to say. I promised."

"That's weird." His face was blank. "That's really weird."

Tanya turned away. She wanted him to ask about her or if she wanted to go out again and where. Wasn't that how a date worked?

He drank some wine. "What's Bri doing tonight?"

She felt like she'd been shoved. "Having a party."

"Huh."

"Our parents are away."

"So, why aren't you at the party?"

Tanya frowned. "Because we're here." So he liked Bri too. Everybody liked Bri.

"Okay. I mean, this is just so weird. Does she have a lot of parties?"

Tanya looked outside again. Bri, Bri, Bri. Enough already. She gave him a hard look. "Does your brother? Have a lot of parties?"

Russ didn't answer right away. "My parents could never afford to take a vacation."

"What, like my mom and dad? They just went to Nova Scotia for a week. They never go anywhere." Because they didn't want to leave Bri. Whenever her parents talked about Bri, what they were really saying was *Don't be like Bri. Don't vanish and turn up two days later, like Bri. Don't drop out of school, like Bri.* Almost anything Tanya did now felt wrong. Being here with Russ. Covering up for Bri. Their parents couldn't find out about any of it. Tanya didn't know what they'd do. They sounded really unhappy whenever they talked about Bri. It wasn't just that Bri's life was ruined. It was that they'd failed as parents and the only thing worse than failing once would be failing all over again if Tanya messed up.

✳ When Tanya was seven and Bri was eight, Tanya took the necklace with the gold-plated flower-shaped pendant from her mother's room and put it on. Her mom had shown it to Tanya a few months earlier and told her it was special because *her* mother had given it to *her* when she was sixteen and it would be Tanya's when *she* turned sixteen. Tanya wore it around the house for a while, under her T-shirt so nobody could see it, and in the afternoon, she and Bri went into the ravine near their house. For a while they sat, tossing rocks into the creek and then poking the water with sticks. Bri saw the chain around Tanya's neck and pulled it out gently from behind Tanya's shirt.

"Where'd you get that?"

"It's Mom's."

"She let you wear it?"

"Kinda. Here." Tanya unclipped it. Bri turned it over and over and then handed it back. "It's mine anyway. When I'm older."

Bri frowned. "How come I don't have one?"

"I dunno." Tanya put it in her coat pocket. She didn't want to wear it now.

When they got home, the necklace was gone. Bri knew to look in the seams of the pocket and in her socks and shoes, but the necklace was nowhere. They walked slowly back to the creek, looking under leaves and sticks and coffee lids.

"Tanya. Stop crying. I'll tell her I lost it. It'll take nothing for them to think it's me. It won't matter."

✳ "Are you staying in band?" Russ asked, and Tanya said yes, she was, even though she knew he was just making conversation; he already knew she was staying in band. The evening was starting to feel spoiled. She liked him, as a friend. Before, anyway. Why did he have to go on about Bri? And why didn't she want to kiss him?

He ordered more wine. Because it was early. Because they were supposed to be having a good time. Because she'd wanted it to be like Bri said, fun. The restaurant made several rotations, and they forgot to time them. Outside it was growing dark. All they could see now were lights, house lights, car lights, streetlights, the flashing red from a police car, the lights of an airplane arriving from the east.

"Tanya?"

"What?"

"I was telling you about being a librarian." He frowned a little.

"Oh, yeah, sounds great."

"If I can't be a librarian I'd like to be a musician, but I don't know how to make a living that way. Maybe I'll just travel for a year, go down the west coast to San Francisco or Israel. I've been checking out these places you can live for free and work—"

"Russ. Listen. This dress. This is not my dress. These are not even my shoes." She reached down and pulled off a pump and held it up. "These are Bri's." She dropped it and slid her foot back into it.

Russ gave her another blank look. "I know." He made a goofy face. "Are you Tanya?"

"Of course I am."

"That's a relief. Why don't we order dessert?" He said it lightly, but he looked confused and small red blotches appeared on his cheeks, the way they did when he picked her up.

"All right," Tanya said.

They ordered one Chocolate Gateau with a Raspberry Ganache. Tanya discreetly checked her watch again. Just past nine-thirty. They had hours to kill. She cut a sliver of cake with the side of her fork and ate slowly. She drank more wine and the wine made her feel like talking, which felt easier than not talking and Russ didn't seem to mind. After a few minutes she shoved the rest of the cake toward him.

Russ said slowly, "You look pretty." When she didn't say anything, he looked down at her cake and ate some of it. He finished the glass of wine and looked at her again. "So you're wearing your sister's dress and your sister's shoes," he grinned. "Are you wearing Bri's underwear, too?"

Tanya sat up straight. "What?"

"At least everything fits," Russ said. He was smiling and looking funny at her now, like he had a hard time focussing on her, but his whole face was distorted, his lips too big, his eyes bulging. His cheeks were bright red. "This is the dumbest thing, both of us, I'm wearing Alan's clothes, you're wearing Bri's. We could be them! Who are we anyway?" He started to laugh, and he laughed so hard and so long the guy behind him turned to look.

Tanya laughed too but she didn't think it was as funny as he did. She knew she was drunk even though she'd never been drunk before. She couldn't wait to get home and rip off her sister's clothes and throw them at her. Little bits of the tune Bri sang earlier were in her head. The ending had a twist. She hated the twist. Something about the sisters and the man. The server brought the bill and she opened the purse and shook the cash onto the table.

∗ When Bri told their mom about the necklace, she didn't respond the way Tanya expected. Tanya thought she'd be really angry. Instead their mom looked at Bri for a long time without saying anything. It took Tanya a while to realize she was crying, silently. The tears just slid down her cheeks, one after another.

Finally she pulled Bri toward her and held her tightly. Bri, her arms dangling at her sides, looked at Tanya as if to say: Don't worry. This will all be over soon.

∗ The bills kept falling to the floor. Finally the server, looking annoyed, scooped up the money and counted it. When Tanya stood up she thought she'd fall over and so when Russ asked if she'd like to walk around the revolving restaurant she nodded quickly. It was strange, making their way along the passage while it moved slowly in the other direction. Maybe it was taking them back in time. She'd like that. She'd like to do the whole evening all over again. She'd come in her own clothes, at least.

"Let's go this way for a bit," Russ said when they finally stepped outside, pointing away from the place he'd left the car. "I don't think I can drive straight."

They walked east, along a quiet street that gave them a view of the river and the city to the south. It was fine until they passed two men in long, loose coats slumped on benches, yelling something mostly slurred that Tanya couldn't make out and swinging their arms. When they tried to get up, they flopped back down again. A little farther along were three girls, teenagers maybe, wearing black fishnet stockings with holes and tiny red shorts and what looked like tiny strapless bras. Their black lips and long snaky tongues and long fingers moved in close to Tanya and Russ when they called out huskily, "Come! Come, my sweeties!" Russ and Tanya turned at the next side street. After a minute they passed a guy turning away from a nook in a tall building, his fly open. He sent a warm, yellow stream over Tanya's bare legs. Tanya hopped out of the way, but it was too late. Russ reached into his brother's jacket pocket and found a tissue, not used, and wiped Tanya's leg.

"My brother said to take one," Russ said. "Girls cry, he told me." After a second, he said, "That was a joke."

They headed back to the car on a different street and halfway there Tanya stepped out of her too-big shoes and said she didn't want to wear them anyway, they weren't hers, did Russ remember? She could tell by how she carried on that she was still drunk and wondered how long it would last and what it would feel like later.

"I remember."

She walked carefully around the crap on the sidewalks, pebbles and cigarette butts, broken glass and dog turds.

When they got to the car, she said, "Could we not go back to my house just yet?"

"I don't care." He started to drive. "How about we just be who we really are now."

He drove slowly through the river valley on quiet streets, up along Ada Boulevard, through Rundle Park, then turned around and made his way to Hawrelak Park, finally stopping in front of the lake on the far side. He flicked off the lights and the motor.

"Someone will probably come," he said. "Officially the park is closed. But let's take our chances."

Russ took off his shoes and socks and they strolled on the grass barefoot. "Maybe we could just start over?"

"The money," Tanya said.

"Oh, the money."

"Yeah." She stopped walking. "My sister didn't want me at the party she's having at the house. Everyone chipped in so I'd stay away and not tell. Our parents." She thought she'd feel better, telling him. But she felt worse. She stopped walking and he continued on. She wanted him to say something. When he didn't, she said, "Can we go back? It wasn't meant to be this way. I could kill her. I could just kill her right now. She does this. She gets me to do things I don't want to do. Or lie for her. Once I even lied when she went all the way to the North Country Fair. You know how far away that is? First she asked me to come and then she said I couldn't and that I shouldn't tell and next thing you know she's gone and my parents are asking me where is she, where is she, just tell us, don't be like her. What's that stupid song about the sisters?"

Russ turned and shook his head. "No idea. I'll take you back home now."

They got into the car and he drove out of the park.

"It's got something about not getting in between them, her sister and her guy, that's it, my dad used to sing it," Tanya said. "I'm gonna kill her. She ruined everything." She wanted Russ to slow down. She felt ill every time Russ turned a corner.

Finally, Russ said, "Why me?"

"What?"

His voice low and heavy, he repeated, "Why me?"

Tanya closed her eyes. *I don't know!* she wanted to say.

"Fuuuck," Russ said slowly.

"Look, I'm sorry!" She shouldn't have mentioned the money.

"This isn't about us. Look."

Tanya opened her eyes. They were on her street. At the far end, in front of her house, was a police cruiser, its red and blue lights sweeping across the trees and the lawns and the road and even Markus-Magnus-Malachy's basketball hoop.

"The last thing I need is to have to take a breathalyzer," Russ said. "In my brother's car. Fuck. I'm on the graduated licence. I'll just stop here." He pulled over three or four houses away and on the other side of the street from the police car. He killed the headlights, then the engine.

"The police car is in front of my house," Tanya said quietly. "Why?"

"Don't ask me. She's your sister."

"Maybe they were too loud and the neighbours called the police," Tanya said.

"Yeah. Probably. Now your parents will find out, I guess." After a few seconds, he asked, "Was it worth it?"

Tanya sat up straight and looked down the street again. He turned, to see what she saw. Two official-looking people, paramedics probably, walked out of the house carrying a stretcher. More flashing red lights on the other side of the police car.

About a dozen people were outside the house, black shapes wandering in the dark, moving every which way, steadily, crisscrossing, not touching.

"Oh, no," Tanya said. She was breathing hard, hugging herself and squeezing her arms.

"Now is when you go and see what happened," he said.

Tanya nodded but didn't move.

"Tell me again how much she gave you?" He said it so quietly she wasn't sure she heard.

"What?"

"Bri. So you wouldn't tell. So you'd find a *nice guy*"—he made air quotes with his fingers—"and stay out all night."

Tanya closed her eyes and whispered, "Two hundred and sixty. Ten dollars each. That's how it works, she said."

Russ nodded. "Twenty-six. Huh. Probably twice that many showed up. We got ripped off. You should ask for the rest. We could split it."

The ambulance gave a shrill cry and pulled away. The police car stayed, its flashing red and blue lights circling the street.

"I can't see Bri," Tanya said.

93

"She's probably inside."

"No. It was her on the stretcher."

"You can tell from here?"

"I can feel it. I just know." She put her hands on her stomach. "I'm going to throw up."

"Whoa, not in my brother's car! Open the door."

Tanya put one hand on her mouth and the other on her stomach.

"Go then. Go see," Russ said.

"In a minute. Not while the police are there."

They watched the two officers speak to people outside the house. It was too dark to see faces. The friends, or friends of friends, or strangers who just happened by and joined in, kept walking in strange patterns, walking like they didn't know how to stop. Then they went one way or the other down the sidewalk. Some got into cars and drove away. After a while nobody was in the front yard.

"This is her dress," Tanya whispered.

"Yup. Know that."

She covered her face. "This is her make-up." She hissed: "This is her hair. I'm her now. I'm her. Don't you see?"

"Nope." Russ stared out front.

"I can't tell them. They'll want to know, but I can't tell them."

"Yup. Got that."

She could see it already, whenever her parents talked about their daughters from now on. Not one daughter, but two, they will say. After a while, they'll stop talking about her, the way they don't talk about Bri. This is how you start to disappear, she thought.

The police cruiser pulled away from the house and crawled up to the Camaro, stopping when the driver doors were side by side. The driver slid his window down and the two officers looked at Russ and Tanya.

"Nice evening," the driver said.

"Yes, sir," Russ said. Tanya looked from the man to Russ. Russ's neck was damp from sweat.

"Looking for a party?"

"No. Uh, no, sir."

"Party's over. Everyone's going home," the officer spoke slowly. "Your girlfriend all right?"

Russ didn't look at Tanya. "She's all right."

"You know the folks who live there?"

Russ looked at Tanya. She shook her head.

The man nodded. "Good thing. They had a bit of a situation. There's quite a clean-up ahead. Go on home now, kids."

"Yes, sir."

When he pulled away, Tanya got out. "I'll walk."

It was cold now, so cold. When she got home she would wrap herself in the red sweater on the bench by the front door.

The
Fainting
Game

THE FIRST TIME I FAINTED, it was a non-event. We were
in Luciana and Mitzi's room. They were helping Gabi faint.
Gabi stood with her back to the wall, closed her eyes, and
took a deep breath.

"Deeper," Luciana said. She put the towel over Gabi's
face. Luciana knew what to do. Mitzi, too. Suddenly Gabi's
legs bent and she started to fall forward. Luciana and Mitzi
grabbed her. Gabi opened her eyes and laughed. We could
see the pink rubber bands on her braces. I laughed too. It
was only the second day of band camp and already they
were my best friends. Gabi especially.

"Now me again," Mitzi said.

Luciana told her no, she was out too long before and
besides she'd already gone, before Gabi. "Liv," she said.
"Your turn. Stand against the wall."

I did.

"Take five big breaths," said Luciana, coming to stand
in front of me. She was taller than me; my head only came
up to her neck. When she moved in close I smelled salt
and sweat. The dorms were hot. "Really big. Bigger. And

slow. Pretend you're about to blow up one of those helium balloons in one breath."

Luciana put the towel over my face and everything went black. Then I opened my eyes and they were all standing around looking at me.

"That's it?" I said.

Their faces were right up to mine, their breath warm on my cheeks, their smiles huge and toothy. I was bummed. I hadn't even fallen over. Probably I hadn't even fainted. If anything, I felt just a little dizzy.

"That's it!" Gabi laughed.

I wanted to do it again but the dorm leader walked past our room and Luciana flicked the towel onto the chair behind her like it was on fire. "Later," she mouthed.

I forgot about the fainting till the next afternoon after sectionals. Gabi was laughing her head off in Luciana and Mitzi's room. She was lying on her back on Mitzi's bed with her arms and legs spread out wide.

"That was the best! The best!" She sat up straight. "How long was I out?"

"Ages," Luciana said. "The longest yet."

"Can I go now?" I asked.

I stood against the wall again, closed my eyes, and took slow, deep breaths. The towel was over my face and the next thing I knew Mitzi and Luciana were holding my arms so tight it pinched, Mitzi especially, even though she was small, like a kid.

Gabi gave me a little punch and flashed her pink braces.

"How long was I out?" I asked.

"Ages," Luciana said.

"Longer than Gabi?"

Luciana gave a little smirk. "Let's call it a tie."

I couldn't tell if she was having me on. It didn't feel much different than the first time.

My roommate, Holly, didn't do it. She didn't do much of anything except come to rehearsals, read, and practice. We had an idea about girls like her. They were better, though we couldn't say how. We just knew they'd be better at everything, when they grew up. They'd figure everything out.

Two days later I made myself faint by myself. Held the towel over my face after five really deep breaths. Woke up on the floor, then the bed after that. When I was out, just for a second, not even, I was in some kind of underground tunnel system. It was completely black but I could see the paths and I wasn't afraid.

✳ I tell Elliott about the fainting game one evening. He's home first, has already started dinner.

"You burned out a few brain cells, did you?" Elliott hands me a glass of wine. "Most people just do drugs."

"Thanks, Smart Aleck. Celia home?"

"No, she's at Anne's. They went to the Goodwill after school."

Thing 1 and Thing 2. Joined at the hip, Elliott sometimes says. Then I remember a dinner-time conversation earlier in the week about finding a dress for some sort of photo-shoot at school. Anne has a new camera with all the bells and whistles.

Elliott's lips graze mine, a half kiss, a whole tease. Garlic and tomatoes.

✳ The next day when I fainted, I woke up out in the hall. I thought I'd be in that tunnel system again, but I wasn't. I wasn't anywhere. I tried again later in the day and got a massive black bruise on my hip. It hurt when I walked. Luckily no one could see it. You could see the mark on Luciana's cheek, though. Black and blotchy. She told our dorm leader she tripped. I knew our dorm leader didn't believe her.

Luciana was the tallest, the oldest too. She was sixteen. Gabi and I were fourteen, almost fifteen. Mitzi was thirteen. The game was Luciana's thing. We all did it because of her. Maybe that was why I kept making myself faint on my own. Because I thought she did too. Sometimes Gabi and I went to her room and did it. Mostly I wanted to know what was in the tunnels. But when I hit my head on the wooden desk in my room and just missed my eye, I got spooked enough to stop. Gabi too.

"Maybe we're not doing it right," she said.

"What else is there to do to get it right?" I asked.

"I dunno."

It wasn't much fun anyway. So she did my hair; she liked to put it in French braids and Dutch braids.

"Let's just not do it anymore," Gabi said.

"Yeah."

It was baking hot in all the buildings that summer. There was no air conditioning. The last day we all complained loudly when we unpacked our instruments in the rehearsal room.

Mr. Forestal, waiting with his baton, shook his head at us. His eyes lit up. "A whole quarter of a century from now, you won't remember the heat. I'll bet you won't even remember this next year or next month even. First rain we get that cools everything off I guarantee you'll all forget this." We all thought Mr. Forestal was funny and cute. He had curly black hair and a sharp nose. His crooked front teeth showed when he smiled. "You won't remember the sweat pouring off your faces. You won't remember your butts sticking to the chairs."

I felt my sweaty butt as soon as he said that, and I knew everybody did because we all started sliding around and giggling.

"You'll only remember what a great time you had." His deep voice was loud in the big stuffy room.

Gabi and I made eyes at each other and tried not to laugh. She was way over in the flutes and I was in the clarinets. Next year was forever from now, so twenty-five years, well, that had nothing to do with us. But still, he was messing with our heads. As soon as you tell someone they won't remember something, they will. So how come he wanted us to remember?

After rehearsal I went to my room to drop off my clarinet. On my way to dinner, I peeked into the small lounge at the end of my hall. Just to see who was there. It was a thing we all did.

Gabi and Mitzi and Luciana were there.

"Liv, I had the coolest blackout!" Gabi said.

"How come no one told me?" I asked. I especially meant Gabi. Because we had agreed not to do it anymore.

"Don't listen to her," Luciana said, meaning Gabi.

"I was, like, this rock star and there were lights and a million people cheering."

"It doesn't happen like that," Luciana said.

"I had big purple hair and funky pants and everybody loved me."

"You're making it up, Gabi," Luciana said.

I was never ever going to tell Luciana about the tunnels.

"Hold the towel for me," Mitzi said. "Please."

I looked for our dorm leader. Nobody was coming.

✳ "I had no idea you're a musician," Elliott says. "Till yesterday, I mean."

"Oh, just in school. Everybody took band. Didn't you?" I know what's happened. Mr. Forestal, Sean Forestal his name was, programmed a timer in our brains that day. When he went on for ages about how we wouldn't remember anything in twenty-five years. In a few months, it will be twenty-five years. My timer went off early. It's the only thing that makes sense.

"Out on the farm? We were too busy driving around in rusty old trucks and getting stuck in the mud."

"Oh yeah," I say, though I know he wasn't. The old trucks and the mud were part of a tall tale his uncle or great uncle told.

Shortly before six, Celia and Anne burst into the house and disappear to Celia's room. Ten minutes later they come downstairs. Anne always looks rosy-cheeked and exuberant and a little out of breath, as if eagerly awaiting what's coming next. Ready to pounce on it. Celia is a different kid, not as enthusiastic about everything. I sometimes wonder if Anne's eagerness will rub off. Wish for it, actually. I envy it, on Celia's behalf. I don't know what to make of it. The enthusiasm. The envy once-removed. They are only twelve.

✳ "Take your deep breaths," Luciana said.

Mitzi breathed. In, out, in, out, like we'd all done a million times. Her reddish hair was in tight curls that afternoon. She'd just showered.

"Slow. And heavy," Gabi said. "So we can hear."

Mitzi wasn't a big girl. She was kind of like my roommate. Quiet and small. We didn't know what she was thinking, ever. We knew she wanted to be like us, though. She wouldn't hang out with us if she didn't.

✳ "Did you find your outfit, Celia?" Elliott asks.

"Yup." Celia piles some spaghetti on her plate.

Anne says, "So. My brother and I used to light matches and throw them at each other. In the basement."

"Oh no," I say.

"That was when my hair was long. Really long." Anne looks at us mischievously. Her round cheeks glow. "Not all of it burned."

Elliott looks amused, not concerned. Not much fazes him.

"How old were you?" I ask.

"Ten, maybe."

Anne looks at Celia. "C'mon, Celia. Your turn."

"What, me?" Celia shrugs. "I never do anything, you know that!"

Something inside me shifts. Elliott teases, "Nothing?"

Celia shakes her head vigorously. She and Anne smile at each other and lock eyes.

Celia must be hiding something. Nothing serious, because of the little smile and the look. If it were anything serious, they wouldn't have looked at each other at all. Or Celia would have made something up. I feel strangely relieved but also a little surprised. They are so young.

* It took a long time for Mitzi to faint that last time, in the lounge. She must have taken fifteen huge breaths.

"C'mon," Luciana said, impatient, looking at her watch.

Then Mitzi slumped forward and we all held her. I was on one side, Gabi the other, and Luciana sort of supported her waist. Mitzi was heavy and floppy. She got heavier and sank more. We were trying not to drop her. Luciana was looking intently at her face but when I looked at Gabi she was watching me. Like I should do something.

Luciana gave Mitzi a little shake. "Open your eyes, girl. It's time for dinner."

"Yeah, wake up, Mitzi," I said. "It's long enough." I tried to make it a joke but I couldn't.

"Yeah." Gabi's voice was croaky. "Tonight's our last supper. We're starving."

Mitzi's head flopped back. Gabi made a sound like she was starting to cry.

"Let's put her on the couch," Luciana said. She held Mitzi by the shoulders, Gabi and I each took one leg, and we sort of hauled her to the couch and flopped her on it. It was hot here, too, and so quiet we heard the buzz of the fluorescent ceiling lights.

"How long do we wait?" Gabi whispered.

"We should just go," Luciana said. "She's just sleeping. She'll wake up and come for dinner. Besides, someone will notice if we aren't all at dinner and uh, it's probably better if we're there. Really, she's just sleeping. She'll wake up. She will."

Luciana sounded so certain, I said, "Okay." I wanted Gabi to say something. I wanted to hear her say "Okay" too. But she didn't. She just looked confused.

"She'll wake up and come to dinner," Luciana said again. On the way to the dining hall she said, "If anyone asks, we haven't seen her since before dinner. No, not since the last rehearsal."

I nodded and when Gabi nodded, I felt better. But she looked scared. I must have looked scared too. I started telling myself things: Luciana's older, she knows Mitzi's just sleeping, Mitzi will wake up, like Luciana says. She'll come to dinner.

✳ Elliott's face fades into the grey light. We're on the couch. We've finished eating; Celia and Anne are in Celia's room. I'm telling Elliott about Penny from work. She torments me with tragedies, local ones and faraway ones. Elliott finds it funny. So I tell him about the new respirator instead. Penny and I are respiratory therapists. As I talk, his nose and eyes and lips slowly disappear into the darkness; we haven't bothered to turn on a lamp. He is no longer recognizable as Elliott. I wonder how I look to him. Whether I am coming to him as a disembodied voice. A floating voice. It's strangely arousing, this disconnection of his voice and his body. I want to be a cat, a mountain lion sort of cat, and mount him right here, right now. I'd let out a yell and leap on him and rip the buttons off his blue and white shirt. And he'd look endearing and puzzled.

✳ On the way back to our rooms after dinner we had to go past the lounge. We knew something was up because the hallway was packed. Everybody was standing outside the lounge, looking in. We tried to get to the lounge door but couldn't. The hallway was too full. Finally I squeezed through and peeked in. I had to know.

Mitzi was still lying on the couch. Her cheeks were pasty and her eyes were only partly open; you could only see the white parts. Someone was kneeling in front of her, holding her lips apart like people do when they are about to breathe into someone's mouth. I looked around for Luciana and Gabi but couldn't see them. After a while I went back to my room. Holly came in and lay on her bed and opened her book. I exhaled. What a long time to hold my breath.

✳ When my eyes are closed I hear the girls from band camp: *Big deep breaths. Deeper. A balloon. Bigger breaths!* Elliott's face is between my legs. Those voices are still there: *The towel, the towel! Watch out, she's falling.* I try to push them away by starting that fantasy about Elliott and me in an old truck, the kind with a bench front seat, but as soon as I picture the truck all I see is Elliott's uncle Ryan, somewhere in rural Alberta, waiting near a rushing river for someone to help him and his girl cross in an old boat, a rowboat maybe, or a small barge someone built, to get to a party in a big red barn. It could turn into a good sex fantasy, but it doesn't because Elliott's head keeps being superimposed with the old uncle's, even though I've never met any of his uncles. It could have been his great-great uncle, for all I know. The face beside me in the truck is toothless and stubbly and the hair feels like straw.

Elliott looks up and says, "My tongue's getting tired."

I switch the great uncle to the age he would have been when he hot-wired the truck, but he was eighteen then, according to the story. A boy. Damn.

"Liv," Elliott says, later. "You're so not here. Are you still thinking about that camp? It wasn't that terrible, that game."

"Maybe."

Elliott closes his eyes. In three seconds he's asleep. He always sleeps more easily, more deeply than me.

✳ Camp ended the day after we went to dinner without Mitzi; the parents came in the afternoon to watch the big performance and then everybody went home. We lived all over the province, so in my mind we spread out in different directions like spokes on a bicycle wheel. Nobody had cell phones, there was no email then, no way to stay in touch. That fall, in the city youth orchestra and the provincial honour band, there was a lot of whispering, intense and relentless, like a hum or a buzz you can't turn off: *Do you remember Mitzi? Mitzi never woke up. She did wake up, but I heard she can't talk. I heard she can't walk. She can so. She can walk and she can talk but she's just not playing the trumpet anymore.*

Only Gabi and Luciana and I said nothing, not even to each other. We didn't know how to be friends anymore.

✳ Friday afternoon when I wake after my night shift there's a note from Elliott under the grey coffee mug he's set at my place at the table reminding me that Celia will be at school with Anne till five o'clock for the photoshoot. I have to think for a minute, piece the parts together. Anne. New camera. New dress. Right. And Elliott wants to swing by the school and take the girls for dinner and a movie.

I turn the radio on and then turn it off again. No need. Penny at work has already filled me in. She has taken to cornering me. It's unsettling, not just what she shares but how, like she wants me to get just as worked up as she does. She listens to CBC radio during her long commute and all evening at home, she consumes the *National Post* on her breaks, and she acts like it's her duty to keep me informed about everything. For my sake. Some days it's the arsenic in rice. The antibiotics in meat. Glyphosate. The habitat of bees, ever more endangered. *When they're done, we're done, Liv. Think about it!* Other days Penny focusses solely on human disasters. She has a pattern: she starts with the other side of the world and works her way close to home. It isn't that I don't care. The other night, three in the morning maybe, Penny went on about the massacres in Syria and moved to the most recent school shooting in the States, the forty-fifth this year. Then she got to northern BC and gave an update on a massive forest fire. She's manic. Or she's been hypnotized and keeps circling disasters. It's suffocating. I don't know how to stop her without offending her and permanently damaging a decent work relationship. Fortunately old Mr. O'Connor, who has acute pneumonia, needed one of us right then and I ran off to help. It's like Penny doesn't want to know what's happening right in front of us. Sometimes I want to take her by the shoulders and tell her to wake up.

When Elliott arrives home from work we drive to the school. It's dusk already; the parking lot is lit by a few scattered streetlamps.

In a few minutes Celia trudges toward us, her backpack slung over one shoulder.

"Hi, Mom, hi, Dad."

"Hungry?" Elliott says. "We thought we'd go to dinner and see the new IMAX movie."

"Yeah, sure."

"How was school?" I ask.

"Fine."

I drive quietly. Conversation with a twelve-year-old. Celia talks non-stop when Anne is there.

In the restaurant, when Celia slips out of her winter coat, I take in the thin lilac-coloured dress. It's snug and short and lacy and has some shape to it. Where was I when this dress arrived? I wrack my brains, try to bring back the conversation. I can't. Was there one? My child is no longer a child. The sleeves are short. The dress is too short, too thin, for late March. For my child, my pre-pubescent child. And yet she looks so beautiful. Her face is still a girl's, unmarked by time and care, a dusting of red on her cheeks and a hint of mascara and eye liner. Anne's make-up? Mine? Who showed her how to put it on? And her hair, not brushed since morning, in disarray, but not like a child's unbrushed mop. Gently tousled. She is both Celia and Not-Celia.

The server comes and I order a glass of red. Only when I speak do I realize I've been inhaling and haven't yet properly let out a deep breath. Elliott orders a decaf. Celia, lemonade.

"How was it, Celia?" Elliott asks. He is looking at her intensely. "The photoshoot."

"Good."

He raises his arms and opens his mouth wide. "I completely forgot about Anne. I feel terrible. Did we leave her at school?"

"No, she left earlier."

"I can't believe I forgot about Anne."

"It's okay, Dad. She left ages ago."

"But wasn't she taking the pictures?" I ask.

"No, it was Mr. Swanson's camera."

"Mr. Swanson," I say. "Who's he?"

"Hang on," Elliott says. "Didn't Anne have the camera? Her new one."

"Mr. Swanson's a teacher." Celia sounds exasperated.

"A teacher." There it is again, that feeling of something shifting inside.

"Celia." Elliott sounds annoyed.

"One of the technology teachers," Celia goes on.

"One of the technology teachers," I say.

"Mom, you're repeating everything I say. This is the dumbest conversation I've ever had."

"Was he taking pictures of Anne, too?" I ask.

"Why so many questions? It was no big deal. I'm starving. Can we order?" Celia looks down at her menu.

I'm annoyed now as well. "Celia, what sort of pictures was he taking?"

Celia shrugs and pokes at the white napkin bursting swan-like from her water glass. "Pictures." Her lips make the smallest smile, the same smile she gave Anne at dinner earlier in the week.

The server arrives with our drinks, and when he asks if we are ready to order, I tell him, "No, we're not ready!"

"I am!" Celia says. "I'm starving. I'll have the linguine with the shrimp."

Elliott orders. I haven't looked at the menu but I've come so often I order the same thing I usually do, something el diablo-ish that the server tactfully pronounces properly for me.

Elliott tries again. "You're sure Anne got home okay."

"Just be quiet about Anne. She's not my friend."

"Celia, what's going on?" Elliott asks.

Celia rolls her eyes. "Mom. Dad," she says. "You just don't know anything."

It's probably nothing. The pictures. The dress. But of course it's not nothing. It wasn't nothing when Mitzi didn't wake up right away, however much we tried to make it nothing. That last time she fainted, I held one side of the towel, Gabi the other. So it wouldn't slip.

And as we pulled the towel snugly across Mitzi's face, in the curious way young, betrayed minds work, I had one, unbreakable thought: Gabi had come to faint again after we agreed we were done. If she wanted to braid my hair later, the answer was no. I didn't look at her. I didn't even look at Mitzi. I just held the towel as tightly as I could.

The Kite

SASCHA AND MAGALIE WERE ON AN ISLAND. Not a big
island. You could walk around it in an hour. They had done
this before, a million times, they'd gone somewhere, a cabin
in the woods, a bed and breakfast in the middle of nowhere,
a spot in the mountains way up above the treeline to camp.
And it had been good. But this time it would be different.
The thought slapped cruelly against the insides of their
skulls, behind their foreheads, in their ears.

Their bed and breakfast, here, was just fine. The couple
who owned it, two guys in their early forties, slept in the
basement when they had guests. The way to the basement
was through a trap door. Magalie and Sascha peered into
the opening left by the raised trap door. It was a hobbit
hole. Below, past the retractable wooden stairs, were a table
and two chairs, also wood, everything a yellowish sheen. The
way the light is in glossy magazine ads. Where the light came
from down there, Sascha and Magalie couldn't tell. Even the
main floor and upstairs were like something in a home décor
magazine. Everything done up with excess, overstuffed
sofas and armchairs with intense paisley patterns, a glass
vase in the living room with the too-big fake bouquet of
puffed-up purple flowers, Persian rugs that clashed with

the paisley, bold reds and purples on the walls and in the faux Picasso art mounted in thick gold-coloured frames. A place you might dress up and pose in. In the right mood.

Sascha and Magalie had booked one large room with two single beds. The house had two other guest rooms across the hall from theirs and a suite that made up the third floor above them (all of which they immediately explored, like mice, scurrying up to closets and shelves, poking their noses into everything), but these rooms were unoccupied. The beds, like the kitchen chairs, like the overstuffed sofas, were high and ablaze with psychedelic floral swirls.

We are strangers in a strange land, one of them joked.

✳ Sascha and Magalie had met almost by accident. They had a mutual friend, Kelsey. Kelsey invited them somewhere. Let's say it was a concert. It was so long ago nobody remembers, and it doesn't matter much anyway. That night, before they went to the concert, or the play, or the bar, the plan was to meet at Sascha's apartment. Magalie was supposed to go with Kelsey but she walked over to Sascha's place on her own because Kelsey was somehow delayed and, as it turned out, Magalie's apartment was only five blocks from Sascha's.

When Magalie arrived Sascha was surprised because she was expecting her friend Kelsey at the door. With a waif. Kelsey was a collector of waifs and strays. Of people missing their people. Sascha, in her surprise, in her pre-going-out and meeting-someone-new giddiness, grabbed Magalie by the shoulders like she was found treasure and pulled her inside, dancing a backwards slip step and laughing.

✳ At the island bed and breakfast Magalie and Sascha set up their music stands on the covered porch on the main floor overlooking the small woods between the house and the beach. They took out their recorders, one of each size and most of them made of rosewood or ebony: soprano, alto, tenor, bass.

Magalie and Sascha had played together for so many years, maybe ten years, all they needed was for one to raise her instrument and inhale and the other knew immediately the tempo, the style. It was uncanny, even to them. They played music by those guys with great names, Valentine and Lassus and Anon., so much Anon., pieces in minor keys, minor in a way that was warm and silky and pleasant, something you could immerse yourself in to your neck, like a hot tub, and stay there, eyes closed, wallowing; something that was full of longing, of something just within reach and always unreachable. Mocking, really. It mocked. It was just music, after all, just notes, centuries-old notes at that, and when they were in tune or, better, in sync, it was fantastic; Magalie and Sascha felt an electric charge run through them, no matter how melancholic the harmonies, how pleading, how desperate. Sometimes when she played, Magalie's mind, Sascha's too, wandered to the lanky master-class dude with the round glasses and the pony-tail and the slight slouch, perched on his stool like a giant bird, one leg bent, the foot resting on the first rung below the seat, the other foot on the lower rung, and listening to them play and then, instead of telling them what they did wrong, instead of telling them how to play differently, instead of telling them to practice more, instead of asking what they thought, asking: What is the colour of that last phrase? Where are you going? Where is the questioning in the ending? They giggled and gave flippant answers: Silky mauve! Terracotta! France! Polka-dotted! Because they were young and didn't see colours. They were young and didn't see anything.

But today the sadness seeped out of them. Today they knew the colour. They wanted to stop, but they wanted to keep going more.

In mere minutes, it seemed, they found they had played through all the duets they'd packed. Normally their cloth bags of music would have been more than sufficient. Because normally they talked. They talked on the drive, they talked when they prepared food, they talked when they ate, they talked when they went for a walk. They talked late into the night. They talked when they unpacked their recorders, they talked when they took out music. They riffed off each other. Like notes running up and down scales, notes approaching cadences with tactful pauses or sudden plunges, notes taking leaps, high-diving, sailing, flying. Notes that softened at times. It had been that way from the first day they met, in Sascha's apartment. When Kelsey arrived, finally, delayed somehow, she gave them both a sharp look. Sharp and stern and then, just before she turned away, hurt. But Magalie and Sascha couldn't stop. It was a crush. A gigantic electric crush.

Today, they said little. As if neither wanted to infringe. To breach an invisible boundary, a shifting boundary whose borders neither could see. Neither wanted to see. When they'd played through all the duets, they played through them again. The ones they especially liked they played three times. Sascha sought out slow pieces, slower meaning longer, allowing them to linger inside the music, to stop time, to stop time from passing. Finally, when they began to make errors, when they left out notes or skipped bars or missed accidentals, when they started over more often than they finished, Magalie said: Let's go for a walk.

They left their recorders out, their music on their stands, a sign that they would come back, they would continue to play, they were not finished, and took a short winding path through the woods to the beach.

✳ After the movie, or the concert, or the club, or wherever it was Sascha and Magalie and Kelsey went that night, they strolled down Jasper Avenue in the warm dark to Sascha's on-again, off-again significant other's. John poured drinks. Something honey-coloured and old and sharp-tasting in short, heavy-bottomed glasses he was clearly pleased with over ice. They stood on the balcony, *twenty storeys up*, John told them, and again, *twenty storeys up*, the valley below creeping with lit-up cars and reflected light moving along the river. Magalie or Sascha started a thought and the other finished. You could almost see the arc of notes running from Sascha to Magalie and back again. Like John and Kelsey were in another piece of music. Or not music at all. The audience, maybe. The back row. Or out in the lobby.

After a few minutes John (his name was not really John), watching and laughing, said, You two sisters? He was really asking Sascha: How come you didn't tell me about this huge part of your life?

John was facing Magalie when he asked it, chest on chest, and something passed between them, some gust, some maleness. He was smiling, but he was thinking something else. Magalie took a step away, felt the hard balcony railing pushing into her lower back.

Kelsey, who had said nothing since the concert, or perhaps had but no one had noticed, told them it was time for her to get home, she had marking to do, an early morning, she'd catch them later. She must have seen herself out.

✳ At the beach they stopped. The beach was sandy and nearly empty and very hot. It was after four. There were a few people near the water. A man and woman, middle-aged and graceful, you could even say elegant, strolled along the shore, where the sand was wet; their bodies were apart but their shoulders grazed from time to time when they walked. Away from the shore, in the dry sand, a young woman in a calf-length colourful sundress sat in a long, low beach chair near a child who looked be about six, on his knees and digging furiously with a piece of broken plastic or a shell.

Sascha turned her face to the sun and closed her eyes and held out her arms in something like a worship pose. She beamed into the sun. Sascha was older by two years. Her hair was short and blond and streaked with purple. She wore a beige bucket hat, the hat she wore everywhere.

Two more things about Sascha: She liked to be seen reading Plato. She was afraid of heights.

Magalie sat on the sand under a huge tree. She sat with her legs stretched out in front of her. She wore shorts and a T-shirt and no hat and felt the heat in the air lift the hairs on her arms and legs as it whispered to her skin. In a minute she lay on her back and closed her eyes. She listened distractedly to the shore birds and the rustling sound the waves made as they slid in and out. She thought of the times she'd played music outside with Sascha. Of how the wind took your notes, no matter how hard you blew, the wind took your notes and did with them what it wanted, played with them, tossed them, swallowed them, spat them out. Erased them, in other words.

What a funny place, this island on the lake, found by accident. The ferry had dropped them off in the morning. There would not be another ferry until tomorrow evening. And they had already played through all their music. Three times.

Two things about Magalie: She did not like to wear colourful, floppy hats. She sometimes rode her ten-speed without a helmet.

✳ And then: The kite.

—Look, said Sascha. —That kite.

Magalie looked. There it was, a huge green and black dragon, cartoon-like, blowing high into the sky, its string bowed below it. The sky was a clear blue strewn with scattered wisps of clouds. The kite's winder was in the water, close to the shore. It was lodged in somehow. Into the wet sand perhaps. The kite, still unwinding, backed into the sky away from the women watching. Backed or was pulled, by an updraft, its pudgy dragon arms waving frantically or doing a backstroke. A visualization of what the wind some-times did to their musical notes.

Magalie laughed. She was content to watch, to see what would happen when the string got to the end. Was the end of the string still tied tight? Or would the kite fly away into the clouds?

Sascha started to move toward the winder. Then she turned and walked over to the small child. —Is that your kite? she asked.

The boy shook his head. He was indifferent to it, and to them; he didn't look at Sascha or Magalie or the woman near him or the sky. He was intent on digging. Where he dug, a few metres from the water's edge, the sand was dry, but not so dry that the sides of his hole slumped in. His hole was so deep now he could lean in with both hands past his elbows. The woman seated near him, a mother, an aunt, a caregiver, turned to look at the cartoon dragon kite. Then she turned back to the boy. You couldn't tell exactly what she was looking at because her sunglasses were so dark you could not see her eyes. What you noticed about her, besides her broad turquoise hat and colourful sundress and dark sunglasses, were her hands. They held nothing. No book. No drink. No phone. They were merely hands, clasped, on her lap.

✻ After that first night, that concert and the visit in John's apartment, spontaneous Saturday morning coffees. And then dinners. And walks. Hikes, in faraway places. And music. Sascha had been a flute player. It was nothing for her to pick up a recorder and play. She preferred Telemann and Vivaldi. But they played other music too, by Machaut and Josquin and Martini. Magalie had been a saxophone player but had played the plastic recorder in school. They joined an ensemble, played consort music and sometimes with small string orchestras. A few years of intense workshopping with guys in ponytails who took it all so seriously. Sascha and Magalie were in their twenties then. Magalie remembers one fellow, from Quebec or Germany or Holland, it was usually one of those places, saying, —Push off each other, push. You got it. Then he'd ask them what colour a section was. —You're in C minor, he'd say. —It's sinister. What colour is it? Or, —This is full of despair. And they'd look at each other and giggle. Despair lived in another land. Another galaxy. For them, playing this music was like wandering with a group of friends in the woods. They'd start out together and within a few seconds everyone took off on their own. Sometimes they crossed paths. Sometimes they called out to each other through the leaves. *Over here!* And: *Look what I found!* Sometimes two would make eye contact, briefly, one would smile, one would poke someone's shoulder from behind. Or one of them would stop and stare, at the grass or the sky or a bird in flight, and then pick up again. And then they'd all come together, abruptly, and stop.

✳ Magalie wanted to let the kite unravel to its natural end to see what would happen.

Sascha got up and grabbed the string and yanked at the winder, at whatever it was lodged in. It didn't come loose. What could happen? The wind could stop and the kite would come down into the water and be tossed about and eventually chewed up by the waves. Or a strong wind could give a fierce pull and wrench the cartoon dragon free of the string and take it far away from here. It might be shredded against jagged rocks. Or it might come to a soft landing on a hay bale or a roof and be visited by a cat or a pigeon.

We are the kite, Sascha realized.

She left the string and came back under the tree. —I decided to leave it, she said. She lay on her back and looked up at the kite. —I decided to leave it, she said again. After a few seconds she turned to Magalie. —We'll be all right.

＊ Fuck, Sascha liked to say from time to time. Or: What a fuck. And: What the actual fuck. Sometimes: Where's John? I could use a good fuck. Or: Fuck him!

＊ The wind by the shore picked up. The elegant man and woman had gone around the corner, down at the end where the dunes were. Magalie, watching them vanish, wanted to go there too.

—Shall we go? Sascha said, her eyes moving from Magalie to the disappearing man and woman. —That way?

The boy was still digging but the woman who held nothing in her hands was standing now and telling him it was time to go. She started to walk slowly away.

The kite string whipped in and out, tensed, bowed. The kite dove a few times, then swooped upward.

—Now! yelled the woman who was with the boy. There it was: A discontented woman, a carefree child.

—Yes, said Magalie, to Sascha.

✳ François or Pierre or Joachim, with or without the long hair, said —What does this part feel like? This part? Will it be a crescendo? Or a diminuendo? And — Plan the perfect ending / aim for a questioning ending / what are you aiming for? What?

✳ An ending: a woman with nothing in her hands. That was where they were, now. Empty. Breathed out. Skeletal but hanging on. Like that damned kite. The wind would get it in the end, they both knew.

✳ The small details are boring. What was it? They don't know, now.

—I need my own thoughts, one said.

—I need my own thoughts, said the other.

They had to come apart. The riffing sounds out of tune, discordant, jarring. You think it is a thing you can put back in tune by giving a little more air or a little less. Make minor adjustments. You try. You have so much air, so much will, you try and try and try. You try till you hyperventilate and black out.

✳ The boy slid into his hole feet first. His legs disappeared. Only his upper chest and his head were visible. He reached down and pulled out more sand and threw it aside. And again. Clouds had filled the sky. Darkness grew in patches, first murky grey, then black.

—Be that way. I'll see you back there, the woman said. She crossed her arms and walked away, not toward the dunes but the other direction, where there were tents.

Magalie and Sascha looked toward the dunes.

—Shall we follow? Magalie asked.

Sascha stood. She shook her head. She watched the boy.

Magalie got up and moved into the space beside Sascha, into the air that moved with her toward the man and woman who had disappeared.

How
to Read
Water

THIS WAS A FRIDAY AFTERNOON toward the end of August.
The last of the sunny blue days, the sky strewn with those
cotton-white clouds, the air fresh, not cold. Cat knelt in the
stern and dug her paddle in and pulled. And again, and
again. There in the bow was a solid mass, a human alba-
tross, look at him, that lug in the faded green life jacket and
too-big beige sunhat.

"You," Cat called to the dead weight. "Your arms broken?"
The lug shifted slightly. "No."

"Then give us some muscle," Cat said. Not unkindly.

The lump, a boy, made a sound like a grunt. He was Cat's
brother, age eleven and a half, competent but indifferent to
canoeing. He alternately stared down at the river bottom
where it was shallow and lily-dipped with his paddle when
he felt compelled to move his arms.

Cat paddled on, her arms like ropes, stretching, pulling.
They were on the Athabasca River, well east of the mountain town of Jasper, Alberta, Canada, North America, The
Universe. She had touched the inkblot splotch of the town-
site on her dad's paddling map that morning and run her

finger along the river from their start—Disaster Point—
to their end, three days by water and less imaginatively
named—the Emerson Bridge Haul Road.

"Hey," Dad called. He was a few boat-widths away, in the
stern of the green Prospector. Mom was in the bow. "Cat.
Jamie. I'll bet you half my Toblerone bar you'll never guess
what the big disaster at Disaster Point was."

He turned his canoe so that it moved closer to Cat and
Jamie's.

Cat didn't want to answer. Dad was about to deaducate
them with a boring lecture. But she said, "Only half?" And
then, "I have my own chocolate bar."

"What? What Disaster Point?" Jamie asked.

"Where we started. The put-in. What do you think it
was?" Dad gave his wide, toothy aren't-I-smart-and-funny
smirk. He wasn't either. He was just annoying. He was
probably born annoying, like Jamie was born jittery. "Not
even going to guess? It's a good chocolate bar."

"Don't ask me," Cat said. "I didn't get to sleep enough
last night. And I'm working too hard paddling this lug."

"I'm not a lug!" Jamie sat up and paddled.

"What do you think happened?"

"Just tell us," Jamie said.

"Probably a train wreck," Cat said.

"A railway guy broke his flask of whisky," Mom said.
"That was the big disaster. Boys and their booze."

"It was a big disaster!" Dad yelled. "It was probably all
the whisky they had for the entire winter! Come on! Use
your imaginations a little. This was back in the day when
there were no roads, no bridges across the Athabasca. You

were way off about a train wreck, Cat," he went on, taking a breath.

Cat rolled her eyes.

"There weren't even any trains back then!" Dad said. "But lots of people think the disaster was something else, something more exciting. Lots of people think the place was named for the pack horses that fell down some mountain cliffs into the river, somewhere around here. But that's not the real story—"

"Check out that bird." Mom pointed. "There."

"Back in eighteen hundred and seventy-two, one Sir Sandford Fleming, a famous Scottish engineer, was trying to find a way to get the railway to the coast. So you're close, with the train wreck. I'll give you two points for that."

"Points," Cat said, "Great. Points."

"Sir Sandford Fleming was waiting for someone to build him a raft to cross the river."

"There!" Mom pointed with her paddle. "See that eagle?"

"Why didn't he make his own raft?" Jamie asked.

"I see it," Cat said.

"He was a 'Sir,'" Dad said. "Sirs don't make their own rafts. Anyway, sometime during that waiting time, Fleming lost his whisky. It was medicinal too, you know."

"A golden eagle," Mom said.

"The eagle got his whisky?" Jamie asked.

"I know, you're not listening," Dad said. "Fleming might sound like an old drunk to you, more interested in his whisky than anything else, but this man, this brave man left his home and took tremendous risks and did many great things, that's more than most of us can say—"

"If he's so famous, how come we haven't heard of him?" Jamie asked.

"Well, now you have!" Dad said. "You can thank your father. When you're old and grey, and nobody has heard of Sir Sandford Fleming, you can say, I know about Sir Sandford Fleming from my father, rest his soul."

Dad stopped paddling for a few seconds to put his right hand on his chest and looked up at the sky dramatically.

"Did they?" Jamie said. Even without seeing his hands Cat could tell he was fidgeting, doing finger acrobatics. She wondered if it was a thing kids outgrew.

"Did they what?" Cat said.

"Fall off the cliff."

"No!" Cat said, maybe too enthusiastically. She didn't know if the story about the pack horses was true or even the one about the old guy with his whisky. "They lost some alcohol. So what. Boring. Whisky burns your throat and makes you want to puke. Anyway, could you paddle a little?"

What Cat really wanted to say was, Dad, I don't care about Sir What's-his-Whisky. Jamie and I aren't little kids anymore; your stories are boring. It doesn't matter, anyway, whether we know these things. It doesn't matter what happened a hundred years ago. What matters is today, tomorrow. One more year of high school. Soon she was going to count the days. Starting next week, with the September calendar. She'd make a diagonal line with a red felt pen through every day.

"They could have," Jamie said.

"Yeah, let's say some guys fell from some cliffs trying to save the whisky and the horses broke their legs and their necks and the whisky flasks broke too. That's a good story, isn't it." Cat knew she was being mean and took a breath, started over. "But that was forever ago," she said, more kindly. "It was probably a story they told around the campfire. To pass the time. Disaster Point is just a name on a map now. Like Brûlé Lake and, let's see, Ogre Canyon, Old Entrance"—Cat recited, from memory, all the names she'd seen that morning on Dad's map—"Swan Landing, Emerson Creek Haul Road."

There it was, she'd learned all those names, and it didn't really matter; those places were just names given by some dead Europeans, just dots really, nothing was there, maybe a bit of old barn board or barbed wire lying hidden in long, gnarly grass, and even if she hadn't memorized the names, they'd paddle down to the car anyway. Where she was off to, next summer, as soon as she finished school, there would be whole villages and towns, real live people doing crazy fun things. Not just dots showing where people used to live.

"Oh wait, one more, Unnamed Sand Dunes."

"Is that a name on a map?" Jamie asked.

"No. I made that one up. There are massive sand dunes coming up that go on forever, and they don't have a name. Aren't I brilliant?" Probably they had a name, from before Sir Whisky got here.

No answer. Cat flicked water at his back.

Back-front. Here-there. Speaking-silent. Cat's mind hopped from one word to the next like a rabbit in a tiny cage. The way Jamie played with the light switch in his bedroom for ages, or till someone came and cupped his hand or led him away: On-off. Up-down. Flick-flick. She called it her yin-yang game, this word-pair hopping. She knew what yin and yang were. Opposites. Like: brother-sister. Father-mother. Parent-child. Wet-dry. Floppy-stiff. Shade-sun. Fidgety-still. She tossed the words around in her mind, silently flipped them from her tongue, sent them spinning into the air. She liked how each one became more of what it was through its other half.

"Anyway," she said, "paddle. Unless your arms are broken. Are your arms broken?"

"Aye, aye, cap'n." Jamie straightened his back and shoved his paddle into the water and thrust the canoe forward. After two good strokes he stopped.

"And there's Brûlé Lake!" Dad called. "Say goodbye to our current for a while."

Cat had seen it already, the widening of the river into the lake. But Dad liked to point out what they could all see. Like they were all clueless. He would probably remind them to go for the main channel. Cat knew that, too; she knew how to read water. The main channel would be deepest; anywhere else would be too shallow. It was always the way, especially by late summer. Rivers dropped toward the end of August. This year the river was especially low. It had been insanely hot in July, glaciers had melted, and some areas had diabolical rains and so the water had gone up a little for a short time, but despite all that, it was mostly a drought, so now, rivers all over the province were low, lower than low. *Extreme* was the catchword every time anyone turned on the radio. Extreme weather. Extreme storms. Flash floods, droughts, fires, all of them record breaking. Cat lost count of the times she heard the word *extreme* that summer. And *climate change*. You could put them together, like it was an escape room theme or a new drink: *climate change extreme*.

"You have to keep paddling." Cat could just make out the main channel in the middle of the lake from the way the sun reflected off the water moving downstream.

"What? I am paddling," Jamie said, though he hadn't been. He sat up again and paddled. He did not like to be left behind, left out, left. And he was desperate to please her. So desperate for her affection. She knows, deep down, it's because when he was born, she wanted nothing to do with him. He must still know this in some way. His body must remember it, even though something changed for her a few years ago. He had grown on her in a weird way. He was a part of her. "Oh, stop, stop," she had said, just last week, moderately annoyed but laughing when he followed her around the house like a pet, wanting to show her something or maybe it was to ask her again about his printing, that was it, was his printing neat.

Jamie was like a growth. A tumour. He stuck to everything. But next year, next June, she would be finished high school. She would be done with all this. With Jamie. With Dad's stupid jokes and his boring history lessons. Mom's endless patience; Mom, who sometimes let Dad go on and on, just smiling, like it didn't bother her, though it did, Cat knew it did, how could it not? When she graduated, Cat would be gone, gone, gone. She'd made the plans, filled in the forms; she was off to a tiny village in Central America to help build a school.

"They could have," Jamie said.

"What now?" Cat said. "Could have what?"

"Fallen off the sides of the mountains."

"Oh, the explorers. The pack horses. Sure, they could have. But they didn't."

"How do you know?"

"I looked it up. I look everything up." Of course she hadn't looked up the story Dad told; she lied because she didn't want Jamie to spend the rest of the day fretting. Sometimes a little lie, in these cases, was okay. It must be. She'd look it up later just to be sure. "This is how you keep people from pulling the wool over your eyes. This is how you reduce risk. You learn more."

"Looking things up doesn't reduce risk. Not doing anything reduces risk."

"But what's the point of that?"

"No risk."

Cat didn't reply. Surely he could see they were just fine. They were like ducks, bobbing along as if they belonged here, as if they'd always been here. She let herself sink into the boat, her knees and shins pressed against the Kevlar. On a river you were out of time and out of place, as in ungrounded, moving, stealing along the surface, the point air and water meet. She'd written an essay about canoeing in English class last year. She wrote about how rivers were a metaphor for life. How water doesn't go straight; it goes where it meets the least resistance. How there are calm days and frenetic ones. Fast-slow. Chaotic-serene. How you left your cares at home, if you had any, when you went on a paddling trip. These weren't all her ideas; somebody from their canoe club talked about it around the fire one night. The teacher gave her an A. Cat felt like a fraud, for using someone else's ideas. Except the part about being out of time and place. That part was hers.

"What's that?" Jamie points down the river.

"What, that sweeper?" Cat laughed lightly. "It's a mile away, Mr. Worry."

"It's not a mile away. I can almost touch it with my paddle."

"Don't then, and we'll be fine. Draw."

Jamie pulled water toward the canoe and they veered away from the massive dead tree hanging over the river on their right. For all his slothfulness and fretting, Jamie could do what he needed to when the time came; he could draw or pry or brace when she asked. Or even when she didn't; they had paddled for so long, she sometimes didn't need to say a word and he would put the paddle blade right where she wanted him to. Telekinetic, that was what it was. She and Jamie were telekinetic. He was hitched to her brain. When they were canoeing, anyway. Maybe he was just so terrified of tipping he'd do anything to make sure it wouldn't happen. She had tipped, in canoe courses, in indoor pools and on slow-moving rivers, on purpose. Jamie, too. "You get wet," she'd told Jamie. "That's all. You get wet when you tip. The important thing is not to freak out or you'll be too hard to rescue."

"Have we been on this river before?" he asked.

"Yep. But not the part we're doing today and tomorrow morning." Cat had looked that up.

"Is it easy?"

"Dead easy."

It was a small lie. Parts of this stretch could be pushy.

"Remember we called it the Athabath-tub one time?" Cat asked. "Because that's how easy this river is. Mostly."

They were younger on that trip. He paddled with Mom, she paddled with Dad. That was before their parents decided they needed their own canoe and their own tent.

"Oh, yeah."

"Easy-peasy. Just close your eyes." She laughed again and the laugh skittered across the water. What was not to love about a substance that picked up sound and flung it about aimlessly?

* Some days Cat felt like an alien. She didn't know when she last cried or got herself into a state, the way Jamie did almost daily. She had a clear picture of their mother scooping Jamie in her arms to soothe him—he was two or three years old—and looking calmly at Cat and saying, "You were just like this, Cathy, and you're fine now." And yet Mom told her later she must have misheard; Cat had not been at all like Jamie. Cat was one of those babies who are born peaceful, Mom said, with an innate sense of certainty that often takes people by surprise. "Nothing fazes you. Nothing upsets you. Whatever you choose to do, Cathy, you will excel," Mom often said. Her mother, clearly, was deluded. Cat sometimes thought Mom described things the way she wanted them to be, not how they were, in the hopes that people might rise to those qualities. Because she never talked about Jamie's worrying, except sometimes in whispers to Dad behind the closed bedroom door. Cat, when she wanted to know what she was really like, who she really was, had eavesdropped, more often than she would ever admit, through the door to hear what they said about her.

"Would you look at that." Dad gestured with his paddle blade toward the bank on the right.

"What? What?" Jamie asked.

Cat looked. The sand dunes had begun. The Unnamed Sand Dunes. She would look them up later. Somebody must have named them. Eons ago. They rose up in an impossible cliff and continued parallel to the lake farther than she could see. But Dad wasn't pointing at the sand dunes. A dozen quads and fat-tired dirt bikes ripped up and down and along the uneven slope, sending a steady, angry RRRR toward the water. The bikes were several boat lengths away, but the sound carried. That was the thing about water. It conducted sound so well. Cat and Jamie stopped paddling to watch a biker try to get up a short, steep rise. The bike got stuck and, in slow motion, flipped the rider onto his back. The rider held his bike and managed to right both himself and his heavy bike and then tried to push it up the incline. The sand didn't give him any hold whatsoever and he slid back down repeatedly while one of his friends watched.

"What's he doing?" Jamie said.

"Trying to get up the dune." She knew Jamie was squeezing his fingers into a fist, releasing them, and squeezing, again and again. "They're having fun. He's probably done this a thousand times."

"Why?"

Cat hardly heard his voice over the roar of the engines. On the side of the lake opposite the sand dunes was a mountain range. The sound rolled across the lake and struck the wall of rock and bounced back at them. She laughed, though the whole thing was more insane than funny. They were paddling through a massive roaring bubble.

"Cat," Mom called. "That laugh! I want to record that laugh so I can hear it forever."

"Let's hope they don't go too far along the sand dunes," Dad shouted.

Cat paddled hard. She wanted to paddle past the dunes as fast as she could and leave the bikers behind.

But the sand dunes went on and on, maybe to the far end of the lake, and so did the quadders and the bikers. Nobody spoke any more except to yell how annoying the noise was. Cat tried to tune out the roaring and focus on her strokes instead. She loved the feel of her paddle. She'd had this one for three years. It was light, made of carbon fibre, it was smooth, it was shiny, it did what she wanted it to do. It had never let her down. Her paddle was like a best friend. There was a family story, one of those that changed a little every time it was told, about how on one of their many trips with their canoe club a family friend had taken her through a set of rapids and she'd somehow been ejected from the boat. Dad and Mom paddled over to her and scooped her up by the loop in the back of her life jacket—and there she was, shivering with cold but beaming and proudly holding her small paddle against her body, Mom and Dad close behind her. Cat has a clear image of this. Maybe someone took a photograph of her, or maybe the story was told so many times. This was before Jamie was born, when it was just Cat and her parents, the three of them in a canoe, Cat crawling over dry bags and barrels between her parents and sitting or lying or reading a comic book wherever she pleased, Cat tucked in between her parents in the tent at night, snug and warm and certain of her place in the world.

"Time to pull in for the night! There's a good spot!" Dad hollered over the roaring. The bikes were some distance away but the sound filled the air like a swarm of gigantic, over-inflated bees. Dad pointed his bow toward a wide sandy beach area. Beyond the beach were flood-level alder and willow, and past those, young aspen and spruce. The quads had left deep gouges in the sand along the shore.

"Where will we sleep?" Jamie asked as he pulled dry bags from the canoe. "They'll run over us in the night."

"Well. That would be messy, wouldn't it?" When Jamie turned away, she said, "How about we go way to the back here. In the trees. Quads don't go through trees."

A few quads zoomed along the beach. The riders waved as they passed. Then they were gone. But Cat could still hear the roaring from all around.

"They'll stop for dinner," called Dad from where he was setting up his tent in the shrubs. "Just like us. They'll want to eat."

In a few minutes he started a fire on the beach. Cat and Jamie finished setting up their tent and hauled their canoe up on the shore next to the Prospector.

"Tie it," Dad yelled. "You never know when a wind will come up. Last thing you want is to wake up to discover your canoe's been blown away. You won't even know it till morning. I've known guys who slept through everything.

Fell asleep to the sound of rapids. Sometimes water drowns out everything. But you never know what will happen in the night. A wind, or rain, or maybe they release some water from the dam and the water rises five feet."

Cat had heard this before, every year. Dad must have no idea he was repeating himself.

"Make it really tight," Jamie said, flicking his fingers every which way and watching Cat wrap the bow painter around the fat log where the other boat had been tied.

"Our canoe's not going anywhere," she said. "See this knot? Here, pull."

Jamie pulled tentatively.

"No, harder! Like you mean it. Like you're a tornado."

Jamie grabbed the rope with both hands and pulled so hard he fell on his butt.

"Good!" Cat laughed.

Mom was near the fire, setting up the camp stove. In the background came the roar of the quads. "So much for idyll," she said loudly. She shook her head and looked across the lake at the mountains and their reflection on the calm water. "This is such a beautiful place to set up camp."

"What's that?" Dad shouted. "I can hardly hear you. It's a bloody dystopia with those goddamn quadders."

"Shane," Mom said. "Tender ears."

"Oh, Mom," Cat said. She was on the edge of telling Mom she couldn't protect her from every little thing. But something about Mom's face stopped her. The way Mom looked at her like she didn't know her. She'd been doing that more and more lately. When she had that look and Cat asked, Mom's face softened and she said, "I'll miss you, that's all."

But it was more than that. Cat knew it was more than that. The way Cat moved near her, tried to be close, close enough to feel Mom's skin, her warmth, and Mom moved away, said she had to start dinner or do an errand.

Cat pulled the bowls and cutlery from the kitchen bucket and set them on the weathered board that was their table. She opened the folding chairs and plopped them on the sand around the fire and sat. After a few minutes, she looked up.

"They stopped," she said. "How long have they been stopped? It's so quiet."

"My ears are ringing," Dad said.

"Mine feel huge," Cat said. When she closed her eyes, she heard bird calls, sounding too loud in the silence. *Kraaa! Dee-dee-dee! Whee-ah chuck chuck chuck.* And the autumn bird, already: *Thief! Thief!* Whisky jacks, nutcrackers, blue jays. Scavengers. A big whisky jack was working its way into the bag of pita bread Jamie had left open when he went off to find a stick to roast his sausage. Mom shooed it away. How strange to hear sounds, the quiet chatter of the water, a playful splash when a wave stood up and fell back down. The rustle of the wind in the yellow leaves and wood hissing and crackling in the fire.

"The quadders must be drinking now," Mom said.

"They'll come along here in the dark, completely drunk," Dad said. "What a gong show that will be." He stood up. "Come on over, kids." He had a stick. He was going to tell them about triangulation. Cat already knew what it was, but she stepped over to him. "Here's the rock." He pointed to an actual rock in the sand. "And here's an object on shore, behind the rock. Here's where you want your canoe to be. To avoid the rock." He made lines. Marked a triangle. Pointed. "Here's where you don't want to be. Always keep yourself in line with that object on shore and you can't go wrong. Tomorrow the water will pick up a bit. There are some slightly more ambitious sections." He looked from Cat to Jamie and rubbed Jamie's head. "But you're up for it."

The air cooled quickly, and dew began to form. A small sliver of a moon preened at its reflection on the water. Dusk fell like a grey bedspread pulled slowly over their campsite and tucked itself in at the far corners. It was slightly overcast. There would not be any light along the shore when the quads zoomed past on their way to the sandy cliffs.

✳ Cat woke to Mom's voice outside the tent.

"Are you two going to sleep all day?" Mom called.

If Cat could sleep all day, she would. Or at least a few hours longer. She did like being on the water. That part she would happily stretch out. She could do most of it in her sleep anyway. But why couldn't they start just a little later? She opened her eyes. There was Jamie, sitting. His sticking-up brown hair. The grey-blue of the T-shirt he pulled over his head. A whiff of his body, warm and smelling of sweat and last night's woodsmoke. And now, out by the fire, hot cereal and a piece of bacon from Dad, in the yellow bowls they'd had forever.

"You kids sleep through everything," Dad said.

"Did you hear the quadders?" Mom asked.

Cat shook her head. It was too early to have a conversation. It was probably not even eight o'clock.

"They came back around two or three in the morning," Mom said. "They stopped right in front of the canoes and started talking. They were so loud I thought for sure you'd wake up. Dad got out of the tent to make sure they didn't do anything to the canoes."

"I can't believe you two slept through it," Dad said.

"It's your age," Mom said. "You need the sleep."

A gust of wind blew up and a slow spiral of air spun around them. On the nearest tall poplar the few leaves that had already turned yellow waved half-heartedly and let go of their branches, falling slowly to the ground. Cat understood.

"Time to pack up," Dad said.

By ten o'clock they were on the water, and an hour later they were at the end of the lake and back on the fast-moving river. The sand dunes were far behind.

The railway ran parallel to the river, on the north bank. Cat saw the tunnel in the distance and, almost as if she'd willed it, heard the blast of a train whistle, long and loud, and then the train appeared.

"Wow! The river is vibrating!" Jamie shouted. He gripped the gunwales.

"Wow is right," Cat said.

"Did you feel it?"

"Yup!" Cat laughed. "It was great."

When their parents' canoe was out of earshot, Jamie told her. "I heard."

"Heard what?"

"Those quadders."

"No way. I thought you were sleeping."

"There was a big fight. I heard Dad yelling. That's what woke me up. I didn't want to go out of the tent. I didn't want anyone to know where we were."

"Were you afraid?"

Jamie didn't reply.

"You can wake me up when you're afraid."

"Mom says I shouldn't. I should get through it on my own." Jamie paddled for a minute and then said, "Mom says you always have a plan. Your whole life is planned." He said it like he was puzzling through it. Trying to understand. "She says your whole life you've known you wanted to get away. Is that true?"

"She told you all that?"

"She says when you leave we'll never see you again. You'll walk away and never look back."

"What? Why would I do that?" Cat frowned and felt her chest stiffen.

Jamie didn't answer.

"I'm just going to Guatemala, Jamie. I'll email. I'll probably send postcards. It's not forever. I'll be back."

After lunch a wind began to pick up. Cat knew it would die down by evening. She paddled hard. She loved this powerful, shape-changing air bubble pushing against her. There was something appealing about this grunt work. But it would end, of course it would end.

The wind backed off after an hour. Late in the afternoon they set up camp on a large island. Cat loved islands; they were cut off from the mainland, where everything was fair game—fields and sometimes dirt roads came right to the water; people could drive right up to the river or a campsite, usually in a four-by-four truck or a jacked-up SUV with fat tires. Like last night's quadders, sometimes people spent the evening driving up and down the shore or riding into the river, their music blasting. Sometimes they had guns and shot at random objects or just because.

The wind continued into the evening, not heavy, but present. A downstream wind. Everybody sat on the upstream side of the fire.

"Here's a crumb for you to chew on," Dad said. He leaned back in his folding chair and sipped his beer. "When Fleming left Scotland he thought he might not survive the voyage."

"Who?" Jamie asked.

"The guy who lost his whisky," Cat said.

"He thought there'd be a storm and a shipwreck," Dad went on. "That probably happened once a month back then. And when people left Scotland or England, it was such a big journey they usually never went back. Never saw their families again. So Fleming sent a message in a bottle, a goodbye note to his family, that he tossed into the sea. Because he was sure he wouldn't make it. But he made it safely to North America, obviously. And in the meantime his family back in Scotland got the message. The message in the bottle! It arrived! Saying he had died in a shipwreck. When he hadn't. Jamie. Cat. Stef. Just wrap your head around that for a minute."

"What?" Jamie said. "How did the bottle get all the way back? How did it get to his family?"

Dad rubbed Jamie's hair. "One of life's mysteries."

"Was it a whisky bottle?" Mom asked. "Did he drink the whisky first?"

"At least *that* bottle didn't break," Cat said.

"Did you make this up?" Jamie asked.

"No, sir, I did not," Dad said. "But c'mon, it's a great story!"

In bed later, Cat heard her parents talking. No words, just voices occasionally blown her direction. She strained to hear something, anything. The way she eavesdropped outside their bedroom door. She strained to hear through the light wind. When Jamie'd said *You'll walk away and never look back*, she tried to remember what she'd once heard, at home, through the bedroom door. Mom telling Dad how she hadn't been able to hold Cat since Jamie was born. Cat was sure she'd heard wrong.

"I thought we were going to get blasted out of the water today," Jamie said.

"What, when the train blew its whistle?"

"And the river vibrated. It was freaky."

"Imagine being a fish." Cat giggled at the sudden image of fish flying out of the water, their eyes bugged out in terror.

Jamie wasn't laughing. "Then why do they do it?"

"Do what?"

"Blast the horn."

"Safety. People and animals walk around the tracks. Into tunnels."

"Why would anyone do that?"

"Maybe people pick berries near tracks. Or mushrooms." She thought also of suicides but didn't say it.

"How do we know a thing is real?" Jamie asked.

"What?" Cat's body tensed a little. How was she going to sleep now?

"Is it real because you see it and I see it? Or is a thing real all by itself?"

"Because we can see it? Feel it?"

"No," Jamie said and rolled on his side, his back to her.

She lay awake for ages. Her thoughts flitted to Jamie and whether their parents would look after him the way she did. She didn't know where that thought came from, but she had the feeling she was the only one who really got him; still, he was a lump, he was a growth, she was ready to shed him, she hadn't asked for him, she couldn't wait to go.

✳ The day he appeared, out of nowhere, in Mom's arms, the arms that had always held her, Cat, who was now six, who had not yet had any need to question anything because everything was just right, asked: "Why?" When Mom said: "Why what?" Cat replied: "Why did you do that?" "Do what?" Mom was smiling still, turning her head close to Cat's, nuzzling, smiling like it was all a game, her sweet little girl was playing a game. "Get a baby," Cat said, taking a step back. What an affront. The baby was not only offensive; he cast a shadow on everything. Cat's world had been just fine till then. And then came this creature that had to be held all the time and cried and cried and cried till the triangle broke, in all the places it had once been so soundly connected it came apart, not all at once, but slowly, painfully, definitively.

"Why did she get a baby?" Cat asked Dad, when Mom, on hearing the question day after day for weeks and then months and finally a year, still cried and looked away. Cat no longer knew why she was asking or what she really wanted to know, except that it mattered to her once and no one had answered her and so, in the way of young children, she understood it to be important and persisted.

Dad looked confused and didn't say anything.

One autumn day her aunt took her to the playground in the next block. Auntie Min never took her anywhere; she was allergic to kids. Cat edged her bottom onto the swing and waited for the push from behind. She sat and sat. She was more than big enough to get herself going, but she wanted Auntie Min to do it. Finally Cat twisted her body around to see what was taking so long. Auntie Min's hands curved around a cigarette she was trying to light and the wind thrashed her long blond hair around her head.

"Fuck," Auntie Min said. She turned away for a few seconds and turned back again, the cigarette between two fingers, lit now, and squinted at Cat.

Cat faced forward again. "Are you going to push?"

"Look," Auntie Min said. Her cigarette clamped between her lips, she took hold of the swing, backed up with it, and let it go with a shove. "Listen. Shane's a bit of a dick. He doesn't know how to talk about this stuff."

Auntie Min never said *your dad* or *your mom* the way other people did.

"You need to stop asking Stef why," Auntie Min said.

Cat frowned and dragged the toes of her runners along the ground when the swing pendulumed to the lowest point, slowing the swing a little. She knew now what the trip to the park was about. The smoke curled around to her face when the swing backed up toward Auntie. Auntie Min gave her a hard shove.

"It's sick, what you're doing."

Cat felt the swing jerk with the next push.

"Women have babies. Sometimes babies die. Do you get it?"

Push. Jerk.

"For some women, it happens over and over again. You wouldn't think it was possible to lose so many babies. But Stef has. Always at the beginning. Four, five times now she's tried. She didn't know this one was going to make it. Didn't even tell me, she was so afraid. But I knew." She pushed. "And he made it, goddammit. The rascal made it."

Shove.

"Every time one goes, a bit of Stef goes too. I know. I've known her forever. She's all I've got, kid. Quit fucking asking. Help them out. Love that little baby."

Cat hopped off the swing and ran home.

✳ The tent was hot in the morning. Greenhouse hot. That meant the sun was up over the trees, had been up for some time. That meant it was late and no one had called them. Jamie's sleeping bag was empty. The heat must have gotten to him. Cat listened. No wind. Yesterday evening's blow had stopped. No morning birds; it wasn't spring, after all. No scavenger birds, even. No rustling of leaves. No voices from near the camp stove.

Cat dressed quickly and pulled on her runners and climbed over the fallen tree outside the tent door, a tree that must have come down in the night. She squatted on the other side of the log and peed. A tree, come down. Now there was a thing. She stared hard. It was a massive black poplar, already dead, probably starting to rot. The tree had landed on a tent peg; somehow it missed the guy rope. And the tent.

More trees were down. One, two. When she got to four, she stopped counting, stood, pulled up her pants.

Jamie's voice came to her from near the water. "Cat. Cat!"

"I'm here," Cat said back, not loudly, not wanting to disturb anything. Her voice sounded strange in the quiet air. "Right here," she said softly.

"Did you hear the wind? In the night?"

Cat ducked under a tree on her way to the shore. There he was, beside the stove. He'd set it up. Had water on the boil, for hot chocolate, for oatmeal.

"No."

"There was a wind. I heard them come down. The trees. I didn't go out."

"Jamie. Where are they?"

"Shhh."

Cat strained to hear something, anything. Her ears hurt from straining. It was too quiet. No quadders. No birds. Just the quiet hiss of the camp stove and the hesitant, intermittent bubbling of the river water, as if they, too, did not want to disturb the strange silence.

She heard a rustling in the shrubs and held her breath. It must be an animal. If she was very still, it wouldn't know that she and Jamie were there. Not true. An animal could smell them. Was it a coyote? A coyote was harmless. It could be a bear. Dad said there were bear in the area. Bear, moose, coyote, elk. Sometimes a cougar. But they hardly ever saw animals. Dad had pointed out the bear tracks in the sand, at the first night's camp, after he'd talked to them about triangulation. Mom had said, "Don't scare them." And Cat had replied, "I'm not scared."

Cat saw that Jamie had set the stove on the same flat rock their parents had used the night before. "You did that."

Jamie nodded. "First you attach the hose, then turn the regulator, and then the knob. Easy. You know how the flame poofs?" His fingers were bending, flexing, bending, flexing. "It hissed and poofed. It's pretty quiet now. It's weird. How you don't think a thing is real."

"Where are they?" Cat asked again.

Jamie looked in the direction of the other tent. Cat looked too. Though she knew already. The tent was flattened by a huge poplar.

Cat looked for a moment at the sky. It was clear. There were no clouds. There was no hint of a wind. It was the kind of morning you wanted when you were out in the woods or on a river. Warm, clear, calm. But she couldn't trust this sky.

She made her way through the shrubs. Under the collapsed tent she saw the shapes of their bodies. "Mom?" she called softly. "Dad?"

No answer.

Cat closed her eyes and imagined the morning conversations. The ones you hear from inside a tent as you wake up, from your parents or other people you canoe with. With her eyes closed and her ears straining, she could hear it all: Good morning. Sleep well? Look at that sky. Thanks, dear. Warm enough? Oh, toasty. When will those two get up?

"Cat," Jamie called. "It's ready."

Cat went back. Jamie handed her a mug of hot chocolate and oatmeal in the yellow bowl. She took them and looked at the canoes. They were on the shore. Upright. They'd rolled over in the night. They'd flipped and the ropes held.

"You saw them," Cat said.

Jamie nodded. Jamie, who was afraid of everything, saw them. Cat put down her mug and her bowl. She kicked the bowl, by accident, when she turned too quickly to go back into the shrubs, back to their parents' tent, and it flipped over. She called out again: "Mom? Dad?" Climbed over a downed tree between the shore and the forest, then stood beside their tent. The zipper already open. Left open by Jamie. The tree across their heads. A tree fatter than a telephone pole.

Cat doesn't remember packing or what they packed. Probably they left the tents and the stove. They might have packed the lunch container. And a jacket and drinking water. Cat has the car key, it's digging into her fist even now, though she can't remember where she found it. In whose pocket. Maybe Jamie pulled it out and gave it to her.

Jamie didn't speak again till they were on the water, well away from the island. He said what she'd been thinking and didn't want to say out loud herself; for all his silences, this is what he is so good at: "How come the trees missed our tent?"

After a long time, Cat said, "I don't know."

"How do we know this isn't a bad dream?"

Cat didn't answer.

"Are we ghosts?"

"No. I don't think we're ghosts."

Jamie didn't say anything after that. She didn't either.

When they got to the road where the car was parked, they left the canoe on shore and Cat drove south on the mess of logging roads to Edson following a map that was on the front passenger seat and drove this way and that way until finally she reached the highway, and eventually found the sign announcing the RCMP, and in the brick building it's all recorded, everything she says is recorded, though later she'll remember very little. Later she'll remember telling someone, a man, someone from the RCMP, that she saw them, both of them, except for their heads; and she'll remember the feeling of Jamie sitting next to her in the small office, his chair pushed up hard against hers and his bottom partly on her seat, slowly inching closer.

"You didn't hear any wind," the man says. "You didn't hear anything?" he asks over and over, scratching his head, until she begins to question her sense of all things, of warmth, of cold, of touch. The palms of her hands are hot and blistery and her shoulders ache. She has no idea how many hours she paddled, without a break, Jamie slumped in the bow. It was still daytime when they got to the car, though the sun was below the treetops by then.

She remembers Jamie asking how you know a thing is real. When did you ask that, she wants to say and: Ask that again. She takes Jamie's hand but doesn't feel it and so she sets it back on his leg like it's an object, a piece of wood or a stone. She expects Jamie to cry. He doesn't cry. She waits. Surely he will cry. His hands are flat on his legs. They don't move at all. She looks around the strange office, a stuffy space with too many papers and filing cabinets and not enough light or sky, and wonders why he doesn't cry. Since he was born he has cried for both of them. She remembers Mom's hug, how full and long it was, after she told Mom she wasn't scared. Of bears. She remembers because Mom hardly ever hugged her. When she saw Mom in the tent this morning, when she pulled the tent away from Mom's body, and touched Mom's hand, and held it, the hand felt just like Jamie's hand does now, cool and smooth, like it was a thing, not a hand. Cat squeezed Mom's hand gently, expecting her to squeeze back. Cat tried again. And again.

And now the man is looking at them intently and saying, "My God. You're kids. Just kids."

Cat has already pointed to the spot on the map where they camped last night. She won't touch the spot. Only point. And after she pointed, the man made a phone call and described that place like he knew exactly where it was, like it was just down the street and somebody would be there in a minute and things would be all sorted out, Mom and Dad would be here in a jiff and they'd all go home to bed. Because you can get it wrong. Like Fleming and his message to his family. The message was wrong.

But that was ages ago. It's dark now. Cat is tired. Her head is so heavy she can hardly hold it up. She wonders if this man, or the people he's sent to get her parents, can take a message to her mother.

Cat has told the man everything, from start to end, but now she tells the man again about Dad pointing out the bear tracks.

"Dad showed us the tracks," Cat says, "and Mom said, 'Don't scare them!' and I told Mom I'm not scared. About the bear tracks," and what she means is: I'm not scared of anything.

She believes this in her heart until the man starts punching numbers into his phone and says, "Just hang on two shakes, we'll find a safe place for you two to bed down for the night. I'll just make a couple calls here. You'll be snug as bugs in no time."

Dear
Hector

MADDIE WANTS TO KICK SOMEONE. She's called for Hector. No Hector. She can't blame him. He comes and goes when he pleases, just like she does. He's good company, though. He purrs when she strokes his jawbone and licks the salt from her shins after a run. Occasionally he bites. He's a cat, after all. Naturally, she'll take him back. Only there's no sign of him, no sign of his intentions even. It seems so cruel. Life is too short for cruelty.

There's a rat-a-tat-tat on the front door. Riker. Coming for their run. He doesn't use the bell. Too intrusive, he says. He bops from one foot to the other on the top step in his shorts and T-shirt while she ties her laces.

"Orange," Riker says into her cheek when she stands and then kisses her. "Orange! Did I get it?"

"Nope!" Maddie laughs. She locks the door and sprints down the steps and to the sidewalk.

Riker catches up quickly. "Coral?"

Maddie shakes her head and runs faster.

"I've done all the standard colours, haven't I? It's not a standard colour, is it? You're more complicated than that. How about turquoise?"

"You haven't told me yours," Maddie says. She turns left at the corner.

"I told you. It's whatever yours is."

He said that at Boun Thai, on their first date, six long-short weeks ago. They aren't in their twenties anymore, after all. Their people-reading skills are fairly advanced. Not only that, each of them has a history. Clean slate, they readily agreed, over the spicy calamari bites. "Let's just go on adventures and have sex and eat. That's all a person needs." Maddie hadn't planned to say that. It rolled off her tongue after a few Thai Pink Ladies and felt right.

They run along Saskatchewan Drive, thud down the wide wooden steps into the river valley, make their way east on a narrow dirt trail through the trees. They hop over big sprawling roots and muddy craters, run past the Low Level Bridge and the *Edmonton Queen*. The late afternoon air has a tenderness to it, there's no wind, it's not muggy, not hot, not cold. The aspen push their tiny, sticky buds out with all their might; there's a hint of new green in the leaves. Maddie smells the earth, pummelled awake from last night's rain, damp and humussy. Their run is perfect. Maddie could run and run and never stop. It's a dream run, and they are in the same dream.

Every three or four minutes Riker tries a new colour, his face bright with hope. "Burgundy?" And then: "Aquamarine?"

Maddie laughs and shakes her head. He reaches for her, tries to grab her shoulders and her hands, but she darts away. He asks as if by knowing her colour he will know everything there is to know about her. It was the only thing he wanted to know, on the first date. Of any relevance, that is. They haven't shared family, birth dates, clothing sizes, keys, work, bad habits, life goals. None of it. Especially nothing about the other people they dated. Or might still be dating. On purpose. Because that meant getting into the core of each other, and getting to the core meant one of them wanted more. Someone always wanted more. Maddie was tired. She didn't want to give anyone anything. But there it was: *Tell me your favourite colour.* Then he smiled slowly and scanned her face in a way that made her skin prickle. Everywhere his eyes paused she felt little nibbles. Like goldfish bites. Or Hector's scratchy tongue. It's a game now. It's like that chase game she used to play with her dad. Wanting to be caught and getting away were equally thrilling. This was the same game. She will not be caught. But she loves the chase. She would be happy for it to last forever.

Before she knows it, the run is over and they're in her shower. Riker gets out before she does and when she steps out he calls from the kitchen, in a heavy, mixed-up French accent, as if he's read her mind, "De vine breeds, madam."

Maddie's in the bedroom, rubbing her hair with a towel. She roots through her sock drawer. No socks. A person can do without socks. She pulls on shorts and a T-shirt

Riker stands at the stove in his underwear.

"*Les crevettes,*" he says, "*avec l'ail et le gingembre.* Sound good?"

"Lay what?" She looks in the frying pan. "Sure."

"Teal?"

Maddie smiles and shakes her head. She goes to the sliding doors off the kitchen and looks out.

"What's up?"

"Hector. My cat. I haven't seen him since yesterday morning." Hector's been with her for three years. Longer than anyone. He was a tiny thing when he arrived. Brown and white-striped, a small scar on his nose, an ordinary cat. He squeezed through a gap in these very sliding doors one long lonely Sunday afternoon and let out a single, tiny, heart-grabbing *meow* and she let him stay; how could she not, the way he rubbed against her leg, purring and looking up at her with such hope. How long he was there, peeking in, watching her every move, she'll never know. An hour, a day, weeks. Time blurs, becomes an amorphous blob in these situations. A creature who came for her, unannounced and wholly unabashed. A creature who chose her. That was it, really. Being chosen. Being wanted. He seems to know her, her wishes and needs. He butts his head against her chest, he kneads the newspaper, he nuzzles the front door till he gets what he wants. Other times, he goes nuts licking her shins. It tickles. Sometimes it makes her a bit horny. Who knew?

"You're a cat person," Riker says.

"No. We never had cats when I was a kid. Or dogs."

The front door opens.

"You expecting someone?" Riker asks. He takes her huge knife and pushes the flat side down hard on a garlic clove.

"Just Hector," Maddie says on her way to the door. Maybe a neighbour has found him.

It's Elizabeth. "Mads! You're home!" She slips out of her shoes and walks past Maddie. "I've been calling! Did you get my messages?"

"Elizabeth. This is not a good time—"

Elizabeth traipses through the living room and into the kitchen. Maddie follows.

"Hel-lo!" Elizabeth sings. "Who are you?"

Riker turns around, shakes her hand. "Riker." He looks at his fingertips, then at her. "Excuse the garlic."

Elizabeth stares at his hand, then his face. "You always cook naked?"

"Elizabeth, he's not naked."

Elizabeth's eyes flick from Riker's neck down to his toes. "You're right, he's wearing his underwear." She takes a wine glass from the cupboard, pours a slug from the open bottle, and sits at the kitchen table. "Well, since I'm here, I might as well have a drink. Thank God, a man who can cook. There's a rare bird. I'm starving. I haven't had dinner yet either."

"Elizabeth, this is a *date*," Maddie whispers loudly.

"Only joking about dinner." Elizabeth takes a long sip and looks from Maddie to Riker. "Nice." She leans back and crosses her legs. "How'd you two meet?"

"*Mes crevettes*," Riker says and turns back to the stove.

"May what?" Elizabeth says.

"Running," Maddie says quickly. "In the river valley."

"Since when do you meet someone running?"

"Every day. How would you know? You don't run!"

Elizabeth likes to work out indoors on equipment she has to sign up for and sterilize and punch personal data into before she gets on. Height, weight, age, how many bites of toast (white or brown) she consumed at breakfast.

"How do I know he's not a serial killer?" Elizabeth asks. "Riker, how do we know you aren't a serial killer?"

"People who run aren't serial killers," Maddie says. "They're too busy running."

Riker turns and nods. "It's true. You need to save your breath when you run." He grins and turns back.

"Riker, she's joking," Maddie says. "Again. She feels a need to look after me and has a weird way of going about it."

Elizabeth gives Riker a dark look. "I'm calling you tomorrow, Maddie. Answer your phone!" She downs the last of her wine and gets up. "I saw myself in. I'll see myself out."

Riker pours two glasses of wine and sits down. "That was fun. Who was that?"

"My sister."

"You have any more sisters?"

"No."

"The coast is clear then. Let's eat." He raises his glass and tings hers.

Later, lying beside him in bed, she sighs happily. There's no bad day good sex won't fix. And sex is way more fun than therapy, other than the massage sort of therapy where you lie face down and spill your guts and someone pushes all the bad karma out of you. When the world comes to an end, by fire or flood or an invasion of those psychotic, biting ants, her plan is to find a safe place and make out till it's over.

✳ Maddie wakes when the phone rings. The space beside her in the bed is empty. No Hector. No Riker. Riker must have left in the night. He does that. Just like a cat, come to think of it. It will be him on the phone. She imagines his warm breath, his tongue in all those little places.

She picks up the phone and says slowly, "Good morning, Riker."

"Jesus, Mads."

"Elizabeth!" Maddie sits up.

"Did you really meet him running?"

"You know how much I love running."

"You met him through a dating app didn't you?" She makes that sound Maddie can only describe as a judgmental huff. "Mads, no one tells the truth in their profiles. They're all hot and financially independent and emotionally stable. And young and super fit. It's all lies."

"I didn't know you browsed dating profiles."

"I don't! I don't need to!"

Elizabeth has always been more grown up, more sensible, wiser. She even goes by her full name, not some shortened form that she insists, as she told Maddie eons ago, keeps a person from actually growing up. Elizabeth is four years younger than Maddie, but everybody thinks she's older. It's not just the name. It's because she knows how to wear high heels and short skirts and those deep-cut silky blouses and, especially, how to do hair. It's all in the hair. Maddie could not care less about hair. She wears it short. Like a pixie. Nor does she care about make-up. It helps that she looks young. She looks twenty-three but she's a decade older. That's how it was with their mother. Their mother always looked young. Maddie assumes it's genetic. One day out of the blue a few lines will appear beside Maddie's eyes and her lips and maybe a grey hair, just one, will show up, but for now there are none, neither lines nor hairs, and so she looks twenty-three. She doesn't really want to be too grown up or too serious. There is a serious side to her, but it's folded neatly and tucked into the far end of her lingerie drawer along with the letter her mother wrote before leaving the family Christmas party and jumping into the river from the Walterdale Bridge, over where the power plant keeps the water from freezing. She was wearing her navy dress, the short one, and her Woolworth's down coat, grey with white trim, the one that went down to her ankles. The note is handwritten, with a blue pen, neatly, and says, "I have to go now. xo." And so her mother did not become old or grown up or serious. When it comes down to it, Maddie is the sort of person who likes smooth lingerie and not thinking too long. About anything. You can't fault her for that.

"He didn't say anything about money or emotional crap," Maddie says lightly. She takes slow, giant, stealthy steps over to the couch and quickly looks behind it. No Hector. Just dust balls. Without Hector, her whole world has been off-kilter. Hector is the one stable life form in her world, other than Elizabeth. She misses his nuzzling nose in her neck and her armpit. She misses his paws pressing on her stomach like it's fresh dough.

"What did he say, then?" Elizabeth asks.

"He said his socks matched." Maddie flops onto the couch and stretches out her legs. Then she remembers she can't find any of her socks these days. Or half her underwear, now that she thinks of it.

"He said his socks matched?"

"Some days. Depends on his mood. And he cooks."
Though he was being a little modest. She does not want
to cook ever again now that she has been fed by Riker.
Sautéed escarole with garlic, chicken tagine, cherry tartlets,
you name it, he can do it. He can do it speaking French or
Swedish and even a bit of Mandarin or Gaelic or Afrikaans
in a pinch.

"What's he do for a living?"

"Something in law enforcement or security. Or maybe
that was his brother." Maddie walks to the kitchen and
shakes Hector's treat bag. "Law enforcement. Maybe he
gives out traffic tickets. Or he said he had a few. Whatever. It
came up after we polished off a bottle of Merlot."

"Oh, Maddie. Will you always be like this?"

"Oh, man, I hope so."

"Mads, life is not all a game. You have to let someone in
sometime." Elizabeth sighs. "Don't forget what I said about
walking away from your drinks. Date rape."

"That's still a thing?"

"Mads!"

"Elizabeth, you worry too much." She wants to be like
normal people and say *You're not my mom!* but that was
crossing a line. And what a thin line it was.

It's Tuesday. Maddie works as a chef in a small hospice.
She's been there five years. At first, it was like stepping into
an altered reality. People arrived and in two or three days,
they were gone. Sometimes they didn't make it through the
first night. Volunteers take the food to the people, so
Maddie almost never sees them. Most of them are very old.
Some use MAID. Once, a year or so ago, there was a woman

who came to the sitting area near the kitchen to eat. She could still feed herself. She was at the hospice a long time. Two months. Maddie got so used to her she cried the morning Suki stopped coming and every morning after for weeks. There was no warning. Maddie can still see the outline of Suki's body in the empty chair, the slump of her back, the flowery pattern on her dress, her rigid face, her shaky hand slowly, so slowly, moving the spoon from the bowl to her mouth. Some days Maddie has to move that chair out of her line of sight. Now she tries not to get used to anyone. Mostly she talks to people through the food as she prepares it. In her head, not out loud. She goes about it slowly, methodically. Because it could be their last meal. Their send-off meal. If only she'd known she was giving Hector his last meal with her. She would have given him an extra scoop of the soft stuff. She would have said something, some kind words to see him through the dark streets.

Today she leaves at three o'clock and walks to her massage therapist, a woman who works tirelessly at all of her knots and globs and rock-hard bobbles. Maddie thought they were just tight spots but no, Jen says they are The Dregs of Unresolved Stuff. The Undealt-with Past. Jen knows about all those short-long flings with men whose names Maddie has since plucked from her brain and flushed down the toilet. Clingy men who didn't give her space, suffocated her, couldn't even let her *read* around them without telling her they felt *shut out*. Bits of them Maddie has shared, over time, and the rest Jen has discovered through Knotty Bobbles. Maddie can't believe she found Jen. A massage therapist is the right sort of therapist for pushing out crap. The other kind is far too earnest. Earnestness suffocates a person's soul.

Maddie's cheeks are pressed into the soft head cradle. The hollow, woody sounds of a pan flute swirl around the room. The world can come to an end now if it needs to. This is not sex, but it will do for the time being and besides, she's warm and nearly naked, she's a comatose gelatinous blob. The pleasure is slow and sprawling. She's just conscious enough to tell Jen about Riker. It's the beginning of something, and beginnings are grand by default. Beginnings can't help themselves; they're laden with hope and lack of sleep and excess.

"What's he like?" Jen asks.

"Well," Maddie says into the massage table hole, "he looks fine. His teeth are a little crooked and maybe his nose is a smidge large for his face, but whatever. He jogs, he rides a bike, he reads. Books, I mean. Oh, he invited me to some kind of dance workshop in Lethbridge this weekend."

"Huh." Jen pushes her warm palms into Maddie's shoulders. "Lethbridge. Ballet?"

"God no." Maddie's mother had visions of adorable, lithe fairies every Christmas and for years Elizabeth and Maddie, who was still Madeleine then, wore pink ballet slippers and short puffy skirts and pink tights and pink body suits and had their long hair pulled up into buns so tight Maddie's head hurt. Who knew there were so many excruciating ways to contort your arms and your legs and your back? Year after year her ears rang with *Madeleine, other way. Madeleine, point your toes. Madeleine, arm higher. Madeleine, point, point, point. Madeleine, what's to become of you?*

"I love ballet!" Jen gushes. "There's nothing like it. It's beautiful, isn't it." She works her thumbs on either side of Maddie's spine and doesn't say anything for several minutes. Maddie hates that. That means she's analyzing but not sharing the results of her analysis. What? Maddie wants to ask. What does this mean?

"Not ballet. Scottish country dancing. It's our first weekend away together. Our true colours will show." Maddie thinks she's clever, saying that, and is just about to tell Jen about the thing with the colours, but Jen speaks first.

"I heard that smile."

Maddie is self-conscious all of a sudden. Jen's been hearing about her forays into dating for eight years or so. Jen is too discreet to ask about any of the previous men once they've been flushed away. This is the sum of what Maddie knows about Jen, after all this time, and it is just enough: Jen has a lovely daughter who's about fourteen, maybe a partner, details unknown, and they have no problems whatsoever. Almost every weekend Jen is off cross country skiing or backpacking or canoeing, she's Wonder Woman or Nike in other words, and when she returns she's glowing with life and energy. Maddie wants some of that glow. She knows that if she comes for a massage often enough, she'll get it, through Jen's fingertips. Through something called osmosis. She will know what to do with a canoe paddle, without ever having been in a canoe; she will know how to get lost and found in the woods, even though she has no idea where the hiking trails are; she will know how to move through the world slowly, without running, like most people. She will one day have no more knots and kinks to rid herself of. But mostly she will *glow*.

"Yow," Maddie says. Jen has found an especially feisty glob. "Sadist."

Jen gets more oil, something flowery, and starts on Maddie's neck, then presses down on Maddie's upper back with her fingers. For a second Maddie thinks it's Hector, gently walking on her back. She sighs.

"You do like him," Jen says, and for a time neither of them says anything.

Half an hour later, the massage is done. Maddie's body is no longer gelatinous but she's still semi-comatose. Her home is a short walk from Jen's studio. It's April and late enough in the day that the low sun gives everything a golden sheen. A band of sunlight streams between walk-ups and just-budding elms, and the air is fresh.

The phone is ringing when Maddie opens her door. It can't be Elizabeth again; she doesn't call twice in one day. But it might be. Maddie replies cautiously.

"Maddie, it's Riker." There's a short pause. "Purple?"

Maddie laughs. "Not purple!"

"Damn. Can I come over?"

"Yes!" she says, then wants to bite her tongue for sounding too eager. Never sound too eager. He'll come, he'll cook, and they'll make love. What will it be? Something quick; it's nearly six. A leafy green salad with a secret ingredient in the dressing, that's it. It will take him twenty minutes to walk over. Enough time to tidy the bedroom and make the bed.

"Great," Riker says. "I've had a hell of a day. I bought new runners and I can't wait to try them out. How about I come around eight and we run along the river for an hour?"

"Eight," Maddie says. She twirls her hair. She won't ask him for dinner, then. Nothing like sounding too keen. He'll get ideas that she's pining for him or something. "Sure," she says. "That works."

Somebody once told her that sex is like salt. You slowly get used to having more and more and suddenly a lot doesn't seem like very much. The same is true in reverse, apparently.

She opens the closet door, the basement storage room door, wonders where Hector is, what he's doing. It's not just his scratchy tongue she misses. He's always warm, even when he's been out in the cold. He goes bat-shit crazy when she makes light birds on the floor or the wall with her watch. And he couldn't make his heart beat softly if he tried.

✳ "Like them?" Riker asks. He jogs on the spot beside Maddie while she tightens her laces. His new running shoes are fluorescent orange streaked with glow-in-the-dark green and yellow.

"Holy Mother of God!" Maddie covers her eyes with her arm and stands up. "Do they come with an off button?"

"I'll take that as a yes."

They run along Saskatchewan Drive. Tonight they head west. The robins are yodelling overhead. A small posse of joggers passes them from the opposite direction and a few wave. Maddie tells Riker about her massage. Riker tells her about the funny woman at the store where he bought his new shoes. Funny ha ha or funny weird, Maddie wants to know.

"Funny demented," Riker says. "She was bringing out all these shoes, just like the ones I said I wanted to try, and everything's going great and she disappears in the back room and I think she's going to come out with my size, because now I have the shoes I like, but she came out with a pair of rubber boots. Size sixteen."

"Seriously?"

"Fuchsia?" he asks.

"Is that even a colour?" she asks.

Riker chuckles.

The make their way down to the river valley and leap over fallen logs and patches of mud. The air is cool and crisp.

"Riker," Maddie says finally. "The sun's going down. We won't be able to see our way back. Even with your snazzy new shoes." What she really means is she wants to go back home and shower with him and take him to her bed because, really, with Hector gone AWOL it's strange and quiet around the house. She hasn't felt this unsettled since forever.

"Let's just get to the footbridge past Hawrelak Park and go back," Riker says.

A huge run, but Maddie's up for it. They run on to the park, cross the river, and pound east on the bike paths and over the river again on the footbridge below Maddie's neighbourhood. They retrace their steps through the woods and Skunk Hollow and slowly make their way up to Saskatchewan Drive. Maddie is fit, but the wooden steps up the hill go on and on; she can't speak, let alone think what she might say if she could. She feels like the aspen buds, pushing with all her might to get up and out and sticky with her body's heat. That's it, she thinks. Everybody must come to this at some point, this stasis, and want something more or something different but not know what, everybody must want to push their way out. At the top she walks slowly, her hands cupping her waist. The Walterdale Bridge is to her right—the one bridge she does not run across. She doesn't even turn; she never turns to look.

At the top Riker gasps, "I kept up with you, didn't I?"

"Just barely," Maddie runs on ahead.

In a few blocks they stop. Maddie's place is east, his is west.

"I'll cut back from here," Riker says. "See you Friday. Ten a.m. sharp." His kisses her lightly, then gives her lower lip a playful nip before he runs slowly down the street.

✻ On Friday morning Maddie carries her blue suitcase down the stairs. She's left out food and water for Hector on the back porch in case he returns. If he's not quick, the squirrels will get it. Or the neighbourhood cats. She's tempted to leave a note. *Dear Hector.* She can't think past *Dear Hector.*

She sits on the front steps. It's cool outside but not cold. The sun shines courageously overhead; pale yellow rays streak through the massive spruce and the overgrown mountain ash on the lawn. Maddie hates the front yard in April. The front yard in April is a thawing sewer. In the shade are patches of mouldy snow and layers of liver-spotted leaves and little mounds of dog turds, and under the mountain ash is a sticky blanket of droppings left by the Bohemian waxwings after gorging on berries. From the top step Maddie stares through the sun-streaked branches at the waxwings. It's like looking through a kaleidoscope at bird-shaped silhouettes. A single bird makes a small turn, and off they all swirl, like they're tightly connected by an invisible cord that pulls one back when it strays too far. They swoosh into the mountain ash en masse, land, and flick their tails coquettishly, then hop quickly from branch to branch as if to say *Can't catch me! Flick, flick*. A-ha—they play the chase game, too. They are in constant motion. Are they exhausted, or do they not know any other life? When they sit still for a few seconds, she sees their colours, the red and black masks covering their heads, their shiny grey wings spritzed with splashes of red and yellow and white. As if they've come to a ball and they're dancing and drinking themselves silly. *Flick!* and they're off again. Maddie laughs. This is the life she aspires to: eat, drink, play, then eat, drink, and play some more. She hopes her mother thought like this.

Riker pulls up in his jeep and honks twice. Maddie shoves her suitcase into the trunk and settles in beside him. A few minutes later they are heading south on Calgary Trail.

"You too warm? Too cold?" Riker asks.

"No. And no," Maddie says.

"Lavender?"

Maddie just chuckles.

"Ha! Lavender!"

"Not lavender." She laughs.

Riker's shoulders sag for a half second and then he sits upright again. "I will get it. One day I will get it."

She can't help it; she loves this about him. She loves how he takes in the highway, the clear sky blue as forget-me-nots, the mucky brown fields. There is still some snow in the fields, on the north-facing slopes, if it can be said that a prairie field has a slope. Every few miles she spots a red-tailed hawk on a fence post, watching over the traffic like a sentinel.

"Mud?"

"That is definitely not a colour."

"Maddie. I want the world never to run out of colours." After a minute he says, "Funny how the hawks face the highway."

"Why funny?"

"All the mice must be in the fields."

"Maybe it's not dinner time?"

"I used to do a great hawk call."

"Do it," Maddie says. "Go on, do it."

Riker shrieks like the red tail. She half-jumps. "Got you! I haven't done that for years. I used to teach summer camp and I'd do squirrels, ravens—I love the raven." He makes a low, gurgling croak. "Weird, isn't it?"

"We're all weird, Riker. This dancing thing you do is weird. What's it called again? Irish country? Spanish country? Old country?"

"Sco'ish, lassie!" he says. He grabs her hand and kisses the back of it and doesn't let go.

After a few minutes he hits PLAY on the CD player. "A few Scottish songs. Some of the ones we'll be dancing to. So you get into the feel of it. The strathspeys, they melt your heart."

Maddie listens. "I like the words."

"Get a load of that fiddle. And the bodhran."

"How do you know all of this?" She's thinking of the bits of Polish and Mandarin too. And his cooking.

Riker shrugs. "I'm a dabbler. A bit of this, a bit of that."

The music is spirited and makes her think of the drunken dancing waxwings.

"No bagpipes," she says.

"Yes, bagpipes. They pipe in the grand march and the haggis," he says. "No haggis this weekend, though."

"You go all this way just to dance?" she asks. "Every year?"

"Most years. Here and there and everywhere."

"How can you actually dance all weekend?"

"We find ways. There's also scotch." He kisses her hand again. "You drive me half mad, you know. Ever since that night at Boun Thai. You drive me half mad."

Maddie's insides dissolve. He's not like the others, not at all. She wonders where Riker has been all her life. Because she feels like she's known him forever. How can that be? She knows so little about him, he knows so little about her. She's about to blurt out a colour. But no. No. Because he wants it and doesn't think he will ever get it.

✳ They drop into the Oldman River valley late in the afternoon. After checking in at the hotel and finding their room, they make their way downstairs to the hotel restaurant. Maddie doesn't want to walk to a restaurant outside the hotel. She doesn't want to go out at all. "It's too windy," she says. "If we go outside we'll get blown all the way to Sweet Grass."

When the food arrives, Maddie lifts a slimy piece of spinach with her fork. "They should hire you."

THIS IS HOW YOU START TO DISAPPEAR

"I'm a terrible cook, remember?" He smirks at her. "It said so in my profile. On that dating app." Riker looks down at the soppy mashed potatoes covered in a thin gravy, limp, over-steamed broccoli, desiccated chicken. "It's pretty bad, all right." He whacks his chicken with the flat of his knife.

They return to their room to change. Maddie's cell phone chugs. A text from Elizabeth. "Hey. Where are you?"

Maddie texts back: "Hey yourself. Lethbridge. Dancing."

"Is that jogging serial killer with you?"

"Of course!" Maddie types. "He will stab me in the heart at the stroke of midnight." Then she enters a heart emoji and turns the phone to silent and sets it on the bedside table. When the phone vibrates, Maddie slips it under her pillow. She's struck with instant regret, though. Why does she still feel the need to torture her sister like this? A sister who loves her unfailingly? It's a bit like the game of tag with their dad, only Elizabeth doesn't play. Even when Maddie, so family lore goes, used to sit on Elizabeth and shake her shoulders and yell: "She loves me more! Mama loves me *more*!" and their mother would gently extract Maddie, still Madeleine, from Elizabeth, take them on her lap, one on each knee, and hug them both tight while they bawled. Even then, Elizabeth loved her.

She walks with Riker down to the workshop registration table. Other dancers pass and call out hello, they give him a light high-five, they squeeze his arm.

"Riker! How nice to see you've brought someone," says the woman handing out name tags. "She looks like a fine lassie. The ceilidh's about to start, go on in now."

Riker introduces Maddie and they fasten their name tags. They walk past the table where a man is selling trinkets with a Scottish theme: toffee, coasters, bumper stickers, ties, charms. Riker grabs her and gives her a quick kiss. He buys two glasses of scotch at the bar.

They sip on their way into the ballroom. Riker had told her earlier about the ceilidh. Easy dances that everyone can do, even people with two left feet.

Maddie watches. So many people, moving every which way, fast, and arriving where they started when the music ends.

The dance finishes. A woman at a mic calls everybody onto the floor for the next dance.

They leave their glasses on a side table and walk onto the dance floor. Riker speaks quietly into her ear: *We're at the bottom of our set. Watch the others. Look at their feet: Skip change. Slip step.*

They're at the top now. When they dance to the bottom of the set and back up Maddie's feet almost never touch the floor. Riker holds her in a way that makes her feel like she knows what she's doing. The dance makes her think of the waxwings in her yard. She's still learning the steps, but she can feel herself flitting, perching, flying, moving in unison, attached by an invisible cord, a lifeline. To what, she doesn't know. Riker is solid and light at the same time. Maddie's never dated a dancer before. Every time he's close to her, he whispers in her ear: *Crimson. Lime green. Meringue.* A warmth spreads through Maddie but she doesn't say anything.

The dances have names that make Maddie laugh: "Marmalade Sandwich." "The President's Dilemma." "Gang the Same Gate."

They walk back to the bar when "Gang the Same Gate" is up; it's not for beginners, Riker says. There's a longer drink line this time. By the time they return to the ballroom to watch, the dancers are well into yet another dance.

"'Postie's Jig,'" Riker says. "One of my favourites. Watch. See the arms going up and down? If you don't know what you're doing, well, you might get injured. But look—a thing of beauty, this, when everyone's in sync. Like colouring within the lines."

Maddie's feet and shins ache a little. She leans in to Riker. "Any more scotch and I won't be able to stand up."

The woman behind them in the line asks, "Is she always this funny?"

"Funny ha ha?" Riker says. "Or some other kind of funny?"

"You know," the woman says.

Maddie wonders if it was a real conversation or if she just imagined it.

In bed that night she climbs on top of him and nuzzles into his neck while he moves inside her. Her cell phone buzzes like an annoyed house fly and she shoves it to the floor.

✳ When Maddie wakes, her legs are entangled in Riker's. She doesn't want to move. Just before the morning class starts, she rolls out of bed and pulls on her dancing clothes and runs her fingers through her hair a few times. Downstairs Riker waves her into the beginner dance class and goes to the advanced. She picks up the patterns quickly. Her body type might not have been right for ballet, but it works in this sort of dance. After half an hour, she knows she likes it. With every dance, she has a new partner and in some dances she changes partners, briefly. No one fusses too much about holding your body perfectly or whether you are pointing your toes just so.

At lunch they sit at a table with some dancers from Riker's home group. A few people joke about what they did in the classes, how complicated the dances were. Byzantine, Judith says. Like those white doilies my great grandmother used to crochet, she adds. I still crochet those, Pierrette says. I need new feet, says Rick.

After lunch Maddie goes to the room to check her phone. Elizabeth's first message reads: "Mads! Are you there?" And the next: "Madeleine!"

"Chill," Maddie writes back. "He hasn't put anything in my drink. Yet." She'll never tell Elizabeth, but she's relieved to hear from her. She slides the phone under the pillow again and goes downstairs for the next round of classes.

That night is the ball. Maddie has a dress. It's yellow with a slightly full skirt, silky but not too. Everyone but Maddie has spent months learning the dances. "You can join in for the easy ones, like last night," Riker told her earlier. "For the others...think of it as a performance with a tiny audience. You'll be part of the tiny audience. There will be others who aren't dancing."

First they have dinner at a big round table. Ella tells a story about Thailand. Trevor describes the new dance he learned. Jackson toasts a dancer they all knew who died. The food arrives and everybody is suddenly quiet. Can't-talk-eating, Riker says between bites. After a minute, the talk starts gain, voices darting here and there, someone erupting in laughter. This must be what normal family dinners are like, Maddie thinks.

Eventually the dances start, and soon most of the tables are empty. The only people sitting are the partners and friends who don't dance. They know Riker, though, and they want to know who Maddie is, what she does, how she and Riker met. She gives the same answer: "Running. In the river valley in Edmonton." They're all friendly. She could love them. All of them.

When she finds herself alone, she watches the dances closely. There are patterns and patterns within patterns. The dances deceive: they seem first like autumn leaves flung into the air, the whoosh of waxwings, the chaos of eating at a table for eight, but they are carefully planned from the first step to the last. People are almost always moving. If they are not moving, their bodies are taut, ready. After each dance, everybody takes a new partner. Dance etiquette. On the dance floor, no one asks anything of her except that she dance. And sometimes not even that.

Riker appears and invites her up to dance. "This one's easy," he says.

After she dances twice with Riker, others ask her to dance. Her cheeks hurt from smiling non-stop. She could dance all night. As long as she can step away.

At midnight, the ball ends. The room is strangely silent. Maddie's heart is heavy. They make their way to their room.

"Chartreuse," Riker says in the hallway, softly, in case people are sleeping.

Maddie shakes her head.

"Well, here we are, gang the same gate," he says when they are a few steps from their suite.

"What?"

"'Gang the Same Gate.' That's one of the dances, remember? It means going the same way." He turns her toward him and holds her shoulders tightly. "You and me. Gang the same gate." Riker gives her an intent look. "Hey. Maddie." He catches his breath and puts a finger under her chin. They step inside their room. "Don't you love it?" he asks. "The dances?"

She disappears into the bathroom to brush her teeth. She takes a very long time. Riker was right; the dances are like colouring in the lines. There are no surprises. No sudden curveballs, blindsiding her. But still. Everybody is attached, by that invisible thread. The weight of it is huge. She does not want to be attached. To be caught. There it is. What is a woman but someone always stepping out, always about to leave?

Finally, she's seen it. She will tell Elizabeth. She will tell Jen. She will tell the soft brown lentils and white rice she prepares in the hospice. She does not need to tell Hector. Hector knows.

Her calves are tight and the balls of her feet cramp. She does some stretches. She does some squats.

When she finally comes out of the bathroom, Riker is spread on his back on the bed, still in his clothes. He's completely passed out. There's no waking him. She can almost see an amber scotch hue rising from him.

She sits beside the bed and reaches for her cell. What to text Elizabeth? She presses the phone against her cheek.

It's cool, like Hector's nose. A vibrating phone is like a purr. Maddie sighs, closes her eyes, and sees Hector. He crawls onto her chest and presses down with both paws. It hurts. It always hurts. Even though she knows he doesn't mean it to. Hector is a cat and cats make their own rules.

She wants to tell Riker how in the morning he'll know, his body will carry the knowledge when he sits up, before he steps into the hall, before he looks for her in the ballroom and the cloakroom. There are things you know before you know them, she wants to say. Before you see the note.

Instead, Maddie dreams, or fake-dreams, that she whispers into Riker's ear, whispers the way he spoke softly into the phone in the mornings, and it's clear: Black, she says, and the dream Riker whispers, Black is not a colour, and she replies, It's what I see when I close my eyes. So you might as well just stay here in the hotel room bed, she goes on, and wait until the room stops tilting and think how the mind plays tricks. How I simply appeared one quiet Sunday in Boun Thai with hope in my eyes.

When
Sleep
Is Easy

CORA MASSAGED A TUBE OF ICING in her palm and
squeezed small pink buds a thumb-width apart around
the rim of the cake. She'd already spread white frosting,
good and thick. It had taken her some time to get the pink
icing for the buds to the right consistency to form shapes,
but now it was pretty near perfect. The buds were an extra
touch for her one grandchild, a little girl named Mikayla-
with-a-K who was coming up to four and almost certainly
loved all things pink. Cora had no idea. She pressed a dozen
fresh raspberries in a small mound in the centre of the
cake and wiped her cheek with the back of her hand. Nearly
professional. The family would love it. They loved her cakes.

The front door banged open and Kelly called out, "Hi,
Mom! Hi, Dad!"

"Kelly, you're early!" Her older daughter usually got the
time wrong. She got most things wrong. Cora looked at
the bag of icing sugar, vials of food colouring, the big red
mixing bowl, dirty cake pans.

"Nice to see you too! You want me to go?"

"Oh, don't start. Give me a hand with these dishes. Your dad's been lying around watching the game all afternoon. Not like the rest of us wouldn't like to do that." Though that was all she and Earl did. Breakfast, lunch, and dinner, they sat in front of the boob tube in the basement. They had their own small tables with the folding legs. "Not like I ever get to see what I want to watch," Cora said loudly, because Kelly was still at the front door, out of sight. "Like a documentary or a comedy. I could sure use a good comedy. Did you hear that thing on the news about the woman from the States and her mother? The mother is dead now and the daughter is alive. Did you? They came all this way. I can't stop thinking about that poor daughter and what she did. How could anybody do such a thing?" Cora felt cold. She turned to check the window by the sink. It was closed. "Are you coming in or are you just going to stand there all day?"

Kelly strode into the kitchen, draping her jacket over the back of Earl's armchair. "Nice to see you too," she repeated quietly. "Dad downstairs?"

"No, he's out back doing a thousand push-ups." Did the girl ever listen? "Where else would he be?"

"Wow, Mom, that's some cake."

"It's the least I can do for my only grandchild."

"Mom." Kelly gathered the mixing bowl and baking pans and set them by the sink. "Lay off. You have kids, they grow up, they move away. And you yell at them when they show up. Why would I want kids?"

"Aren't you in a mood." There had always been something different about that girl. Maybe there always would be. Kelly was thirty-five but still acted like she was nineteen.

What was that new expression for people like her? *Failure to launch.*

Kelly turned on the hot water. "When will Alana and Rob be here?"

"You know them. They're always late."

"They have a three-hour drive. And a kid who's probably puking or having a tantrum about her sock."

Earl emerged from the basement. "Kelly! I thought I heard your voice." He rubbed her head hard. "That's my girl!"

Cora watched Kelly scrunch her eyes and move close to Earl. She and Earl had a cat once, a brown and white thing. More Earl's pet than hers. He used to rub the cat that way, too, and it would purr loudly and move in close.

"Hi, Dad. How's it going?"

"I keep on keeping on. Not getting any older, not getting any younger."

"You sound like a stuck record," Cora said.

"Just don't trade me in for a CD."

Kelly chuckled. Cora didn't see what was so funny about it. He'd said it a hundred times by now. "You cut your hair, Kelly," she said.

"Yeah, you like it?" Kelly ran her fingers up her shaved neck.

"It's just so short," Cora said. "There's almost nothing to it."

Kelly shrugged. "Who's winning, Dad?"

"Oilers. One-nothing. Hey, we should take in another game sometime."

"You don't ask me what I'm doing," Cora said to Kelly.

"What are you doing, Mom?"

THIS IS HOW YOU START TO DISAPPEAR

"Making dinner for my family! Isn't it obvious?" Cora felt them staring, like something was wrong with her. It was the other way around. First they ignored her, then they completely overlooked what was right in front of them. What was with everybody?

"So, what's for dinner, Cora?" Earl asked.

"I told you. Lasagne! I went to the store to pick one up so I didn't have to spend the day cooking. This proves it. He never listens to anything I say, Kelly."

"Tell us what's new, Kel," Earl said. "Miss ya."

Kelly squeezed dish soap into the sink. "Nothing really."

"Playing your guitar?"

Kelly turned to him brightly. "Yeah, lots. I've had a few good gigs and I have five students."

"Five!" Cora said. The girl would never make it at that rate.

Kelly turned back to the sink.

"That's hardly a living, Kel," Earl said. "Anyway, bring your guitar next time. You're the only one of us with any talent. Don't let it go to waste. One day you'll look back and wish you'd played more."

Cora flicked on the oven light and looked in. "Alana'd better get here soon or we'll have dried-out lasagne."

The front door burst open and Cora hurried to the entrance. Mikayla flew past her and shrieked. Rob scooped her up and held her against his side while he pulled at her shoelaces. She flapped her arms and legs like she was swimming. Alana stood calmly inside the door.

"Alana," Cora said. "You're always so well turned out. How I ended up with two such different daughters I'll never know."

"Oh not again," Alana said over Mikayla's squealing. "I forgot my 'boring daughter' badge at home."

Kelly and Alana laughed, though Cora had no idea what was funny.

Cora covered her ears. "Does she come with a volume button?"

"Hush," Rob whispered in Mikayla's ear. "We're at Grandma's." He set her down and she tipped her head back and stared up at Cora.

"Hi, birthday girl," Cora said. "I suppose you have no idea who I am. How can you get to know me when your parents live so far away? Your grandpa grumbles every time I ask for gas money, so how can I come and visit you?"

"Oh, stop, Cora," Earl said.

"I know who you are. You're Grandma." She looked at Earl and pointed. "You're Grandpa."

"Hi, Dad," Alana said.

"Hey," Earl tousled her hair. "Beer, Rob?"

"You see? There's always money for beer around here." Cora turned and walked back to the kitchen.

"Give it a rest," Earl muttered after her. "A man is entitled to a beer once in a while."

"Sure. I brought a few," Rob said, following him.

Earl opened to the fridge and pulled out two cans. "To the birthday girl," he said.

"To volume buttons." Rob tapped his can against Earl's. "We'll see what we can do about that," he joked. "Cora, anything I can do?"

"I could use a hand," Cora said. Somehow Alana got lucky with her Rob.

Earl said, "Cora has it all under control. I stay out of the women's realm. Safer that way."

"Need a dish dryer, Kelly?" Rob asked.

"C'mon, let's go catch a bit of the game downstairs," Earl said. "This kitchen will get pretty tight soon."

"I'm fine," Kelly said. "Go on."

"I left you some puzzles in the living room," Cora said to Mikayla. The girl stood beside Alana and flicked the skirt of her dress back and forth, back and forth. Cora forgot how irritating small children could be. "I'll need some help setting the table," she went on, to nobody in particular. "How six of us are going to squeeze in I don't know. Do we have enough plates?" She was feeling off. It must be because of that thing on the radio. "Did you hear the news?" she asked Alana. "The daughter had a long interview on CBC. Didn't anyone hear it? The two of them planned it. The mother and the daughter. They set up their tent and went into town for propane, then came back and let the propane run into the tent while they slept. Wouldn't." She stared at Mikayla's face. She was still trying to work it out. "Wouldn't the propane evaporate? Or seep out the tent walls? A tent is so thin."

"Mikayla, Grandma left you some puzzles." Alana took Mikayla's hand and walked into the living room.

"The mother died right away," Cora went on. "She must have been eighty or eighty-five. The daughter went back three times for more propane and lay down in the tent beside her mother. Trying to die. Three times! They had a pact. They had no money, they'd been evicted, they both needed medical help but they couldn't afford it. That's how

it is in the States. You have to pay through the nose. You
have to sell everything you own till you have nothing left.
Even the dogs died, in the tent. But not the daughter. Good
Lord." Goosebumps broke out on Cora's arms. She gave
them a hard rub. "She sounded like a regular person, on the
radio. A regular, sensible person."

"I think I heard something about that, Mom." Alana
stepped into the kitchen. "It's terrible."

"Do we have enough plates?" Cora asked again. "I could
use a scotch."

"It's not even one o'clock," Kelly said.

"Don't worry." Cora laughed. "Your dad's so cheap
he won't buy any and it's not like I have extra cash lying
around. Don't look at me like that. You don't know your
father the way I do. He's a different person when you're not
here." Cora walked down the hall to her bedroom. Were the
pills still beside her bed? Sometimes they weren't where
she thought she'd left them. They could be anywhere. But
they were beside the lamp. She half-filled her water glass in
the small bathroom off the bedroom and left it beside the
pill bottle.

On the way back to the kitchen, Alana said, "What have
you been doing since—how long has it been—Easter?"

"Nothing," Cora said loudly.

Alana giggled. "I meant Kelly, Mom! I've talked to you
since Easter."

"We don't even go to the movies," Cora said. It wasn't her
problem than Alana hadn't seen Kelly since Easter. "We just
sit and watch the news. I'm so sick of the news. It depresses
me. The same thing over and over. Everything going to hell

in a handbasket. But that thing on the radio that really got to me, that woman and her mother and their dogs—"

"But you have a car. You can go somewhere," Kelly said. "Mom, just do something. Get out. You always did whatever you wanted."

"A car takes gas. You watch gas prices? We're on a pension. And a pension is not very big. You'll find out. If you even get one." Kelly certainly wouldn't, at the rate she was going. Not even a husband to help her out. Kelly was twenty when she told Earl and Cora she was gay, and Cora assured her it was all right, she'd grow out of it. But Kelly was stubborn. Always did things her own way, never open to suggestions. "They should call it peanuts, not pension." Cora looked at the cake. She wanted to hurl it out the window. A chocolate raspberry layer cake, for a grandchild she saw once or twice a year. A grandchild who didn't know her and would never know her. Why did she do it? No one had ever made a cake for her. Not her own mother. Not her daughters. They were too busy with their own lives. Would they ever do anything for her? Take her somewhere beautiful to help her die? Not likely.

"Is that why Dad never comes to my shows?" Kelly asked.

"What?" Cora asked.

"I was wondering why Dad doesn't come to my shows."

"Your dad does what he wants when he wants." Cora peeked in on the lasagne again. Not long. She opened a bag of salad and shook the loose greens into a bowl. Pricey stuff, not even fresh, probably full of pesticides, but less work than making a salad and fussing with a dressing.

Cora had simply been unlucky. That's all it was. First, unlucky in love; the man she loved had loved someone else. Earl was not the man she wanted to marry, but he wanted to marry her. They had married late in life, by the standards of their generation. She was thirty. He was close to forty. All her friends were getting married or were already married and having children and one day she noticed she was the last single woman. Nobody ever said it outright, but if you were single, people thought you were a lesbian, and if you weren't a lesbian, you were an old maid, and everybody she knew would rather be dead than either of those. So she settled with Earl. Settled. Like dust. Because something about it felt unclean.

And then, she was unlucky in childbirth. Her first child, a boy, had stalled in the birth canal and died. They gave her so many drugs she didn't feel a thing. Just the pain, later, where they cut her open and stitched her back up. Nobody wanted to hear about it, so she went right back to work, didn't talk about how it hurt. Nobody named the child in those days. Nobody held the baby. Nobody talked about the baby. That's how it was then, not like now when everybody tells everybody everything, even strangers. She knew something wasn't right about this but she didn't question it, nobody questioned much then; she trusted that it was better to just try to forget. Of course she didn't. She learned how to not talk about him. Sometimes in the night, when Earl was out for a few drinks with Lord-knows-who, co-workers maybe, he had so few friends, she let herself cry. She even held a blanket, rolled like it was a baby, and talked, sang, kissed. That's when her heart hurt the most. When she sang. Everyone said the next baby would take away the pain, make it easier, but she didn't want a next baby. She wanted him. So Kelly was a surprise when she arrived, a few years later. And then Alana. Cora wasn't ready. That's what she told herself, when she didn't feel for them what she felt for the boy. She just wasn't ready. When Cora thought back to that time, when she was a mother of young children, that woman she saw in her mind was a stranger. She could picture her clearly: the woman who got up and got dressed and made breakfast for her daughters and dropped them off at school on her way to work. The work she loved. By then she was done with those boring office jobs and was at the humane society working for the vet. No matter what you did, animals loved you. Even the ones that had been abused. And her daughters, of course she loved her daughters, that was a given. But was it love; was this assumed love really love? Because it wasn't like what she felt for the boy, a love that hurt inside her chest. She couldn't bring herself to sing to her daughters.

Now Mikayla was at her side, peering up at her, saying something nobody could make sense of.

"I can't understand you," Cora said.

"She wants to help, Mom." Alana stood by the table, arranging the place settings. "Maybe just try to connect with her."

"Oh. Well, everything's done," Cora said.

Mikayla went back to the living room. Cora set the salad bowl on the table and wandered after the child.

"You're dressed up pretty," Cora said. The girl wore a velvety red dress with a big bow tied at the back.

Mikayla rubbed her left eye. "Mom said to."

"Did she. Well, it looks nice."

The girl pulled at the tag in her neck. "It's itchy. Mom forgot to cut it off."

"Did you do the puzzle? I used to love puzzles when I was your age. I could never do one now. Can't concentrate the way I used to." Cora was just too tired. There was a time when she thought sleep would come easy. When her daughters were young, she accepted the lack of sleep as part of living with babies and toddlers. She expected to return to normal sleep once they grew up. The kind of sleep where you wake feeling rested and alert. But normal sleep never returned.

Mikayla pointed. The two puzzles Cora had left out on the coffee table were done.

"You put them together already!"

Mikayla nodded.

"I guess I got that wrong, too. You've already outgrown the puzzles. I might as well get rid of them. By the time I see you again, you'll be much too old for baby puzzles."

"Mom, something's burning," Alana called.

"Oh, the dinner."

There was Alana, pulling the lasagne out of the oven. A few black spots on top, but it would do. Cora wasn't hungry now anyway. Thinking about that American woman, the daughter, made her feel off. That woman was awaiting a trial. For taking her mother to the most beautiful place on earth and helping her die. Because they'd run out of all their options. They were at the end of the road. No going back. Now that woman was in a psychiatric hospital. The food was probably mushy and bland in those places. None of it homemade. No real cakes for a birthday. Cora could take the raspberry cake to her.

"Go call the boys," Cora said to Alana. "It's ready."

Alana went downstairs and came right back. "Dad wants five minutes. The game is nearly over."

"Dad wants five minutes," Cora repeated. "Everything on his schedule. What about Mikayla?"

"It's okay. She had a snack in the car. She'll be fine for a bit," Alana said.

"It'll be fifteen, just you watch. What did I make this food for anyway?" Cora yelled.

"Mom, you bought it all at the store," Kelly said.

"What difference does that make?" Cora stomped down the stairs. There were Earl and Rob, slouched on the couch. "Look at you lazy bums." She marched up to the television screen and stopped in front of it and crossed her arms. "Earl, we are eating now!"

Earl put his hands to his face and moaned. "Christ Almighty, Cora, that was the final goal!"

The man was always complaining about something. "You can see the replay ten times later. Your family is here for a birthday dinner. You never see your family."

"I'm seeing one of them now. We were having a perfectly good time. Weren't we, Rob?"

"I'd say we've been called, Earl."

"What's with you, Cora?"

Cora was already starting up the stairs. In the kitchen she took out a large knife and started hacking the lasagne. It had come to this. Store-bought lasagne for people who didn't want it anyway. Someone she used to know years ago, from work, had the nerve to ask why she didn't leave him. Back then he was away a lot or going for those long lunches with people he worked with, men and women, whoever. And doing who knew what else. Cora had her suspicions. She had a good nose for different scents and a certain look Earl had some days. Why don't you leave him, Cora, in that snotty voice, like they knew better. Everybody knew better. As bad as it was now, she did not want to be penniless, on the street. On her own with two children she hadn't been ready for. Like that woman and her mother. Not even able to buy a carton of milk or a loaf of bread. And nowhere to sit and eat if she could. And to have people look at her with pity. Almost nothing worse than pity.

"Mom." Kelly put her arm around her mother hesitantly. "We're all here. We're all hungry. We'll eat."

"Let's eat then." Cora carried the lasagne to the table.

"Sit down, Mikayla," Rob said. Mikayla sat beside him on the far side of the table, against the wall, and Kelly and Alana sat across from them.

Cora and Earl took their seats at the ends. "Just like when Kelly and Alana were little," Cora said.

"What's that?" Earl called.

"The way we're sitting. You and me at the ends," Cora said, louder. "The kids along the sides. Back then you girls used to say, 'I love you from my toes to my nose. I love you even when I am sleeping.'" Cora looked at Kelly and Alana but they just stared at their plates. Where did those little girls go? They were gone. Poof. Nobody told you about this cruel trick of nature. How the wriggling bit of flesh you gave birth to transformed, so slowly you didn't notice, into something that had nothing to do with you. The boy, he was still part of her. The ache was still here, in her chest, in her womb. Because he had never left.

"Lasagne anyone?" Earl was ready to dish out.

"Lazagany!" Mikayla yelled.

"What?" Cora asked.

"That's what Dad calls it." Mikayla said.

Cora couldn't eat hers. Mushy pasta. The sauce had no flavour. It was like baby food. The men ate it, at least. Men will eat anything. They ate and nobody said a word. Except the girl. She chattered in her high voice, most of it gobble-dygook to Cora, but Rob and Alana seemed to understand everything.

Alana cleared the dishes. It was time for cake. Candles! Cora hadn't thought of candles. She searched the kitchen cupboards and drawers, the telephone table, her bedside table, even the bathroom drawers and behind the mirrors. Took one of those pills beside her bed while she was there, couldn't hurt. Not a single candle, anywhere. She hadn't bought candles for so long. Not for Earl's birthdays, not hers of course. As if the day wasn't already ruined, the way Earl had carried on in front of the television, the way Kelly had gone on when she arrived.

She walked back to the kitchen and everybody belted out the words to "Happy Birthday," Mikayla included, as loud as they could. They were laughing so hard they almost couldn't get the words out.

"Alana, you might as well cut the cake," Cora said when the cacophony was over. Her ears rang and her head ached.

It wasn't fair. She had wanted them all to come today. She used to like it when they were all here.

"Sure." Alana cut. "Looks great. Is this the cake Kelly and I made you a few years ago?" She put a small piece on Mikayla's plate. Then she began to scrape the icing off the slice and whack it off her knife onto a little plate. Like it was a giant slug. All that icing Cora had made earlier. Even the pink flowers she had worked hard to get just right.

"What are you doing to my cake?" Cora asked.

"It's the icing," Rob said. "Mikayla goes ballistic with too much sugar."

Her daughters always loved cake. Cora slammed her hands on the table and stood up. "Oh, for God's sake!"

Mikayla put her hand on Cora's arm. Cora saw her, but her hand was so light Cora didn't feel anything. What was wrong with her that she could not feel the child's hand? She wanted desperately to feel it.

"Mom," Kelly said. "It's only icing."

Cora shoved back her chair and walked to her bedroom and pulled the door closed after her. She meant to pull it quietly but it slammed. From the bottle on the dresser beside her bed she shook out a few pills, pills to help her sleep, swallowed without water (but hadn't she left water earlier for this very purpose? She was certain she had), though when she did that the pills sat in her throat for ages, lumps slowly dissolving and pressing into her throat. The pills burned. She wondered if she'd taken any pills when she came in before, or if she'd just looked to see where they were. No matter. She'd simply sleep better. Longer, anyway. She'd just sit on the bed for a minute first.

Sounds came to her from far away, muffled, like she had cotton balls in her ears. Talking, chairs scraping, footsteps. After a time, the front door opening and closing, voices calling out goodbye from a long way off. The van starting up and driving away. Faint talking from the kitchen. And then, sweet, heavy silence.

✳ When Kelly opened her parents' bedroom door, she saw that the curtains were drawn; it was early evening, and the room was tinged in grey light. It was cooler here than in the kitchen. Cora lay on her back on top of the bedspread, her hands resting on her stomach. She was asleep and snoring faintly. Kelly moved closer, then sat on the bed. She had never been on this bed. In the other house, the house Kelly had grown up in, there had been a different bed, smaller and saggy but fun to jump on when she and Alana were little. Sometimes they curled up in the middle, hugging, pretending to be their parents and wondering how close to get, whether bodies touched all over or just the lips or whether they should lie as far as possible from each other, one side of their bodies just about to fall off the edge of the bed. They'd tried everything.

Kelly lay on her side. This mattress was comfortable. It was one of those new memory foam mattresses. It felt like a gigantic hug. It felt like heaven. What she wouldn't give for a bed like this. Sleep would come easily on a bed like this.

"Mom," Kelly whispered, almost soundlessly; she didn't really want to wake her. For a long time she looked at her mother's face and listened to her cloggy breathing. Cora's forehead was crinkly and her lips were parted a little.

There was a flush in her cheeks, but the rest of her face was pale. Kelly moved so that her cheek was against Cora's and there it was, the night-time hand cream her mother wore. She closed her eyes. She was back in her small bed in the old house, under the heavy wool blankets; the air was still; she heard the creaky house sounds, the neighbour's Jack Russell barking himself hoarse, sirens from the late-night television news. Her mother came to check on her. Kelly smelled the cream, even in her sleep, and woke up. Cora stood in the doorway for a few minutes, then walked quietly to the bed and lay beside Kelly and rested her cool hand on Kelly's forehead. She didn't say anything. Kelly tried hard to stay awake because she knew that as soon as she fell asleep, her mother would leave. Without her there, the room was big and dark and empty. But she fell asleep anyway. After her mother left, Kelly sometimes woke again. That was the worst part of the night, waking to that cold, hollowed-out spot in the bedspread.

Kelly slept. When she woke it was dark. She didn't know where she was. In bed, that was it. The bed that was an enormous hug. Maybe her mother would come, like she used to. Kelly was so cold now. If only her mother would come.

The Night the Moon Was Bright and We Ate Pigs and Brownies and Drank Fizzy Beer and Didn't Remember Much at All, in the End

WE DROVE TO THE PIG CAMP on Thursday. The next morning we took our tent down and drove to another place to camp. It wasn't what I thought, Mom said, the next day, when we were all in the car driving away. I mean, I had an idea. But not that. Dad laughed and said: Oh, you knew. You don't go to a thing like that and not know. I sat beside Evan in the back seat. He stank of smoke and sweat and beer.

✳ We'd camped somewhere else the night before and got to the pig camp in the morning. It wasn't a normal camp-ground. It was just a big clearing in the woods in the middle of nowhere. Dad drove right into the clearing and stopped.

Holy! Evan said. Lookit all the tents! Is there room for ours?

There'll be room, Dad said. There's always room. That's how these parties are. We'll all be piled on top of each other. Like pigs in a pen, ha. I hear they got two little pigs. They'll roast faster.

Mom said she was not going to watch the pigs cook. She couldn't bear to see a pig run through with a spit. It looked too much like a human baby. She would go for a long walk instead. With Marlene. Do you see Marlene and Bill anywhere? she asked.

There was a girl by the fire pit in the middle of all the tents. She looked like she was the same age as me. Eleven.

Not yet, said Dad. Bill's probably stocking up at the liquor store. There's Arnie, by the fire.

You can count on Arnie to be making the fire, Mom said. He likes to keep himself busy, doesn't he.

Hey, there's some boys, Evan said. Up in that tree.

How long are we staying? I asked. Because we never stayed long enough. We just got to know the campground and then we had to leave.

A few nights, Mom said. Over the weekend probably.

Good.

Dad drove on the grass and stopped between two tents. We were going to put up our tent right there, beside the car.

* I can tell you what she looked like because she stood right next to me and Arnie when Arnie opened a beer. Half the beer fizzed out the top. He made a face at the beer like something was wrong with it and his eyes flicked from me to her and back to me again. Flick, flick.

Here, kid, he said.

He handed me the half-empty bottle and went for another. I don't know why me and not her but I took the beer anyway and looked over at my tent before I had any. It felt a bit funny that I had beer and she didn't. Because we were pretty much the same. Her hair was just like mine, brown and tangled. Summer hair. But she looked into the fire pit like we weren't there. Her eyes were closed a little, like her eyelids were heavy. Her glasses slid down her nose, and her mouth hung open a bit. She was bony and her bones were hard. Her shirt was loose and her jeans looked too big. Because she was so skinny. Her jeans had a belt, a thin pink one with a butterfly for a buckle. I wanted that butterfly buckle.

Cute, Arnie said to me. You're cute. It didn't really mean anything, the way he said it, but I waited for him to say, You, too, or something like that to the girl, and when he didn't I expected her to pipe up, I'm here too, ya know, you blind or what? Cuz that's what I would've said. I would've, if it was me. But she didn't say anything. She didn't even look at us. She was just shy. I get like that too.

I looked at the beer and back at the girl. I've had beer before. Dad gives me sips of his sometimes. This was just the same, fizzy like pop and bitter. I didn't really like it, but I wanted to like it.

Arnie had a beard, longish and brown and a bit like wool, and hair pulled back in a ponytail and a small scar above his left eye. Behind him, next to his case of beer, were three huge piles of firewood, organized by size: twigs, branches, small logs. I wanted to make a joke and ask if he was collecting wood for the three bears, but then he would have to make one of us Goldilocks, her or me, and I already knew what he would say.

∗ I can tell you her name. Randi.

∗ Arnie stuffed some crumpled newspaper into his tower of twigs, not the comics because I took them to read later but something from the news. I never read the news anyways, he said, nothing worth reading in the news. It's all bad and it's all stuff I can't do anything about.

He knelt down and lit a corner of the paper. It flinched and curled and blackened. Red and blue flames shot up. I love that about fire. He added to the tower, slowly, starting with more small sticks. Look at 'er go, he said. Look at 'er burn. He was happy with his fire. Really happy. I backed up. I was wearing shorts, cut-offs from old jeans. I could already feel my skin getting hot.

I know what to do with a fire, he said. I can just mind my own business here. Not get in anyone's way.

I was so thirsty I drank the beer in two minutes. My whole face tingled.

Mom called and I dropped the empty beer bottle next to the case. When I tried to run to our tent, I nearly fell over. I put my hand on the side of a green truck to stay upright.

Where on earth have you been? You can unpack the mats and the sleeping bags. Where's Evan? I could use a hand. Your dad's off drinking with Bill already. It's not even eleven! He'll be wasted before the pig is done! Sheesh. What a mess if he throws up in the tent. It already reeks.

I opened the mats and left them to inflate, then yanked the sleeping bags from their sacks and tossed them into the tent.

I see you met Randi, Mom said. Sherry's daughter. Nice you found a friend.

She's not a friend, I said. I couldn't say why, if Mom asked. Probably it was because she didn't say anything.

There's food in that box, Mom said. If you want some lunch. I'm going for a walk with Marlene.

✶ The next day, when we were taking down the tent, everybody looked funny. Even Mom and Dad. Mom wanted to camp somewhere else for the rest of the weekend. Nobody slept, she said. We can't stay here. There are some unpredictable elements in the group, she said. Most everybody is fine. It just takes one, though. Which one? I asked. Pick one, she said. Good grief, said Dad, it was just a pig roast.

✶ Arnie was good at fires. He kept adding wood. He wanted coals, he told us. Coals make a cooking fire. There were two sets of metal spikes already set up for the spits to rest on.

Arnie stood with his legs a little apart. There was a rip in his jeans under one knee, going side to side, and another up near the crotch, going up and down. I sneaked looks at that one when he wasn't looking, just to see what he was like in there. When he moved one leg I could almost see in. He had the hairiest arms I have ever seen. He watched the fire and drank beer.

Where's your tent? Who you with? Who're your mom and dad? Arnie asked. I pointed at our blue and white dome. You could just see a bit of one side.

Wendy and Greg, I said. And my brother Evan.

I got a brother, Arnie said. Back east. Bugger never calls. I coulda used his help a while back and he acted like I was dead. Good riddance to brothers everywhere, I say. He took a long swallow of beer.

I sneaked another peek. Nothing. Just some white cloth.

Gonna be one helluva party tonight, he said and looked around at all the tents.

I counted fifteen, and more cars were driving in. You could hardly walk without tripping on guy ropes.

Where's yours? Arnie asked Randi. She turned and pointed to an orange tent behind us. A pup tent, for two. Then she turned back to the fire.

Miranda! called someone from inside the tent. Randi didn't say anything, she didn't even turn to her tent, but I could tell it was her mom calling. When she said Randi's name, I had two thoughts. One. Miranda is sure a grown-up name for a kid. Two. She should go to her mom.

She didn't move. I went off to find Evan.

✳ This is what happened. We went to a pig roast and ate pig meat and brownies and watched the adults drink beer and talk funny. The next morning, when most everybody was still asleep, we took down the tent and drove even farther into the forest and set up our tent along the river where nobody else was camped. On the drive to the new camp I was thinking that nothing happened. I was thinking it was all a long, strange dream.

On the drive Mom said: It wasn't what I thought. I mean, I had an idea. But not that.

Oh, you knew, Dad said. You don't go to a thing like that and not know.

But that girl, Mom said. What about that girl.

They'll find her.

Evan and I didn't look at each other. My arms were so sore I could barely lift them.

Mom threw up her hands and said: They called it a pig roast!

That's what they do at pig roasts, Dad said.

There was pig! I said. I ate pig!

Mom yawned. Well, she said. I could sleep for two days. She looked at me and said, Ali, you kept me awake half the night. How many of those hash brownies did you have?

There was hash in those brownies? Evan asked. He looked both surprised and excited. I wish I'd known. I woulda had more!

What's hash? I said.

You tromped around the tent all night, Mom said. She laughed softly.

I didn't tromp around the tent.

Dad hooted and said: You were all over us. He drove slowly and peered up at the snowy peaks through the gaps in the pines. There wasn't much in those brownies, he said to Mom. Unless Ali ate about twenty-five, she wouldn't have felt anything.

You were probably sleepwalking, Mom said.

I don't sleepwalk, I said.

Evan laughed, too long, and finally he looked at me. I wanted him to look at me. I wanted to see what he was thinking. He was scared, too. Somehow we agreed, yesterday, not to say anything. I don't know how we did that without talking about it, but we did. We were afraid of those boys he met. Johnnie's words were stuck in my head: *You did it. You did it. I didn't touch her. No, sir.* The *No, sir* was especially stuck in my head, because he was so definite about it.

But I was mad at Evan, too.

✳ This is what we did at the pig camp. After I helped Mom with the sleeping bags, I went off to find Evan. He was way up in a poplar tree. I climbed up to him and we watched people drive in and set up tents. When we got bored we went back to the car and made peanut butter and jam sandwiches. We went from our tent past the fire pit and watched the pigs hiss and splutter on the spits for a while and then went over to the tracks. The tracks were on the other side of the pines. We didn't go straight through the pines. We went way around to the left between a few tents and then into the trees to make it look like we were just going into the woods in case anyone was looking. Then we doubled back to the tracks. One of the boys Evan met was there. Zach.

Look at this, Evan said. It was an old hand car. Look what we found. Before, he said.

The hand car was small, maybe big enough for four or five kids. The car was just wooden boards on top of rail car wheels. There was a lever in the middle. You could sit on either side or the front or the back. Evan and Zach sat on one side, dangling their legs. I sat on the back. We could see the fire pit and all the people.

The next thing we knew Dad was strolling over to us with Bill. Bill tipped his beer toward us and said, Look what those kids found.

That's a relic, Dad said. Looks like it's in great shape. Does it work?

Don't know yet, said Evan.

Don't go too far, Bill said. The pigs are coming along.

They went back to the fire pit.

Evan stood up and put his hands on the lever.

She's a girl, Zach said. He didn't look at me. He didn't even move his lips when he talked.

She's my sister, said Evan.

Zach looked away.

We thought the tracks weren't being used. No one would leave an old hand car sitting on a track when a train might come along. It would be in the way of a train. And anyway we hadn't heard any trains all day. So we got the car going. Evan and Zach and I took turns pumping the lever and rolled along the tracks a short way. It was hard work, especially going up the little hill. The car never got going very fast and the lever was heavy and squeaked and sometimes stuck so it took a ton of work. We had to take a lot of breaks.

You even like pig? Zach said after a while. We'd stopped beside a slough. Zach had a bag of sunflower seeds that he didn't share. Every few seconds he'd pop a seed in his mouth and work it with his tongue, frowning the whole time, and then spit out bits of shell. He showed his tongue when he spat. It was fat, like a pig's tongue.

Never had it, Evan said.

You have too, I said. Pork chops. Sausages. Ham. Ham is pig.

I mean pig-roast pig, idiot, Evan said. My sister thinks she's so smart.

He had to say that because he was just thirteen and Zach was older than us, maybe fourteen, and he wanted Zach to be his friend.

Zach spat more shells. She's a girl, he said again. If Zach was my age, or younger, I would have said something but because he was older, and bigger, I pretended I didn't hear.

After a while we went back the way we'd come and when we got back to where we'd found the hand car, Mom and Marlene were there. They'd changed into their long hippie dresses, the ones with too much colour. That meant evening was coming on. It would get cool and the bugs would come out.

Come down off that, Mom said.

They're just sitting on it. Marlene's words slid all around the way Dad's do when he's had too much beer. They're not going far.

Evan and I went back to the camp and grabbed food, handfuls of pretzels and carrot sticks and brownies, and went into another part of the woods, near the river, and ate and tossed pebbles into the water. Zach wasn't with us. It was starting to get a little dark. After a while Evan and I went back to camp for more food. Everybody was drinking something. And smoking. Not cigarettes. Something they called weed that smelled like old dry mushrooms. Where's the weed? they said. Any more of that weed? Nobody spoke normally. Nobody looked straight at you. The adults thought everything was hilarious. And they were loud. There were empty beer bottles everywhere. The pigs were on a picnic table, done now, and cut up. You could smell the pig for miles, that's for sure. Like bacon or stew. Evan and I ate pig meat and brownies and white buns that we pulled the insides out of and squished into balls and rolled around in our mouths till they turned gluey. We could eat whatever we wanted because no one was checking. We could even take beer. Evan took one and drank half all in one go and then made a face and laughed and gave me the bottle and I had some too, maybe I had a long sip and gave it back or maybe I had it all and he grabbed another. Nobody was keeping track. We went back to the hand car. We didn't even bother going the long way. The adults were too distracted. The sweetness of not being watched came over us.

Zach and the other boy Evan met earlier were there. Johnnie. Randi was there, too. I could tell that Zach and Johnnie had asked her to come. I knew by the way she stood close to them, like she was with them, and they were looking after her, like they were her friends now or something. More like they were in charge of her. Zach was the tallest and probably the oldest. He even had tiny bits of black hair on his top lip. Johnnie was short and had short brown hair, cut in a straight line across his forehead. He was chubby too. They didn't look like boys you could get into any kind of conversation with. They didn't say much. They just looked at you in a way that made you feel picked over and icky.

We all got on the car except Randi. Randi couldn't hoist herself up. She kept trying, but her arms weren't strong enough. The boys just watched, even Evan. So I reached down and pulled her up. It was like she was a big rag doll. She hardly weighed anything. I didn't know if she was my friend yet. But I wanted her to come. I didn't want to be the only girl.

Randi and I sat at the back, Zach and Johnnie at the front. Evan stood and moved the lever. Whenever someone took a turn, the person who was pumping took that person's place on the car. Evan and I passed a beer back and forth.

We pumped along the stretch of track we'd gone down earlier and then back. When we neared our camp, we looked through the trees toward the fire pit. Everybody was moving slowly and laughing. Somebody played a guitar, someone played a drum, lots of people were singing. Everybody talked loudly. Some people were glommed together and touching each other all over and kissing and making funny sounds.

One big orgy, man, Evan said. Gross.

We made the car go the other way, into the pines, above the river. There was a long drop on one side. I sat very still when we moved past the drop. It was steep, not steep like a cliff but steep enough and mostly open, with bushes and rocks and big trees at the bottom. It was a long way down. We couldn't see where it ended. We kept going.

It's getting dark, I said after a bit. I want to go back. We were too far to hear the singing from the camp. I felt woozy. The moon peered at us over the tops of the pines, a big, worried face with scarred cheeks and a round O for a mouth.

We're going to stop here, Zach announced all of a sudden. Take a break. He stopped the car and hopped down. Randi jumped down beside him. Then Johnnie and Evan. They walked a few steps toward the forest. I stretched out on my back, now that I had the hand car to myself. The sky was clear but it looked deep, like a swimming pool full of dark blue water. Stars began to pop out and dance. A star picked me up and I danced with it through all the other stars. When I said *Stop!*, the star set me back down. It wasn't that I wanted to stop. I liked dancing in the stars. It was that something wasn't right. It was too quiet.

I sat up. The boys had their backs to me. They were facing Randi and making a wall between her and the hand car. They stood like Arnie, their legs spread into upside down Vs. Their hands were on their hips. I slid off and walked over.

When I was close, I could see Randi's face. That was when I saw how huge her eyes were.

Zach pushed at the butterfly clip on her belt and she took a few steps back and curled in a little. Like the newspaper, when Arnie lit it. Curled in and shrank. C'mon, Zach said. We just want to see. Just give us a look.

What, you don't like us? asked Johnnie.

The way he said it, nobody would like him.

Evan didn't say anything. But he wanted to be like Zach and Johnnie. I could see it in the way he looked at them, the way he tried to stand like them and turned up one side of his mouth. But he wasn't like those boys. He was just trying it out.

Johnnie flicked his fat lower lip with his finger a few times and said, Don't cry. We don't want you to cry.

You're cute, Zach said. Anybody ever tell you you're cute?

That was what Arnie said, but Arnie wasn't creepy. He was just Arnie, minding his own business, and there were other adults all around. By the fire, I knew that if I yelled for Mom, she'd hear me. But nobody would hear us way out here. We were far away and the air was thick and heavy and made everything slow. I felt slow, too. Because I just stood there.

Zach touched Randi's butterfly clip again and she backed up.

I'll tell, Randi said.

Johnnie tugged on the butterfly again. Yeah? he said. Who you gonna tell?

I looked at Evan, willing him to say something, to make them stop. He looked a little scared, too.

Hey, I said. Guys. Maybe there's dessert. Maybe there's cake. Let's go back.

The boys turned to me. Their eyes were bugged out and shiny. Who's she? Johnnie said. Evan looked at him but didn't say a word. I wanted to give him a punch.

His sister, dolt, Zach said finally.

Johnnie took a step toward me.

They don't want to play, Zach said. Let's go back.

But Johnnie stayed right where he was, staring hard at me.

I think they do, Johnnie said. His eyes were small and mean and he was smirking like somebody made a joke. It's a party! he yelled.

Something happened in Zach because he sort of sighed and shook his head. Nah, he said, Nah, let's go back. I told you, that's his *sister*.

Johnnie made a disgusting sucking sound and spat a huge glob of spit onto the ground near his feet, then shuffled past me to the hand car. He was too fat to run. Last one on's a rotten egg! he yelled and hoisted himself up.

I ran over. Evan and Randi were right behind me. Randi put her hands on the car. C'mon, I said, pulling her up as Zach started the car.

Past midnight I bet, Zach said after a minute. Anybody got a watch?

No, said Evan. But I bet the party's still on.

Of course it's still on, Zach said. It'll go till the sun comes up.

How do you know? I asked.

That's how these parties go. Don't even try to talk to any of the grown-ups tomorrow. They won't make any sense till the afternoon.

Johnnie's shoulders were slumped and he didn't say anything. He didn't help move the lever. Randi took a turn, but she could hardly get the car to budge. You gotta pull your weight, Johnnie said, though she was. You can't have a free ride, he said. No one told him that he was getting a free ride. I could see he was still bothered. He squinted at me and Randi. His shoulders twitched and his left leg shook. Like a dog about to snarl or bite. He was so big the whole car wobbled.

It felt longer going back. Maybe it was the dark. Maybe there was more uphill. Evan took a long turn, and then it was my turn. This was how we were: Johnnie and Zach sitting in front with their legs dangling down. Evan on the side, behind Johnnie. Me pumping now. Randi at the back, partly behind Evan, partly behind me.

When we got to the drop, Johnnie stretched out slowly, even though there was no room to stretch out, and bumped into Evan just enough that Evan's shoulder bumped Randi. It was a little bump, hardly a bump at all, more like a tap, like a Hey, guess what?, and she should have stayed where she was, anybody else would have just stayed put or grabbed onto something, she could have grabbed me or Evan or anybody on the car, but she didn't. She fell.

✳ I can tell you what she looked like. Because she stood right next to me when Arnie opened a beer. Most of the beer fizzed out the top. Did I say that already? Standing by the fire, at the pig camp, was the best part of the day. It was before I went on the hand car. Everything was just right, by the fire. Maybe someone shook the beer. Or maybe it was just warm. Arnie made a face at the beer bottle. He made the face you make when you are puzzling over a complicated math problem. When you know you won't get it right away. You might get it tomorrow or next week, but not right now. I wanted to tell him he'd get it. I wish I'd told him he'd get it. Because he was kind. He made a face and said Bloody hell and then Oops, pardon my French and looked at Randi and me and said Here, kid, and gave me the beer. His face looking like he was trying but still hadn't figured out whatever it was he wanted to figure out. It was funny, about the beer. Why me and not her? This is what we did: Arnie lit the fire and I drank his beer and Mom called me to the tent and I went and later I ate pig and the next day we left the camp. That's what happened.

✳ I saw her hand first, up high, and then the hand was gone, and legs and blue running shoes were in the air instead. She was doing a cartwheel. There was a crack like a rock hitting another rock and then a snap like a dry stick breaking. She didn't cry or yell or say anything. She skidded over the rocks and the roots and the shrubs. Then she did a slow somersault. She had time to yell or grab something. Anybody else would have. We all had time to do something, it was all so slow. Then she was through the trees at the bottom, she must have been, but I couldn't see her, it was too dark or she was too far.

She should have just come back up.

We kept going. No one said to stop. Johnnie turned his fat lips to Evan and said loudly, You did it. You did it. I didn't touch her. No sir.

I pumped us over the top of the hill and then there was another downhill. For a minute I did not have to work hard. The lever squeaked loudly the whole time. At the bottom of the hill was a long flat stretch and then another uphill. Evan was just sitting there not saying anything and looking at the track in front of us. I could hardly move the lever anymore, but I held on and finished my turn. I wasn't going to be like Randi, who couldn't even get up on the car on her own, and I was pumping so if I was pushed I'd have something to hold on to. I wasn't going to be shoved off. I looked at Evan. I wanted him to say something. But he was being like the other boys.

The moon was high and it shone down on us like a spotlight. Finally I heard the camp noises. They drowned out the squeaking of the hand car. Guitars, drums, singing, howling like coyotes, laughing. And sparks from Arnie's bonfire shooting up into the sky.

I stopped and hopped off and ran as fast as I could. I zipped around the dark shapes that were outside the light of the fire. People dancing. Smoking. Heads tipped back drinking. And from tents, moaning sounds. Like people were sick maybe, from too much pig, or too much beer, except they were giggling too.

Hey, kid. Someone grabbed my arm and for a second my legs kept going. It was Arnie. He must have been there all day, feeding the fire and drinking beer. Hold up there, he said.

My heart thunked in my chest. I wanted to ask him to tell me where I was on the hand car. How I knew her bones were so hard. How I felt them. How I knew how much of a bump it was, that it was a little tap, just a little tap on the shoulder, no more. I wanted him to ask why I didn't grab her. He would know because she had been right here beside us in the morning and in the afternoon, she had been right here looking at the fire with her mouth open a little and her glasses slipping off her nose, she had been so close we could touch her if we wanted to, but we didn't want to, did we, because she acted like we weren't even there, that was it. He would ask after her though, wouldn't he. Someone would ask. Soon, they would all ask. And we wouldn't remember much at all, in the end. Arnie. He would ask.

Kid! Arnie said. Long time no see! Where you been all this time? I've been all by my lonesome here. Want a beer? He held out a beer to me, close, right up to my cheek so I could feel his rough fingers and smell smoke and wood. I shook my head and looked right into his eyes, willing him to see everything that I had seen so someone else knew. Here, he said. Take it. There's more. Have a sip. You'll see. After you have that sip, you won't care about nothin'.

The
Golden
Rice Bowl

IT'S SAM'S IDEA to drive to Marta's from his parents' place.
Sam never suggests anything. It's not that far, he says. Once
we're on the road anyway.

Okay, I say finally, Okay. But I'm not keen.

And then, too soon, the day arrives. I didn't sleep
much last night. I gave up counting puppies and started
conjuring daisies and tearing off petals. *Go. Don't go.*

We pack enough clothes for a few days. I tell him I will
drive first. Before we get to the end of our street I see that
the air conditioning conked out. We are driving into a heat
wave. "Sam. I don't know why I'm doing this."

"You sure do," he says quickly. "Someone named Marta."

Yes. Marta. But his parents' anniversary. "I can't believe
your parents have been married for thirty-five years." I
nearly burst out crying. *Thirty-five fucking years*. Sam and
I will not make it to five. Today we're driving to Creston
for their big whoop-up. Together. To avoid the questions.
"How'd they do it?" Besides not being a dumbass like you, I
want to say.

"Lots of scotch?"

"Do they know?"

"I already told you. No."

"Who's coming to this party? Will we know anyone?"

"How would I know? It's not my party."

"You didn't ask?"

Sam throws up his hands.

I used to think it was funny, his not finding things out. He'd look at me lamely, and I thought it was cute. Now it's annoying.

By ten we're on the outskirts of Calgary. The wide, flat, nearly empty highway unfurls in front of us. It's the first of August, one of those dreamy summer days: blue sky, no clouds, no wind. Soon it will be unbearably hot.

"Can I put on *Bob the Builder*?" Lily asks.

"We just got going. Not yet," I say.

Sam turns to set up the DVD player. Lily belts out the theme song: "Can! We! Fix it?" and Sam joins in for the next part: "Yes! We! Can!"

For a moment I want to murder these two people. I'd make it painless. And temporary. They are too loud, and the party will be too loud. I am mostly going because a part of me wants to see Marta. Because of what happened. Because she might get it. And it's been so long. Eight years. She found me, wrote a letter, invited us to visit, to stay overnight even. Of course I said yes. Sam was thrilled. Because he wants me at the party so he can pretend everything's normal and he's convinced his parents' place is just down the road from Marta's. What's normal, I said. Just try, he said back.

"Sam, talk to her."

"Are you tired? Want me to drive from High River?"

"No, I just want you to talk to her."

"Hey, Lily," Sam says, "what do you want to talk about?"

"Bob!"

"Ask her where Grandma and Grandpa live," I tell him.

"Where do Grandma and Grandpa live?" Sam says.

"In that place with all the flowers! Right? Now can I watch?"

"Creston, Lily. C'mon, Jen, she probably doesn't remember their place. It's been a year since Alex's wedding." He turns on the DVD player.

"I do so remember!" Lily says.

I could have gone to Marta's on my own. But there's my pricey massage course; Sam's working at the gym; money's tight. And of course Lily, who would look after Lily, no one can look after Lily now. What if I'd come home a bit later that night and missed it all? This whole road trip would be different. And how strange it would be, me not knowing and him acting like everything's the same.

"Hey, Lily, the famous crooked tree," I say.

"That's the ugliest tree in the world," Sam says.

"It's not ugly!" I glance back at Lily through the mirror. She's glued to Bob. "Let's show her Frank Slide."

"She didn't care about the crooked tree."

So we don't stop at Frank Slide, we never do it seems, but I pull off at Burmis for a leg stretch. At Crowsnest Pass I want to get out. I want to be on a mountain. Every way I look there are mountains and it's killing me not be on them. Before I met Sam, I spent nearly every weekend in the Rockies, hiking, scrambling, climbing, backcountry skiing.

Those scrambles up Temple and Rundle, first walking
for hours to get to the climb, then the rough, warm rock
face, my fingers reaching for something to grab, my skin
bleeding, always just about to collapse near the end but
every time, the moment I saw the top, I had energy, so much
energy, and I bounded to the peak, the peak that was never
pointy the way I imagined but flat and sometimes even
hollowed out in places. I lay on my back and breathed in the
air at the top of the world or sat with my legs dangling over
the edge, wondering about who had come before me and
what they made of this peak that wasn't a peak after all.

"Want to hike around here?" Sam asks.

I nod. Sam and I have never hiked together, never been in
a canoe together.

I drive through Sparwood. In Fernie we stop for lunch
and Sam takes the wheel. Lily falls asleep and I stare grog-
gily out at the wall of trees, the Doug firs and poplars, the
larches and Ponderosa pines trundling up and down the
mountains, the scattered plumes of smoke from forest
fires. Then, way too soon, the big green highway sign
announces the last few kilometres to Creston. Sam slows
down. I almost say thanks but hold back. I don't want to
thank him for anything yet.

"Not quite four-thirty," Sam says. "Enough time for a
shower before everything gets rolling."

"They can't complain that we're late."

"They can try." He laughs lightly. "We haven't seen them
since before," he says. "Before—"

"What have you told them?"

"How come you keep asking? I don't like her. I hardly know her. I don't know how to explain anything about it."

"I wish I could just forget. Like you." He told me she was okay with it and I sort of believe him; he tells me he doesn't like her and I sort of believe that, too, but still I want to know why. Especially if he doesn't even like her.

"I haven't forgotten." Sam says flatly. He turns into his parents' street and parks in front of their house. Lily scrambles out of the car, squealing, and does a somersault on the front lawn.

Gus and Arlene are on the sidewalk, waiting. They're even taller than Sam. I'm not short, but I feel a little diminished around them.

"Look at that child!" Gus watches Lily run in a wide circle. "Like a weed, is that how the saying goes?"

"Like pigweed, Dad," Sam says.

"You need to visit more often." Arlene says. She says this every time we come. "Lily is our only grandchild."

"I'll take your bags," Gus says. Sam pops the trunk and hands a small suitcase to his dad and takes the other. We've only got two. I shoved Lily's clothes in with mine.

"You're lightly travelling," Gus says.

"Where's the party?" Lily yells.

"Trip short," Sam chuckles. He imitates his Dad's quirky speech pattern when we visit.

"Around back," Arlene tells Lily.

"As I say always, a rest is as good as a change, son," Gus says. "Let's put the bags in your room."

"You made good time," Arlene says. "Jen, you can give me a hand, once you're ready. I'll catch up on all the news."

I reach for Lily's hand, but she's already running on ahead with Gus. Arlene has made up Sam's old basement room for us. Except for the country cottage-style bedspreads, the rooms are still teenaged boys' rooms. The *Jaws* and *Ghostbusters* posters are still up, Sam's bedside table has his orange plastic lamp, I'm sure I smell sweatpants.

Lily runs into the bedroom. When she sees the crib squeezed into the tight space between the bed and the wall she wails, "I'm not a baby!"

"We'll take the sides off," Sam says. "We'll figure something out. Can! We! Fix it?" he sings.

"Yes! We! Can!" Lily shrieks.

Gus puts my suitcase beside the bed. Lily takes Sam's hand and starts to pull him out of the room. "C'mon, Dad, let's go find your bed. C'mon!"

Sam stares down at her and tries to laugh, to make it look like Lily's being funny, but the sound he makes is somewhere between a throat-clearing and a cough. Sam's been on the couch since That Night. Three months is forever. Not just for her.

Gus pulls at his ear lobe. "What I don't hurt won't know me," he says, slowly. "Like that something. Take your time, kids. Meet you in the garden." He makes his way through the rumpus room and up the stairs.

"You might as well take the first shower," Sam says.

After I've dressed for the party I head up to the kitchen.

"There you are," says Arlene. "I thought I'd never see you kids again." She looks intently at me. "When I was your age I never thought we'd make it this long. Thirty-five years. My old aunt told me something a few years after Gus and I, you know, tied the knot." She puts her hand on my arm, just hard enough that if I pull away it would be awkward, and gives me a huge smile. "There are always bumps along the way."

Sam's lying. He has told them something. "Where's Lily?"

"Outside helping her grandpa. Be a dear and take this punch bowl out with you."

The punch has orange slices and strawberries and even rose petals floating on top. I cradle the bowl in my arms and step out the side door. The back yard is not a yard, it's a garden. The grass is the same colour everywhere, the edges are neatly trimmed, there are no weeds. The garden is green and full; nothing's dead. The flowers are as big as my face, and trees grow things to eat: apples, plums, apricots, cherries, even nuts. Glass things, swans maybe, with tea lights are spaced evenly near flowerbeds, ready to be lit later. The air is warm and heavy with scents from the flowers. I feel light-headed all of a sudden. It's not a real garden, is it. It's a garden you'd find in a fairy tale, in the part before things go wrong. Or maybe it's the place you'd fall asleep, after everybody leaves, and not wake up for a long time. I look for a quiet corner. I don't want to talk to strangers and pretend everything is normal with Sam and me.

Lily is under the big tulip tree, twirling, trying out cart-wheels, doing somersaults. She's in the very spot where I went through all the motions, saying "I will" at just the right time, pregnant with Lily but not showing, knowing but not believing any of it, Lily, Sam, the vows; none of it felt real, because it couldn't be real if Marta wasn't there. I was floating along that day with a sort of blissful detachment and a small ache, hidden, invisible, like the not-yet-born Lily.

Gus walks into the garden with a few guests and they keep coming, in small clusters, talking loudly and carrying plates piled with cheese, thin meats rolled tightly and held together with toothpicks, stuffed olives and garlic shrimp, puffy pastries.

"It's a party!" Lily yells, running in a circle around the huge lawn with her arms outstretched. She pulls her arms in and dives into a sea of skirts and slacks near a cherry tree and out of sight.

Sam walks up beside me.

"You know anyone?" I ask.

"Parental units, check, you and Lil, check. Oh, and my bro. And here's the devil himself."

Alex and Carmen stride over to us. They have a look: Alex freshly shaven, hair gelled; Carmen's skin an orangey-brown tan, her red hair done up above her head like a fountain.

"Long time no see, little brother." Alex high-fives Sam. They grip each other's hands and tug. "I haven't seen you so swish since our wedding day. Ready for a beer?"

"Sure," Sam nods.

They saunter across the lawn jostling each other.

Carmen watches them briefly and then turns toward me slowly. "Any summer trips planned?"

I know she's going to tell me they've been to Cuba or Jamaica and are flying to Europe soon. "We're off to Vernon tomorrow morning. How about you?"

"Vernon! That's a good one." Carmen snickers.

"Is it funny?"

"Well, sure." Carmen looks offended. As if I'm laughing at her. "Oh, you *are* going to Vernon. What's there in Vernon?"

"An old friend."

"Does this old friend have a name? Oh. An old lover! I don't believe it! You?"

"No," I say. How to explain Marta. "She's from Marsh."

"Oh. Marsh." She doesn't have to say, "What's there in Marsh?" I hear it anyway and just like that, Marta is a fly under her thumb, flapping her wings, gasping for air.

I turn and walk in the direction Sam and Alex went, squeezing between clumps of people. After a few squeeze-throughs I see them, drinks in hand. Sam hands me a glass of wine.

"I'm off to find Lily," I tell him.

"She's fine," he says.

"I know."

A woman takes my hand. "Which one are you, dear?"

"I'm Jen, I'm with Sam, he's the younger son." I've said it this way at other gatherings at his parents', quickly, as if Sam and I are other people. We used to laugh about it in bed later. Hold our hands in the bit of light coming through the window and bob our fingers at each other, making giant shadow creatures on the wall. We'd repeat the questions and make up silly answers. We'd come up with stranger questions. Do those wings come off? Have you always been employed as a scuba diving pizza delivery person? Sometimes, we made large, grotesque shapes come up behind the people asking the questions and the people ran away in terror, whisper-screaming, so Lily, sleeping, wouldn't hear. Our fingers airy, weightless beings on the wall, then pressure points on skin, gentle, warm, arousing. This was before That Night.

"Where do you live?" the woman goes on. She's old. They are all old. Maybe everybody here has been married thirty-five years, like Sam's parents. I am probably surrounded by a combined total of a thousand years of married life.

"Calgary." I forget the other questions; work, hobbies, what? Doesn't matter. I push past her. "Excuse me."

Arlene waves me over from one of the food tables.

"Have you eaten?" she asks. "I'm sure you haven't. Here, take this plate. Lily's fine, if you're worried about her."

I pick out a fat green olive stuffed with an almond, a blob of soft white cheese, a cracker.

"We've missed you three. Tell me about the massage course," Arlene says.

"So far so good."

"Everything all right? In Calgary?"

I look at her face, try to see what Sam told her. This is the part where I have to pretend everything's normal. "Yes."

"Lily is growing exactly as she should be. You're doing everything just right."

Sometimes I know when people are being kind for no reason and when they are pushing me to share something personal and then holding it tight. I don't know what Arlene wants. Sometimes I think she just really wanted a daughter and has an idea of what a daughter is like and

wants me to be her. The more she wants that, the more
I want to get away.

"I need to find Lily." I don't think I'll find her, but I
slowly make my way toward the wine, flicking my hand up
a little every time someone asks me something: "Jen. Sam.
The younger son. One child. Three years old, almost four.
Calgary. Fine. Yes, I'll have more wine, that one." Every flick
is like a little stab in my side, my gut, my breasts. I try not
to look up. No matter which way I look, I see a long, wide
branch of the tulip tree. Maybe Sam was going through
the motions that day, too.

I eat, refill my glass, drink, feel pathetic. The sun goes
down, and the lights glow from their small glass homes.
The sun sets so early this far south. In Marsh the sun is
up till eleven in the summer, and twilight lingers for ages.
Some warm clear nights Marta and I canoed well into the
evening, not hard, not fast, just drifting.

Lily's asleep on the wide swinging chair under an apple
tree. I carry her inside. Gus is in the kitchen, wrapping his
finger in a bandage seeping blood.

"Gus, what?"

"Those little tea light holders," he said. "Trying to
arrange them just so. Not sure what happened. I didn't
want them anyway." He sighs. "Arlene's idea. All right I'll
be. Take the little one to bed." This is the most he's ever said
to me in one go. He's not very talkative. Like Sam.

A small mat is on the floor beside the bed and the crib is
gone. Sam must have taken it away. I lay Lily on the mat and
snuggle beside her. The room is cool and dark. A relief, after

our baking apartment and the hot, crowded back yard. Lily snuggles closer. She smells of pickles and peanuts.

When she falls away, asleep, I pull off my dress and lie on the bed. The walls shift, this is what wine can do. Shift walls. Beds. I close my eyes and in my sleep there is Marta, at the Golden Rice Bowl, and we're shouting "Shanghai! Singapore!" Now we're backpaddling to avoid a rock or a ledge or a log but before I can see what it is I'm sitting on a chair at the restaurant again beside Marta, and George is talking to the guys at the next table over about the Roughriders or his new tires and then he's telling Marta and me something and Rosa turns into a giant raven, opens her wings wide, and caws "*George!*" so loud I wake up.

It's not the dream that woke me but voices from the other basement bedroom on the far side of the bathroom. I can't make out words, just angry talking. Carmen goes on for a while, and then Alex, then both at once. I look at the walls. They only move a little now. It's too dark for shadows, too dark to make shapes on the walls. I slide to one side of the bed so there's plenty of space for Sam when he comes. He could sleep out on the couch in the rumpus room, but somebody will see him and ask questions. They will ask and ask, picking away at us till we are sore all over. My tired brain generates those white daisies again. They skitter past and I grab one and pluck slowly. *Stay with him. Don't stay with him.* And then: *Get over it, get over it, get over it.*

Lily wakes early, like always, singing and hopping on Sam and me like a baby robin. I laugh and try not to throw up. Upstairs Arlene has a big breakfast for us and keeps Lily talking and eating and giggling to make us stay longer. Gus has replaced his bandage. The blood isn't leaking through anymore.

"Gus," I say. "How's your hand?"

"It's nothing," Arlene says. "Sam. You don't really have to leave yet. Where are you off to? A friend of Jen's? Could it be tomorrow? You want to stay, don't you Lily?" Lily nods. "You just got here. It's summer."

"But work, Mom, work," Sam says. "And Jen's in her course."

I take Lily downstairs to wash her face. Finally, the suit-cases are loaded, Lily is buckled. Sam drives. We head west and then north through the Okanagan in sweltering heat. It's a good hour shorter up the east side of the lake but Arlene convinced Sam to go past some of her favourite wineries on the other side. We know nothing about wine, so it doesn't matter really, but Sam likes to do everything Arlene says and tell her about it later.

I roll down my window and the air makes a loud, steady flapping. Lily watches *Bob the Builder* with the volume up as high as it goes. Every few minutes she yells "Can! We! Fix it?" and Sam joins in with "Yes! We! Can!"

Eventually she falls asleep and I turn off the machine. We drive past gift shops, huge wineries, outdoor markets selling hats and colourful dresses and fruit. On one side of us are lakes; on the other, dry, mostly treeless hills. The wind sends a steady *whom-whom-whom* through the windows. I think about what to tell Sam about Marta. I try different opening sentences in my head: Sam. We had a canoe. Her parents gave us a tripping canoe. We were always in it. We were always on the water. It was my home. The canoe and the water both.

"Sorry, who? What?" Sam says.

"Oh—I'm thinking about Marta. And canoeing."

"Oh, that."

Sam doesn't like being outside. Too many summers at his grandparents' farm when he was a kid, he said. Some people are afraid of the outdoors. Maybe he is. I didn't mind, at first. Sam was like the mountains, after. A distraction.

"Why wasn't she at our wedding?" Sam asks. "Hang on, is this the person you knew in Marsh?"

"Yes."

"And you'd go to that Chinese place."

"The Golden Rice Bowl." Her dad would ask us what noodles we wanted and we'd shout *Shanghai! Singapore!* We went all the time, for birthdays, after exams, after we got our drivers' licences, after every canoe trip. I thought we'd go before leaving Marsh to go to university, but she said no, she was sick of it. We weren't about that place, though. We were about canoeing. Being on the water. We used to practice tipping canoes on lakes because for a long time I was afraid of capsizing. Tipping when you want to is hard, so usually we jumped out and pulled the boat over. But one day we tipped for real, on a river. We yelled at each other while we got the boat and all the stuff to shore. One of our paddles broke and we yelled about that too. But a strange thing happened after we collected everything and changed into dry clothes. We sat on the rocks, eating something, a piece of chocolate or some jerky, and looked up at the clear blue sky and, at the same time, yelled "That sucked!" as loud as we could and, after a few breaths, we started to laugh, hard, with tears pouring down our cheeks. We could laugh everything off. I never forgot why we tipped, though. We tipped because we were both certain we were right about something. I have no idea what. I don't tell Sam any of this. Since That Night, I don't want to share anything like this with him.

Sam rolls his window down further. My ears feel bruised and swollen. Sweat seeps from my neck, behind my knees, my armpits, my eyeballs. I close my eyes after a while. The scenery never changes anyway; it's all lakes, souvenir shops, ice cream stands, fruit.

Sam pulls off the road and stops. The sudden quiet is almost painful. My ears throb.

I look out. We're parked next to a big, bright orange building with curled trim on the roof and colourful tiles along the front wall. "Where are we? Why are we stopping?"

"A winery," Sam says.

The winery sits in a dusty, dry parking lot all on its own, like it's been plucked from the other side of the world, from the Mediterranean, and dropped here.

"You wanted to pick something up for Marta."

"Oh. Yeah."

"It's not one of the places Mom recommended but I'll just tell her it was and she'll be happy. She'll never know," Sam says.

Lily flings her water bottle down and cries out that she has to pee.

"Go on," Sam says. "I'll take her. We'll find you."

The inside is huge and cold. It's like stepping into a cave. A woman calls out from the far end of a long counter. She pours wine, four kinds. I want her to go away while I drink slowly so I can figure out on my own what I like, but she goes into long descriptions of the wood the wine aged in and what the flavours will do to my palate and something about notes and fruits and who knows what.

I sip and the woman pours and prattles on earnestly, and now Sam and Lily are here.

"She's done," he says.

"Okay." I finish quickly, then buy a bottle for Marta. My head buzzes a little, just enough. The feeling lasts till we step back out into the furnace.

"Noooo! Too hot!" Lily cries when Sam tries to put her into the car seat. She clings to his neck, her body slumped against his like all the life has been sucked out of her. She's wearing that little blue onesie, no sleeves, no legs, thin as a tissue but still too warm. Naked would be too warm. Her hair sticks to her forehead. Her cheeks are flushed.

"We need to find some water, Sam. We need to cool her off."

Sam drives a little farther north and stops at a small lake. Lily runs from the car and splashes into the water and I join her, wading in to my knees and then my waist and finally falling backwards and dunking my head. I didn't know I needed this, too. She shouts for Sam, again and again, and finally he comes in, reluctantly, as far as his ankles. He lets Lily splash him. He's doing this for her; anyone can see he's not loving this. He stands stiffly, won't splash back, won't even get in as far as his calves. Probably no swimming lessons when he was a kid. As soon as we can afford it, Lily will have swimming lessons. She jumps up and down, flings water over her head, and laughs hysterically.

Finally Sam tells her we have to go. Lily protests loudly but is too tired to resist being carried.

In the car, we sit in dripping clothes. After driving a few minutes, Sam asks, "Are we bad parents?"

The water has washed away the layer of sweat that clung to my skin. I feel different. I shake my head. "No. We're like a river. After the rapids, there's always a quiet spot. You see the leaves on the trees again. And smell the earth. George told us that."

"I wish I'd met this George."

He rounds a corner and we see the largest lake of all.

"It's the ocean!" Lily yells.

"What a long bridge," I say.

"It's Okanagan Lake," Sam says. "This is a pontoon bridge. It's floating. We're just going to float over the ocean, Lily. You. Me. Mama. Hang on tight. We might get bucked off. Wait for it," he says as we approach the bridge. "Wait for it. Casting off. And...floating!" he shouts when the rear tires are on the bridge. He slows a little on the ascent, slows so we can take it all in, the lake so long on either side of us we can't see to the end, the sailboats and houseboats, the windsurfers, the sun sparkling on the water, and some-where out there, the lake monster. For an instant, in my groggy state, I am bobbing along the waves. Lulled. The way I was with Marta, with her family. The best feeling in the world. "Lily. Say Ogopogo."

Lily giggles. "Dad's an Ogopogo."

Sam growls. "I'm a monster who's going to eat you up!"

"Can! You! Eat! Me?" Lily shouts.

"Yes! I! Can!" Sam yells back.

I'm laughing, too, before I notice, before I can stop myself.

"Jen," Sam says.

✳ It's after five when we get into Vernon and close to forty degrees in the shade. I look for a tree to park under, but there's nothing on Marta's street except a few sickly looking junipers and pines with dry, reddish-brown needles, sucking whatever bit of moisture they can find underground.

Lily is asleep, her face cotton-candy pink; bits of her hair are plastered to her forehead and cheeks. When I turn off the engine, my ears throb. I cover them.

"What?" Sam asks.

"All day. The air going *whom-whom-whom*."

"She's home. I saw her at the window."

Marta's house is the colour of pale lilacs. I can't decide if the flower garden out front is overgrown or just playfully wild. I hope wild. Like George and Rosa's.

"Sam. Could you take Lily to the lake for an hour?"

"What?" Sam frowns. "I'm dying. I could use a cold beer right about now."

"I know. I need a little while alone with Marta. And Lily needs to cool off again. Look at her."

"You could have told me sooner."

"I didn't know till now."

"This is a bit harsh." Sam's cheeks are flushed pink too. "Whatever. Go."

I take the wine. The main door is open. I can see down a hallway to the back of the house. Marta strides toward the screen door and pushes it open. She has on a bright sundress and looks the same except for her hair. Her hair used to be long like mine and in a ponytail. Now it's short and bleached with bits of red.

Now what. Go first, Marta. You invited me. You sent the card.

"Oh, Jen, here you are." Marta smiles. She steps aside and looks past me. I'm glad of the wine, a thing to hold. "You didn't bring Sam and Lily?"

"Sam took her to the lake for a bit. Our air conditioning died yesterday."

Marta laughs. Her laugh is bigger than I remember, fuller. Or maybe just older. "Welcome to the world of ancient rental houses. We don't have any air conditioning either. Come on out back. It's a little cooler there."

I follow her down the hall, past a small living room, neat and tidy, nothing out of place, no Lego or child's underwear strewn about, then the kitchen, also neat, no dishes in the drying rack even. It's just hot, so hot. Marta puts my wine in the fridge, pulls out a bottle, takes two glasses from a cupboard, all in one go. Now we're outside, under a gigantic tree. It's shady but warm. The back yard is larger than the front and nearly as wild looking. I want to tell Marta about Gus's garden, how it's completely different. How Sam and I were married there. In a garden, just as George imagined it for his girls. She might like to know that. That something turned out the way her dad wanted, the way we imagined.

There are four plastic Adirondack chairs in bold colours like giant Smarties—blue, red, orange, green—set at a round table with a yellow umbrella. Near the table is an old barbeque. Marta sets down the glasses and pours, slowly. We didn't drink wine the last time we saw each other. It was a grown-up drink and we were not grown up.

She lifts her glass. "Welcome to Vernon."

I look at her eyes. Nothing. Just here-you-are eyes, but with so much life, like always. Maybe because we are both older. Maybe Marta doesn't care anymore. Maybe I shouldn't either. That must be how it works. You both just stop caring.

"You first," Marta says. "What have you been doing? Tell me all about Lily."

"She's a kid. You know. Typical kid."

"Oh, Jen, come on!" I hear Rosa in her voice and look away. I miss Rosa, too. "Brag about her! How old is she?"

"Almost four. She's a normal kid. Everything functions. All the body parts. She has tantrums, she sleeps." I try to make it sound funny. There's no evidence of a child in Marta's house. I've had these conversations before. I've gone on about Lily with someone who listened nicely for a long time before telling me her son was stillborn. And another time, the woman listening, acting like she was interested, then saying: Don't you have a life?

"Does Lily love canoeing? She must!"

"Sam doesn't canoe. I haven't taken her."

"How'd you meet? What's he like?"

"At the gym, where he works."

"So, you met and then you got married." Marta speaks slowly, precisely, her voice lilting a little, her intense eyes moving across my face. "Just like in a fairy tale. Sweet."

Her words, even her tone, are both light and not. I stare at the big trees along the back fence; the wildflowers and tall grasses in the browning lawn, the overgrown shrubs along the side fences. Even weeds; I am glad of the weeds. Flowers grow randomly. It isn't messy, just full. It's the garden George had.

I pretend she's joking and try to joke back. "And here we are in a fairy tale garden."

Marta sighs. "The renters before us spent all their time making the yard look nice. What you see is the result of benign neglect, other than what I've done. We're both too busy working and having fun to bother with it. Oh, Les will be along in a bit. Wait a sec. I have some snacks." She goes inside.

✳ Our last summer in Marsh, before we went to university, Marta and I went on a month-long paddle, our longest. The sun was still up when we crawled into the tent at eleven our last night. It was so warm we lay on top of our sleeping bags. After four weeks, I wasn't sore. I wasn't tired. My whole body vibrated with happiness. I couldn't see past the first few days of university, but I knew I was going to come back every summer and paddle with Marta, forever and ever.

Noisy frog chatter surrounded us, echoed off the lake and made the frogs seem gigantic in the empty night. There must have been a hundred frogs. We laughed quietly, listening.

"Keep it down out there!" I called, and my voice echoed back.

"Frog Mama speaks!" Marta laughed. Another echo. She sighed happily. "This was the best trip ever."

"You say that every year," I teased. "This was better than the best." I couldn't believe how my body felt. I loved bracing, pushing, leaning against water and water pushing back, pushing lightly or hard, teasing. I loved bobbing along, sometimes pulled by the current, sometimes not. I could float on water all day and all night.

"Better than the best." Marta made a giddy humming sound. Her cheeks were red from the sun and the wind. Mine probably were too. "This is going to sound dumb. Remember when we were thirteen and promised to be forever-ever-ever friends?"

"Yeah."

Through the tent we saw the shadow of a bird fly past, something big, an owl maybe.

"Now you're going away." Marta said quietly. And then: "I'm going away."

"We'll write." I listened to the frogs for a minute. I was going to Calgary, she was going to Saskatoon. At first, we didn't think anything of it. We were busy finishing high school and canoeing. Now it was starting to sink in how far apart we would be. "We'll be back next summer. Right? And canoe? We'll be working for those outfitters. Right?"

"It's not the same."

A loon gave a long, clear, mournful call, and another replied from the far end of the lake. Even the frogs stopped to listen briefly, then started to chatter excitedly again, but we didn't laugh.

"But." Marta turned on her side and touched my hair and twirled it a little. "Will we always be best friends?"

"Yeah, why?"

A barred owl hooted *Who-cooks-for-you?* It sounded so sad, the owl.

Marta turned onto her back again and stared up the top of the tent for a minute or two. "Jen."

"Marta?"

"Nothing."

✱ "You did an Outdoor Ed degree, didn't you." Marta sets down the plate of cheese and crackers and tops up our wine glasses. "You were Mizz Outdoor Girl, last I saw you."

"Hey, so were you."

Marta shrugs, swirls her wine, drinks. "It was what Dad and Mom wanted. Dad mostly. Good grief, he wanted many things, didn't he." She shakes her head, her lips pressed together, stares into her glass before taking a sip. "I'm glad you did the degree anyway. You loved it."

"I didn't. I quit." Now we are getting to it. I dropped out after the first year. After my last trip home. I tried to stay in the program, even with my new friend Alice rallying, dragging me up and down mountains. But all I wanted to do was sleep. "I'm studying massage therapy now. Not—Hang on. You really didn't like canoeing and camping?"

"I can't believe you quit the outdoor program. It was your thing. It was you."

"You're messing with my head. It was *you*."

"You will be a fabulous massage therapist. You're very strong." She sounds exactly like Rosa again. My heart whirrs and then tightens. Marta grins widely. "We did crazy things, didn't we? Remember Otter Rapids, the first time?"

"How could I forget? We aced them."

"We were sixteen," Marta says. "Kids."

"We did it twice that day. First you were in the stern—"

"Then you. We lined the canoe perfectly."

"Both times."

"We nailed it." Marta raises her glass.

"We dodged car-sized holes and huge rollers!" I clink my glass against hers. For a few seconds it's almost like we've just done the rapids and are at the Golden Rice Bowl in our canoeing clothes, sunburned, windburned, bug-eaten, exhausted but buzzed, sitting across from Rosa and George and both talking at once and getting louder and louder until Rosa calms us. Almost. Something is not right but I don't know what.

Marta slaps her knee. "Remember the Mother's Day cake we made for my mom and used baking soda instead of brown sugar?"

"Because someone had abbreviated it BS. But Rosa was so great, she ate it anyway. She was cool with everything."

"Thank God," Marta says.

I look around. I can feel Rosa. I've come all this way, I have to ask, and I have to ask now, before Sam and Lily arrive, before Les comes. Before I lose my nerve. "What happened?"

Marta gets up and moves toward a patch of wildflowers. "Come, have a look." She kneels and pulls a weed.

What? Flowers? I want to say. But I get up.

"See this one?" Marta tips a long flower to show me its reddish top. "And this one? And these. Come. Walk along and have a look. These are all native. I tried to grow some others. The ones that aren't from here just don't thrive. Or I don't have the knack, I don't know." She laughs softly. "All of these, they're thriving."

"Marta." I stop walking.

She turns and takes my hands loosely in hers. "Okay then. Sometimes you have to start over. It was stupid. Whatever. I was stupid. Anyway, it was a long time ago. We were young. We were kids." I don't know what she means but all of a sudden she seems much older than me, much more laid back or assured, in the way she can dismiss whatever happened. She wants to let it all go, wants me to let it go, but at the same time it's as if she's covered in a sheet of Saran Wrap. Like she's put one self forward and left the real Marta behind the plastic.

I used to go over in my mind what I'd say if I ever saw her again, after I asked her what happened. Things like, I wanted to canoe with you again. I wanted you there when Lily was born. I wanted you to be her favourite aunt. I wanted you to meet Sam. But everything I imagined I would say seems pathetic.

✳ The first fall and winter at university, I wrote long letters to Marta, and she wrote long replies. By mail, we planned our summer canoe trip: first, short sprints to wake up the paddling muscles, and when the ice melted in early June we'd drive up to Missinipe and paddle till we started our jobs with the outdoor expedition company.

April arrived. I finished my exams, packed my bags, and rode the bus to Saskatoon. Marta and George and Rosa

were waiting at the depot. Not my parents; they'd moved to
Mississauga when I left for university. Marta and her parents
swooped over me in a huge hug. I smelled home: sausages,
cinnamon buns, hand cream. I didn't want them to let go,
but eventually George announced it was time for a bite.

"The Golden Rice Bowl!" I yelled.

On the drive to Marsh I talked about the dorm, my
classes, pounding up and down trails in the Rocky
Mountains, in hiking boots or on big wide skis; it wasn't
the Churchill River, I told Marta, but it was what was there,
Marta should come, she'd love it; and there was a guy,
Eric, I'd been hanging out with, since January, okay maybe
dating, who was in the same program I was, he'd like
Marta, I knew he would, how could he not.

It wasn't until we were at the restaurant that I saw how
quiet Marta was. On the way to our table, George high-fived
the guys sitting at the big table, said something about football maybe, then started to whisper about them to Marta
and me when we sat down even though Rosa tried to cut
him off with a sharp *George!* and a quick shake of her head.

The server arrived and because Marta seemed to be out
of sorts, I didn't even ask for the noodles I liked; it was only
fun if we both played. We ordered all of Marta's favourites,
Shanghai noodles, spring rolls, fried rice for George, green
tea for Rosa.

Marta was slow to get going the next morning. It was
late when we set off. I didn't care. I was home. Home was
in the canoe with Marta, bobbing through the current,
hearing the water burbling, smelling wet earth and peaty
tree trunks, being lulled along, hypnotized, almost.

The plan was to paddle for three days on the South Saskatchewan. I started out in the bow. Marta was still quiet. After a half hour, she finally spoke. "C'mon, Jen, paddle! You're not putting any muscle into your stroke!"

"I am." I paddled harder and let it go; Marta would get in the groove soon, I told myself.

"You're not moving the boat forward. I can feel it." And then: "Pry, Jen, pry! Didn't you see that rock! Oy, brace! Do you want to tip us on purpose in freezing water? Can't you see the chunks of ice?"

"I'll go in the stern, then."

"Fine. I need to pee anyway."

Marta turned us into shore and hopped out. I took the stern. When we were afloat again, I thought things were better. Marta didn't say anything for at least five minutes.

"Point the bow to the left. You're catching the wind."

I angled the bow slightly left.

"You put me right into that huge wave! Watch out. Rock!"

"We were nowhere near that rock. What's going on?" I whacked the water hard with my paddle blade. "Marta. What's wrong?" Marta didn't answer, but she might as well have said: You. You are all wrong.

Instead Marta said, "It's late," calmly, like I was having a bad day. "Let's just find a place to camp."

I wanted a fight, so Marta could vent and we could carry on. That was how it was sometimes. We'd yell and then not say anything for an hour or a day and then one of us would say something and it would all be fine. Though I dreaded what Marta might say. Once I joked to Rosa that I'd rather be bucked out of a canoe and thrashed up against jagged rocks in an icy river than fight with Marta. Rosa shook her head, her eyes glistening, and said: *Zwillinge*. Twins.

We pulled into shore. Marta didn't say anything when we unloaded the canoe. She looked alternately bored and irritated.

"You're not going to tell me what's up, are you," I said.

We sat on a log with our bowls of salty noodles. I wore my heavy fleece and a windbreaker. It was overcast and the wind was cold.

Marta didn't look at me. She didn't say anything.

In the tent later, after we'd been lying in our sleeping bags for ages, neither of us able to sleep, she said, "Jen."

"Marta."

I waited a long time and finally rolled onto my side and fell asleep.

The sun was up early, even in late April, and as soon as Marta was awake the next morning she got out of the tent, yanked off the fly, and began to shake the dew.

"Let's just paddle out to the car," I said quietly. I felt ill. It was two leisurely days to the car from the camp, but if we paddled hard all day and into the evening, we could get out tonight.

"Whatever you want," Marta said.

The sky was grey when we loaded the canoe, and soon there was a light drizzle. Ducks huddled by the shore, flicking their wet tail feathers and hiding their beaks in their wings.

The paddle out was a long, quiet slog. I waited for Marta to say something, but she didn't. Nobody was at the take-out; we'd left Marta's car there. When we came ashore in the late evening, I was so cold and tired I couldn't stop shaking.

"Could you just take me to the bus," I said.

At the station, I bought a ticket to Calgary. Marta stayed in the car, didn't come out for a goodbye, didn't even look when I got on the bus.

I was sick for two months with some sort of flu that lingered. In all that time I didn't hear from Marta. I found a room in a house with other students and, eventually, a summer job at the nearby grocery store. I didn't pass on my address to Marta and her parents. For months and months, even on sunny days, the sky was dark grey, as if someone had switched off a light.

It was nothing, really. It was nothing. I repeated the words over and over, felt them fall like heavy rain on my skull till I didn't feel anything when I thought of Marta. On Fridays my friend Alice suggested a scramble or a climb and I went. At first I went because I didn't have anything better to do. Soon I went because I couldn't get enough of those long, hard days. It wasn't the trail or the peak that wasn't even a peak or even the scenery that I liked at first. It was being able to walk far enough and long enough to make my body and my mind go numb.

One day I met Sam and latched on. When I discovered I was pregnant, his parents threw together a wedding and we moved into our little apartment. I tried not to think about Marta. But she was always there, like an itch in the middle of my back where I couldn't reach.

* "So where are they? Sam and Lily." Marta says.

"Kalamalka. Lily likes water. Sam will have a hard time extracting her."

"Just like you." Marta sips her wine. "Les and I met in Vancouver. We lived there for a bit. Think you'll stay in Calgary?"

"We're not sure."

Marta's eyes scan my face. "Things are good with you and Sam?" She tops up my glass, then hers.

It comes out before I can stop myself, in a rush: "In May he made out with a girl we hired to look after Lily." I don't know why I say it. Maybe it's because I want things to be the way they used to be with her. Maybe because of what Marta said about starting over. Or maybe saying it will help me figure out what to make of it. Because I haven't told anyone yet. When Marta doesn't say anything, I go on, "Not a girl, she's nineteen or twenty. But still. She lives in our building." Sam thinks we should go on like we were before, just put it behind us. Huh, just like Marta. Like Arlene too. Maybe this is what she means by bumps along the way. "They were on the balcony. I was at my course. I got home, she saw me and came inside, trying to, oh man—" This is the first time I've said it out loud. I've been so mad I didn't see till now that it's a bit funny. "Trying to hide her bra in her fist and make her shirt straight and get out of our apartment. You should have seen her face." I start to laugh.

Marta takes this in. After several seconds she says loudly, "That sucks."

"It so sucks," I say.

The air in the garden shifts, loosens. Marta becomes the Marta I knew, the Marta squatting beside me on the riverbank after we capsized, both of us soaked through and pissed and scowling. We both yell "Oh, fuck!" and laugh

hard. We laugh till our sides hurt. Then comes the feeling
I had after the swim earlier today, the little pull of hope.
It's the line down the river, the downstream vee. The water
smooth and buoyant. We've come through the rapids
without capsizing and now we're bobbing along.

We're still laughing when Sam and Lily run into the yard
from the side of the house, and there's introductions and
chaos; Marta goes inside for food; and when she returns a
few minutes later holding a green salad, Les is beside her,
in a long dress like hers and with short spikey blond hair, I
see what I haven't seen before, and now George is here and
Rosa is shushing him.

Les is holding vegetables and dips and sausages; in
a few minutes, sausages are on the grill, a plastic cup of
lemonade arrives for Lily and cold beer for Sam and more
wine for the table and a fifth chair. Sam's so hot and tired
he drinks the whole beer in one go and starts another. The
crown of the orange-yellow sun peeks over the hills beyond
the back fence, as if having one last glimpse at us, as if
saying *You are on your own now, ha ha!* before sliding away.

Lily watches Marta and Les closely, then inches toward
them and puts a hand on Marta's leg, rests her head on it
while Marta absently runs her fingers through her hair.
Now Lily plays some sort of hand clapping game with
Marta and Marta sings Rosa's songs in Rosa's voice. George
has gone to check the flowers.

"Good," Sam says, waving a piece of sausage on his fork.
"This is so good."

For a few minutes while we eat, it's quiet. The air cools
a little and smells sweet, like the perfume smell of the wolf

willow. The crickets trill and the thrush make their night-time call, that long drainpipey echo. Now Lily is telling Marta about the lake, Les talks jovially about her work, Sam chimes in about the drive, and Marta mostly laughs or says something unrelated or confusing, and drinks more wine. I look everywhere but at Marta.

"Lily looks tired," Les says.

Lily's in her chair, her head back, mouth half open and eyes half closed.

"Sam, come, I'll show you where she can sleep," Les says.

"S'more wine?" Marta opens another bottle without waiting for me to answer.

"Are you okay?" I ask.

"Wha? Yes. Course." She finishes her glass while Sam and Les are gone with Lily and pours another.

When Sam and Les return, Sam opens a beer and sips slowly. After a minute, he says, "Jen said you girls used to go to this Chinese restaurant up in Marsh." His eyes and lips are starting to turn a little red from all the beer. "Is that really the name of the town? What sort of name is that?"

"Oh, hardly ever," I say quickly. I will him to stop.

"What?" Sam says. "You said you went every week practically. You loved it. You two couldn't agree which noodles to order, right?"

"What's this all about?" Marta asks, carefully, not slurring, and just like that, everything changes. The air is brittle. The wolf willow loses its scent. The thrush stop singing.

"Hey." Les touches Marta's arm. "It's okay."

Marta's body is taut, like a cat about to spring. She turns to Les. "Oh no. This is how it was." She stands.

"Marta," Les presses down on Marta's arm. "I left the meringues in the kitchen. The ones you made especially for Lily. And Jen and Sam too of course. Why don't you get them?"

Marta pushes Les's hand away and shakes her head. She crosses her arms and slowly turns to Les, then to Sam, and finally to me. "You don't know how much I hated that place." She's looking right in my eyes but what she's saying is for Les. "But she insisted. And Mom and Dad gave her whatever she wanted. That was. That was—" She downs her wine wobbly. "And me. And Dad. And you. Gloating about what's his name, before Sam here. Eric! Thought I forgot, didn't you? Did you make up Eric, just for Dad? So eager to please him, like a little kid. You never saw what an asshole he was. Shaking hands with those guys in the restaurant, giving them high-fives, and then turning around and telling us they weren't good enough for his girls. They could hear all that. You didn't get it. Oh! Maybe you did. What Dad always said—" She speaks with a slight German accent, "'*My* girls are not going to marry someone from this small town, *my* girls are going to find a nice man from a big city and make a vedding here and bring home some grandchildren, *ja*?'" She looks exhausted, speaks softer. "At first, I thought Sam and Lily were made up too. Like Eric. Ha, joke's on me." She closes her mouth, opens it, picks up Les's glass and drinks it down. She holds the glass out and Les takes it carefully.

"Well." Marta's like a rag doll; she can barely hold her head straight. "It's past. Ancient history. It's nothing. There's no test or anything. Nobody will fail. C'mon, laugh, it's a joke." She speaks more quietly and even more slowly. "You wouldn't stand up for me, would you?" She shakes her head, puts her hand on her chair to steady herself. Her shoulders sag. "Jen. You were my best," she pauses, drags it out, "Best. Forever. Friend. Remember?" She raises her head and shoulders up and looks around. "And then you weren't," she says quickly, dismissively. "Just couldn't do it, could you?" Her face changes, goes from looking upset to calm, and then she gives us a big smile. "Aren't I the buzz-kill. I think we need more wine to liven this party up. You brought a bottle, didn't you, Jen? What do you say we crack it. Celebrate, the way Dad wanted to. You brought home the man, you brought home the kid." Without waiting for an answer, she walks awkwardly toward the house, foal-like, stumbles on the porch steps, stops herself with her hands, and goes inside.

✳ Sam and I are side by side on the guest bed. The bedspread is on the floor.

He is a few inches from me but I can feel the heat radiating from his skin, and surely he can feel mine. It's not just the heat of the room. It's everything.

Marta broke the glass right after her long speech, after she went inside for the wine I brought, insisted on opening it, insisted I have some, then put the glass down hard on the table when I said no. The long thin stem broke and then the rest of the glass, wine splashing over the table and my bare legs. I washed, but my thighs and shins are still sticky and now the fruity scent fills the air.

Les swept the shards, wiped the wine; Marta said she was sorry and left and didn't come back. I wanted to leave, to find a motel, but Les insisted we stay, said it was too late, we wouldn't find a motel, she couldn't let us drive with everything we'd had to drink, it would be irresponsible of her, and Lily, after all, was sound asleep; and Marta—Marta wouldn't remember anything in the morning anyway.

"Please stay," Les whispered. "I brought this on." We were in the small dark space at the top of the stairs. "She's not really a drinker. She's never done this before. You can go before she gets up. It's my fault, all of this."

"What is?" I said.

"After Rosa died. She kept talking about you. The canoe Rosa and George gave you two. All the trips. It was her, I don't know, identity. Who she was. When Rosa died I suggested she just write to you. Invite you here. It was me. I'm glad we met. I can see why she—" She stopped, took a breath. "The guest room faces east. You can pull the blind down if you want."

"Rosa died?"

Les nodded. "Four years ago."

Sam and I forget the blind. The room isn't fully dark when I lie down. I feel like I've been bucked from a canoe. I'm still in the water, fighting the current, trying to see the shore in the dark. It's not just finding the clear line, moving forward, after all. It's not always about getting on with things. You can repair the canoe you smash against the rocks, but it's never the same canoe. You will always know where the break is. How easy it is to be lulled along.

"Jen," Sam whispers.

"Sam."

"Jen."

"Sam." I will myself not to fall asleep. Now he will tell me what happened That Night. I wait. He will tell me what I missed, what I hadn't seen, what I should have known.

"Jen. You would have loved the lake."

Acknowledgements

DEEP GRATITUDE to Betty Jane Hegerat, Jasmina Odor, Tatiana Peet, and Julie Robinson, for reading when these stories were disoriented little hatchlings; to Leslie Greentree, for helping the stories take flight; to Fran Kimmel and Audrey Whitson for the Great Manuscript Swap; to Deborah Willis for careful editing and insights near the end; and to Christine Wiesenthal for reading and rereading (and rereading) these little rascals, for patience, for thoughtful feedback. Every one of you: thank you for rallying!

For many decades, my writing home was Strawberry Creek Lodge, where Brenda Kshyk and Tena Wiebe created a welcoming hearth for writers near and far to practice their craft in peace and (mostly) quiet while a vast, caring community slowly grew. Thank you both.

Thank you to the editors of *Prairie Fire*, *The Dalhousie Review*, and PRISM *International* for publishing earlier versions of "These People Have Nothing" (Winter 2021–2022), "The Night the Moon Was Bright..." (Summer 2016), and "Devil's Lake" (Winter 2014).

Songs referenced in this collection include "Don't Worry, Be Happy" by Bobby McFerrin, from his 1988 album *Simple Pleasures*, and "Sisters" by Irving Berlin, from the 1954 film *White Christmas*.

I am grateful for the financial and other support from the Alberta Foundation for the Arts, the Banff Centre for Arts and Creativity, the Edmonton Arts Council, and the Writers' Guild of Alberta.

A huge thank you to everybody at University of Alberta Press for your enthusiasm.

Most of all, thank you to my daughters and to Herb Taylor, for answering random, seemingly spontaneous questions about trees and rocks and soil and water, for patience and understanding, and, especially, the space to write.

Other Titles from University of Alberta Press

You Haven't Changed a Bit
Stories
ASTRID BLODGETT
Full-fledged characters positively crackle in the deliciously realistic situations of these thirteen short stories.
Robert Kroetsch Series

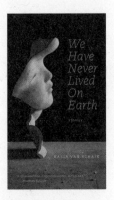

We Have Never Lived On Earth
KASIA VAN SCHAIK
Balancing an ambivalent relationship to the past, and fear and hope for the future, Kasia Van Schaik's portraits of female interiority, immigrant identity, dislocation, and desire trace the transitions from girlhood to adulthood, grappling with the struggle to understand what it means to live on earth.
Robert Kroetsch Series

Annie Muktuk and Other Stories
NORMA DUNNING
Fifteen Inuit stories portray the unvarnished realities of northern life via strong and gritty characters.
Robert Kroetsch Series

More information at uap.ualberta.ca